Letter of

Marque

Michael Aye

BOOK TWO, THE PYRATE

PYRATE

Letter of Marque

Book 2

Michael Aye

Published by Boson Books

An imprint of Bitingduck Press
Formerly an imprint of C&M Online Media, Inc.

ISBN 978-1-938463-07-5
eISBN 978-1-938463-75-4

For information contact
Bitingduck Press, LLC
Altadena, CA
notifications@bitingduckpress.com
http://www.bitingduckpress.com
Cover art by Mike Benton

Author's note

This book is a work of fiction with a historical backdrop. I have taken liberties with historical figures, ships, and time frames to blend in with my story. Therefore, this book is not a reflection of actual historical events.

Books by Michael Aye

Dedication

This book is dedicated:

to all my Bullock County High School classmates. God's Speed.
to Buck Jewell, a great friend who drives an awesome 'Vette,
and to Pat...for more reasons than words can express.

WEST INDIES.

Scale
50   100   200   300 Miles

Tropic of Cancer

Explanation,
The Spanish Islands are coloured   Yellow
English   Pink
French   Blue
Dutch   Orange
Danish   Purple
Swedish   Red

A T L A N T I C   O C E A N

FLORIDA

BAHAMA or LUCAYOS ISLANDS

New Bahama

HAYTI or ST. DOMINGO

PORTO RICO

LEEWARD ISLANDS

ISLANDS

G R E A T E R   A N T I L L E S

JAMAICA

Santiago

Havannah

Tropic of Cancer

Windward Passage

C A R I B B E A N   S E A

L E S S E R   A N T I L L E S

MOSQUITO SHORE

G U L F   O F   M E X I C O

PROLOGUE

"It's war...it's war." The cry rang out through the streets and down to the waterfront. John Will and Michael Brett looked at each other, and then they both looked at the calendar on the wall...June 18, 1812.

"The colonel was right," John said. The War Hawks in Congress would have their way.

Michael looked into space, deep in thought. "It will be the war for sailor's rights," he finally said. John nodded his agreement. This had been the theme the War Hawks had pushed from the onset.

Michael and John, along with their "not so silent" partner, Eli Taylor, owned a shipping business that had grown considerably in the last few years. They now had no less than twenty-four ships. Over the past year, a number of their ships had been stopped by British warships searching for "deserters." The Brits, with their large navy, were always hungry for seamen. Whether they were British or not, they always seemed to find at least one seaman. The only exception was when Eli Taylor's ship was stopped, he held the young lieutenant under rifle point and ran out his larboard side guns. He sent the cox'n of the boarding party back to his ship with a note. The note said:

To the Captain of the British ship, Mars:

I, Captain Eli Taylor, am personal friends with Sir Robert Basnight, Governor of Antigua, and both Lord Gilbert Anthony and Vice Admiral Sir Gabriel Anthony. I have no British subjects under my command. With your apology for detaining my ship, we will forget the whole matter.

Should you persist, your boarding party
will be held until we reach the island of
Antigua and you can answer to your admiral and the governor. You have a quarter
of an hour to make up your mind. The time
will start when your boat reaches your
entry port.

Eli Taylor

According to Taylor's crew, the Mars' captain had been standing on deck when the boat's cox'n climbed through the entry port with the note. The captain snatched the note from the seaman's hand and stomped when reading it. He quickly called for his clerk and writing materials. A hasty apology was written and sent back to Taylor. Releasing his hostages, Taylor had his ship underway before the Mars' boat made it back to the ship.

Other captains didn't have the audacity Taylor had, who as a pirate had dealt with the British navy for years. He had never raided any ship from the United States. His past was kindly ignored by Savannah's people because of this. Taylor, like his friend, Colonel Lee, had predicted the war. He was so sure President Madison would give in to the War Hawks in Congress, he had put together a group of investors and commissioned the building of a small frigate to use as a privateer.

Colonel Jedidiah Lee, who now owned a small part of the shipping business, owned twenty-five percent of the ship. Eli and Colonel Lee had merged their small fleet of traders into the Savannah Import, Export Merchants and Ship Chandlers; a company that Eli already owned stock in. John Will and Michael Brett together owned twenty-five percent, as did Eli Taylor. The remaining twenty-five percent had been given to some of Savannah's most prominent politicians. Men who could obtain a Letter of Marque from both the State of Georgia and the Secretary of War.

The captain of the small frigate had already been chosen. A man who had saved Taylor's life when it was Taylor who had stopped his ship. A man who had proved to all his ability not only as a fighter, but a shrewd tactician and leader. The crew on Taylor's old pirate ship, Raven, had watched as young Cooper Cain had ascended the ranks from landsman to captain. Not a man would question his authority and all would follow him. These were the men who had given up their lives in the brotherhood of the sea and would now become legitimate privateers. Some would say they were still pirates, but pirates with a license. Taylor's only concern right now was when would Cooper get back?

Cooper had fallen in love with Vice Admiral Anthony's daughter, Maddy, and had gone to Antigua to marry the girl. Much to Maddy's mother and father's chagrin, she frequently called Cooper, 'Sir Pirate.' Cooper had rescued Maddy, her mother, Faith, and Sir Robert Basnight from another pirate known to all as Cobra. Maddy had been taken to a tent, bound, stripped naked, and was about to be raped when Cooper intervened. His intervention and rescue had forged a bond between himself and the Anthony's. Now he and Maddy were to be married. How would the news of the war affect their marriage and the relationship between the families? Taylor hoped that things would work out. Cooper deserved some happiness, after losing his home due to a lie by a relative, and then being exiled from England due to that lie. The exile caused him to be separated from his mother, and he lost his first wife to death at the hands of a previous suitor. Taylor thought to himself, that boy definitely deserves some happiness. The ship lying in wait, the raider, was named in honor of Cooper's first wife…Seafire.

Taylor felt a pang of guilt. Was it right to send Cooper back to sea, back in harm's way? Would Cooper have it any other way? The boy had become a man…a man who loved the sea, and born to command. Time, and only time, would tell if it was the right decision…time and God.

CHAPTER ONE

NOTHING MOVED OR STIRRED; even the flag at Government House hung limp...limp and wet. Lingering drops of rain dripped from the riggings onto the deck of the flagship at anchor in English Harbour, Antigua. Only an hour ago, the wind had been brisk, the sky dark, and rain had fallen steadily for nearly half an hour. As was usual in the West Indies, the storm had moved on quickly, and the calm was followed by calamity. A ship was entering the harbour.

The flagship's captain presented to his admiral's cabin. The marine sentry announced him and he entered. Captain David Davy had been a young midshipman on board *HMS Drakkar* when his admiral was the senior midshipman and then a lieutenant. Now he, David Davy, was captain of *HMS Minotaur* and the flag captain to Vice Admiral Sir Gabriel "Gabe" Anthony. It was a position...a job that Captain Davy loved. He had served with Gabe under Captain, and then Admiral, Gilbert Anthony, Gabe's brother, since he was a young boy. The old admiral had retired as the Governor of Antigua and been replaced by Sir Robert Basnight.

Entering the admiral's cabin, Davy was not surprised to see the admiral and his cox'n, Jake, playing cribbage. The relationship between the two went much further than admiral and cox'n. Jake had saved Admiral Anthony's life when he was a captain, and not long after that he became the captain's cox'n. The admiral's son, Captain Jake Anthony, was named after the cox'n.

"Morning, sir," Davy greeted the admiral. "The *Sparrow Hawk* has just entered the harbour, and before the anchor was dropped the captain was over the side and his gig is approaching."

"It must be important news," Anthony said.

"Aye, it's possible our fears have come true, Admiral."

Anthony gave a sigh and then said, "Bring him on down, David. Jake, if you will get my coat for me…and Jake, don't lose that score sheet. You've ten shillings owed to me, so far, I'll not be forgetting."

Jake and Captain Davy both smiled. "Ten shillings, indeed! You're lucky it's me and not Bart," Jake replied. "It's you who'd be owing, and not your poor cox'n."

"Humph, nobody but a fool plays with Bart," Gabe replied.

"There are plenty of them about," Jake replied.

It had become a challenge to the plantation owners and their sons to beat Bart. Some of them had, but that was rare. Bart had even won a sugar cane plantation one evening, but in the end he gave it back to the planter. Bart had a reputation of being honest. He usually beat you, but he'd never take advantage of anyone. He owned two taverns now that he was retired from the navy. One of them was for the common sailor and was named Twenty Fathoms. The other one was a more upscale tavern that catered to the island's upper crust residents, and was named Island Paradise. Bart could be found at either tavern at any given time, but at bedtime he was at his quarters at the Anthony home.

From outside the admiral's cabin, the *Sparrow Hawk's* captain was being piped aboard. He was soon announced at cabin's door. Upon entering, the young captain gazed about him. He never failed to be amazed at Admiral Anthony's cabin.

"Sir Gabe," the captain said in greeting. He'd been a midshipman to one of the admiral's captains not too many years ago, and he'd learned how the admiral preferred to be addressed if he knew you.

"Captain Lacy," Anthony returned the greeting and Jake nodded at Lacy.

Lacy had learned the hard way that nothing was kept from Jake. He'd made the mistake his first visit when he'd brought in a sensitive dispatch. When asked to report he'd said, "Perhaps the admiral would like for his cox'n to be excused."

Anthony had risen and said very sternly, "Perhaps you'd better report as ordered and let me decide who is to be present. Something that you'd do well not to concern yourself with." Lacy had mumbled his apology. Since then he'd done his best to get back in Anthony's good grace.

"I'm afraid I bear grave news, Admiral. We are again at war with America," Lacy reported.

Hiding his disgust, Anthony only nodded. It was the first war that had ensured his career, his reaching high rank very quickly, and had made him a rich man. It almost cost him his marriage. He had a son, James, his first born, who had taken after his mother's family and loved the soil and not the sea. James now owned two large farms, some would even say plantations. One was in Beaufort, South Carolina where his mother, Faith, was from, and the other in Thunderbolt, an inheritance from Faith's uncle. Faith would not appreciate his going to war with her and their son's country. Jake, his second son, was a new commander of a small eighteen gun sloop-of-war. And Maddy…she was to marry Cooper Cain. A British gentleman who had been treated so badly that he'd become a pirate and raided British ships with daring, like no other Gabe had come against. Would he become active as a privateer? Cain had given his word to give up his life as a pirate. He'd even been given a pardon signed by the king. Sir Robert Basnight and Hugh, Anthony's brother-in-law, had seen to this. But now it was war. Would they be enemies? So damn many ifs. There was one sure thing: wherever Cooper Cain went, so would his daughter. Should he resign, retire. Damnation…damn Parliament…damn those navy captains who raided American ships for seamen. He'd unofficially forbade the captains under his command from doing this.

"Captain Davy!"

"Aye, Sir Gabe."

"Please provide Captain Lacy with some refreshment," Anthony said as he looked out of the stern windows. They were all open to catch any little breeze that might happen to favor them. He could see no fewer than six American ships and there'd be more at Saint Johns. "Captain Davy, if you'd also be kind enough to send your first lieutenant to personally inform the American ships, here and at Saint Johns, that our countries are now at war. Tell them they will be allowed one week in port to complete any business that needs to be done and also take on provisions and water. At such time, they will be given a letter to provide safe passage to their home ports without fear of being taken."

"Aye, I will see to it, Admiral," Davy replied.

When the two captains left, Anthony read his dispatch and then handed it to his cox'n. "What to do, old friend?"

Jake looked up, "It might be better for some if you remained in authority, sir. Otherwise…" He did not finish his statement. They both knew what 'otherwise' meant. "Should I call for your barge, Sir Gabe?"

"Yes, we'll notify the governor of these unpleasant events first, before we tell the family." His cox'n nodded his head. "Faith and Maddy are visiting Coop's mother and Jean Paul. I believe that young Jake is there, as are Lord and Lady Anthony."

"Jean Paul has agreed to give Jake lessons in the 'manly art of fencing'," Jake Hex said with a smile.

Young Jake, the admiral's son, had quickly learned how lacking he was when fencing with Cooper Cain. It was Cooper who had persuaded Jean Paul to offer his new friend and soon to be brother-in-law the lessons.

"I hope he has the chance to finish those lessons," Anthony said.

"Aye," his cox'n agreed.

The thought that Jake and Cooper might soon be facing each other broadside to broadside made Anthony shiver. Jake saw the shiver and knew that Gabe was worried. Where was Dagan? He should have been here already? He'd sent word that he'd be here for the wedding.

Dagan had previously met Cooper and visited with him. He thoroughly liked the young man. What would Dagan's reaction be to the war? Did he know yet…yes, Dagan always knew. His ability to see the future was uncanny. He did things nobody else could do. He'd even saved Jake's life from some thieves in England once. Jacob Hex was in awe of Gabe's uncle. Some called him a soothsayer. Jake called him friend. Would Dagan be able to ease some of their worries or would it be gloom…gloom and possible doom?

"Damn the government," Jake found himself saying. He must have spoken aloud, as Gabe replied, "I agree."

CHAPTER TWO

Jacob "Jake" Anthony was wiping the sweat off his face. He had just completed an hour of intense instruction from Jean Paul de Giraud, who was a fencing master of some renown. He had at one time been France's greatest maitre d'armes. That he was a master swordsman was an understatement. While young Cooper Cain bested him two of five matches, that only meant he'd survived twice and died three times were it combat. Jean Paul walked over to Jake with a towel in his hand as well. He liked the way Jake listened to his instruction. "You have promise, Master Jake. I think, in time, you will hold your own with most anyone who should draw his blade against you." Jake was really pleased with Jean Paul's praise, yet he knew he'd never match Cooper Cain.

"Thank you, but I wouldn't stand a chance with Coop," Jake replied.

"Ah," Jean Paul said with a smile, remembering his year with the young Cooper Cain. "I must admit, Jake, that Cooper was a most adept student. He had a natural flair for the art. I feel its doubtful many men would stand toe to toe with Cooper and win."

Jake nodded his agreement. He was going to ask Cooper about some of the tricks he'd learned, with Jean Paul or in actual combat, when his thoughts were interrupted.

Jacob Hex walked under the small archway to the grassy area where the three men were gathered. Uncle Jake, as he was known to Anthony's children, had a very stern look on his face. "Sir Gabe has some very concerning news," he said. "He'd prefer to speak to everyone at one time." Cooper and Jake Anthony both knew from Hex's voice that the news would not be good.

Walking through the rear door into the kitchen, the men made their way into a larger great room. This was the house where Cooper had been born. His mother and father had lived here until the place had been nearly lost in a game of chance. The property had been deep in debt when Cooper's father had been killed in a duel. His mother's brother, Lawrence, had assumed the debt and paid it off. However, when his uncle had died, Cooper's dandy of a cousin, Phillip, had incurred more debt on the plantation. Cooper eventually bought the mortgage with the help of Sir Robert Basnight. When the payment was forfeited, as Cooper knew it would be, the plantation became his again. Free of debt, he'd given the plantation to his mother and Jean Paul as a wedding present. It had gone from near ruin to a productive plantation once again under Jean Paul's management and Lady Deborah's recommendations.

Everyone was gathered in the great room, with his mother standing next to Maddy and Jake's mother, Faith. Lady Deborah sat in a chair with Lord Anthony standing by her on one side, and Bart leaned against the doorway.

Seeing that everyone had arrived in the room, Gabe came right to the point. "The dispatch vessel, *Sparrow Hawk*, has just arrived with some grave news." Looking directly at Cooper, he continued, "It seems our two countries are again at war."

It was Faith, who responded first. "You'll retire. You will not be part of another war where we fight against my country or countrymen. It's your sons' country now, Gabe."

Gabe didn't respond until Faith got a handkerchief and started wiping tears from her eyes. "I thought about that," he said.

"Jake and Lord Basnight both agree though, that I might well be more able to help our people if I were to remain in a position of authority, one of influence."

Maddy instantly knew what her father implied. She knew her man would fight. He would be a privateer. Should he be captured, her father's rank might prove to be the difference in his living or hanging.

Faith was not done, however. She looked at her son, "Jake, what will you do if you see Cooper and you are broadsides to broadsides? Will you do your duty?" She almost spat out the last word.

Cooper answered before Jake could gather his thoughts. "I'd never fire on a ship on which Jake was aboard." He said this with all conviction in his voice. Maddy, who'd been holding his arms, hugged him closely.

The front door opened and, surprising everyone, Dagan stepped in. He had arrived for the wedding but his words were of steel and caused a silence in the room. "It's a war where brother shall rise up against brother," he said. "It will test the resolve and convictions of every family member. A man has to live his convictions and a woman has to support her man, understanding that love will once again stand the test of times. Now is not the time for Gabe to haul down his flag. Neither is it a time for young Jake to try to climb the ladder of promotion and prize money. Cooper, you have adopted America as your new home, as I have, but you can't forget your ties to England…to your wife's family." He had walked in speaking as if he'd been in the conversation from the start, and everyone remained silent.

It was Hex who walked over and shook Dagan's hand. "We've been wondering when you'd arrive."

Dagan smiled, and then Gabe embraced him, simply saying, "Uncle, I've longed for your companionship."

Maddy ran across the room next and with tears in her eyes said, "I wasn't going to marry Sir Pirate until you gave me your blessing."

Dagan leaned in and whispered, "Liar. A battleship couldn't keep you from marrying Coop."

"You like him, don't you, Uncle?" Maddy asked.

"I do very much, little lady, but remember what I said. This war will test your resolve. It's not easy on a man, but it's worse on a woman."

"We'll make it through though, won't we, Uncle?"

Dagan looked into Maddy's misty eyes. "That will depend on you, my dear. Coop will certainly need you to support him in the days and years to come. Just remember, who it was that went against the brotherhood to rescue you and your mother; something that made him a marked man by others of his trade. He did this after only having met you and Faith once. He risked it all and nearly died because he knew what they planned for you. Each time you feel your resolve weakening, remember what Cooper did for you and Faith."

Memories flashed back in Maddy's mind. How Cooper took on the three rogues to save her, and when the fight was over he stood staring at her nakedness. She recalled the words that passed between them. The excitement she felt as he gazed upon her nude body. She remembered saying something like, 'Am I that hard to look upon that you frown?' And his reply, 'No, my lady, were I not a married man I'd fight a hundred such as he, if I thought it'd gain favor in your eyes.' She'd fallen in love instantly. She also remembered the voyage back to Antigua. He'd revealed that he was a pirate, but it didn't matter to her. She was deeply in love and she'd said as much to her mother.

When Maddy and Cooper next met, his wife had died. While she would never have wished death on anyone, she couldn't help but feel it was an omen that she was to be Sir Pirate's wife. She would have run off to sea with him if he'd asked but he was too much of a gentleman. Sir Robert, her father, and Uncle Gil had gotten a pardon, signed by the king, for Cooper, so that his past life would not impede their life together. What would happen if he were captured while being a privateer? Dagan and Uncle Jake were right. It was probably best that her father remain in the navy where the Anthony family held a considerable degree of influence. Hopefully, it would not be needed. She was suddenly very determined to support Coop. She would have run off to sea with him as a pirate, a rogue. He'd, at least now, have the blessing of his country…no their country. She was not so flighty a girl not to believe Dagan's words, though. She knew she'd be tested as her mother had been. She thought, like her mother, *damn these politicians, why can't they find a way to get along.*

CHAPTER THREE

THE WEDDING WAS FAR more lavish than anything Cooper could imagine. His first marriage had been aboard the *Raven* and Captain Eli Taylor had performed the ceremony. Cooper understood that with Gabe's status and social standing, this wedding would be nothing like his first one. What he didn't understand, nor was he prepared for, was the island's society. The wedding of a daughter of such a prominent figure was also an event...a great event. The wedding was too large for the Government House and far too large for any of the churches. A large gazebo with an arch had been set up for the rector, bride and groom to stand in. Cooper's best man was Jean Paul de Giraud, and his groomsmen were Jacob Anthony, Doctor Beau Cannington, Dagan Dupree and David MacArthur.

Maddy's matron of honor was Ariel Davy. She was a strikingly beautiful woman who, though several years older, was Maddy's best friend. She was also Dagan's ward and Captain Davy's wife. Cooper couldn't remember all the other bridesmaids' name. He had been introduced to so many people his mind was in a swirl.

All of Vice Admiral Sir Gabriel Anthony's captains and first lieutenants were there, as were Commodore Gardner and his wife, Greta. Lord Anthony and Lady Deborah were also attending, along with their daughter, Macayla, who was on the arm of a plantation owner. Governor Sir Robert Basnight and his wife, Sheila, were there as well.

So many people, yet Cooper felt a void and emptiness; Eli and Debbie were not there. "Son, I've tweaked the British's nose so many times they'd clamp me in irons soon as I came ashore," Eli had said. "No, I'll stay in Savannah. A wedding reception will be planned and given once you've returned."

The wedding ceremony was a blur. Cooper couldn't believe how beautiful his bride looked coming down the aisle. 'Radiant' was the word. He was so caught up in her beauty that he had to be prompted to say I do. He was then told he could kiss the bride.

The reception was at the Government House with Sir Robert graciously opening the doors while Jean Paul and Lord Anthony paid for the reception. After what seemed like an eternity, Maddy and Cooper were placed in a carriage and taken to a cottage on top of a hill that overlooked much of English Harbor. Lady Deborah had whispered to Maddy, "It's where Gil first made love to me."

Maddy was, of course, intrigued and wanted an in depth description of what it was like. She admitted to Deborah that she feared she'd not be able to please Cooper as his first wife had, a woman who'd been taught the art of providing pleasure to a man from a young age. Deborah smiled and said, "Be yourself, Maddy, let your love guide your actions. Cooper isn't concerned about anything but loving you."

THE WIND WAS BRISK with a slight chop to the waves. The sails were full as the small ship, *Ruth*, made her way into the open waters, with Buck Jewell as her captain. He had been the first mate when the ship had arrived in Antigua. A man with years at sea, and who, like Eli Taylor, had spent some years under the black flag. He, also like Eli, had decided to give up the trade before it was too late.

Ruth's captain on the voyage out had been Cooper's good friend, David MacArthur. During their time on the island, Mac had happened on several of his old navy comrades. One, now a captain of a sloop-of-war, needed another first lieutenant, as his present one had become a drunk and was to be put ashore. Mac had asked Vice Admiral Anthony if his offer to return to his commission was still open; it was and Mac had returned to the life that had been taken from him. He had been advised not to mention his involvement with pirates. He was to keep hidden his pardon as a pirate and only produce it if it became necessary. It had been a sad parting for both Cooper and Mac.

"What can I say, Mac...you've taught me so much," Cooper said, trying to overcome the emotions that were building up inside him.

"We had some good times, didn't we?" Mac responded, also trying to put down his emotions.

"Aye," Cooper replied with a smile. "You've been able to put the past behind you and you're back in the navy where you want to be, at least."

Mac smiled and then suddenly his face grew stern. "Give it up, Coop. You're a rich man. You don't need to go back to sea. You could stay here...or go back to America, if you wish, but don't become a pirate."

"Afraid we'll meet?" Cooper asked jokingly.

Mac was not joking though. "Aye, Coop, that's the one thing I do fear. I'd never knowingly fire on you, but I will not be the captain."

Cooper felt a chill. Mac's words were true. Now he had to worry not only about Jake Anthony but Mac as well. What was it Dagan had said, 'Brother shall rise up against brother.' Taking a deep breath, Cooper shook Mac's hand, "Should I see a navy ship, I will do my best to run." As they departed, both men did so with dread. Would they be able to avoid combat with each other?

Newly promoted Captain Buck Jewell approached Cooper. "We've a good ship in, and a good crew, Captain," he said in deference to Cooper having been captain of the pirate ship, *Raven*. "We're making ten knots," Buck continued. "Your friend says that we'll have squalls by tomorrow." By 'your friend', Buck meant Dagan.

Dagan had decided to return with Cooper and Maddy, understanding that it might be the last ship headed to America for some time, or as he still called America, "the Colonies."

Seeing his wife walk out on deck, Cooper excused himself but said, "Dagan is an old salt. I would not disagree with anything he said, Buck."

Walking to his wife, Cooper thought of their wedding night. Candles had been lit and offered a dimly lit path through the cottage to the bedroom. A large canopy bed with the covers turned down and large pillows awaited them. A sheer mosquito net hung over the bed and citronella burned in a small pot giving off a gentle fragrance. Their kiss had been long and passionate. Stepping back from her husband, Maddy had undressed… slowly, watching Cooper's eyes as he stared at her, in awe, anticipation, and longing for this woman…this goddess.

She was removing her last garment and letting it fall to the floor, when she asked Cooper, "Would you still fight a hundred such as that rogue to gain my favor, Sir Pirate?"

"More," Cooper replied, as he took her in his arms and kissed her again.

She pushed Cooper back and began to undo his buttons. "I've wanted you since that night," Maddy whispered. "I've dreamed about it. You slaying those rogues and then taking me."

"You little vixen," Cooper whispered. "I'll take you now." His clothes came off quickly after that. He sat back on the bed and Maddy sat on his lap, her legs straddling him. He kissed her forehead, her eyes, the tip of her nose, her lips and neck, and then her breasts…young, firm, proud breasts, and they were also jutting out. Her nipples hardened as he took first one and then the other between his lips. After a moment, she pushed him back and took him inside her. Their first round of lovemaking was done in frenzy. Her lips were cold as she kissed him as she had become so excited and near breathless. After collapsing in his arms, they slept the contented sleep of lovers, of husband and wife.

They awoke later and made love again. This time, it was a slow deliberate lovemaking. Their hands were touching and feeling each other, while their lips were exploring each other's body. Exhausted, they slept again. At daybreak, they woke up and tended to nature. They then started the new day making love once again. Before they fell asleep in each other's arms, Maddy whispered, "That's the way I want to start each new day." They had, so far.

CHAPTER FOUR

"SAIL HO," THE LOOKOUT called down. Cooper, Dagan, and Maddy were having their breakfast when the cry was heard.

"British warships," Dagan announced, between bites of his toast and preserves.

Maddy looked at her uncle. "You sure?"

Cooper smiled and placed his hand on his wife's hand. "Of course he is, honey. These waters are probably full of warships waiting to pick up a prize since war has been declared."

He had instructed Buck to not run from any British warship. The boom of cannon was heard just as they finished their breakfast. "Not to worry, dear, that was just them telling us to heave to."

Going up on deck, Dagan and Cooper watched as a longboat approached. A young, smartly-dressed lieutenant boarded with his armed boarding party, made up of marines and sailors. The lieutenant walked to the mainmast where Captain Buck Jewell waited. The captain was barely able to contain his anger at being stopped.

"Are you the captain?" the lieutenant asked abruptly.

"Aye," Jewell replied.

"It's my duty, sir, to inform you that war exists between our countries, and your ship is now a lawful prize."

"I'm sorry for your troubles, Lieutenant," Cooper interrupted, "but this is a protected ship. I have letters guaranteeing us safe passage."

"On whose authority?" the lieutenant asked.

"Vice Admiral Sir Gabriel Anthony," Cooper snapped back.

"What ship is that?" Dagan asked, joining the conversation.

The lieutenant looked at Dagan. Gray hair that was almost white, a face burned by years in the sun and crow's feet at the corner of his eyes. This was a man that was used to being obeyed, the lieutenant realized.

"It's *HMS Racer*, sir, thirty-two guns," he replied.

"Captain Hawks, Richard Hawks?" Dagan asked.

"Yes sir," the lieutenant responded.

"You go back and tell your captain that Dagan and Sir Gabe's daughter are taking passage on this ship. That should be enough."

As the lieutenant was rowed back to his ship, Buck approached Cooper. "Get underway, Captain?"

Dagan responded with one word, his eyes never leaving the British ship, "Wait."

In just a few minutes another officer, in addition to the young lieutenant, boarded a ship's boat and was making its way back. "It would be good if you could line your crew up similar to quarters," Dagan recommended.

"Why?" Buck asked.

"To show an element of respect," Cooper answered.

The bosun, an old British seaman, nervously watched as the naval captain climbed up the battens. Ordinarily he'd be concerned, but it seemed the passengers on board had little fear of the British Navy. As the British captain's head came even with the entry port, the bosun piped honors and Captain Jewell called attention to the gathered crew.

"Captain," Richard Hawkes bowed and doffed his hat. Seeing his old friend, his face broke out in a smile as he shook the offered hand. "Dagan, old friend. What a pleasant surprise."

"Aye," Dagan responded. "It's a joy to see you've climbed the ladder, Richard, and a frigate no less."

Hawkes agreed, "Aye, and much due to your tutelage."

"Lieutenant Hinds," Hawkes addressed the young lieutenant. "You're having the pleasure of meeting one of the finest sailors you'll ever meet. He was my mentor and my friend when I was a new midshipman." Dagan shook the lieutenant's hand.

"Would the captain like a bit of refreshment?" Cooper interjected.

"Certainly," Hawkes responded.

Dagan quickly introduced Hawkes to Cooper and Buck Jewell. Cooper led the way to the captain's cabin, which in deference to Cooper and his new bride, Buck had given up.

The gentlemen were entering the cabin when Maddy called out, "Richard!"

"Maddy! Have you been taken hostage by Dagan?"

"Aye," Maddy replied, trying to sound like a sailor and deepening her voice. She then added, "Cooper and I have just been married."

"My congratulations," Hawkes responded. "You know, sir," he said, addressing Cooper, "you've succeeded where most of the young naval officers and islanders have failed."

"Just the young ones?" Maddy asked slyly.

"Some of us not so young officers as well," Hawkes added.

"Pooh," Maddy replied. "I've seen how the ladies look at you on Antigua."

After refreshments had been served and they'd had an enjoyable visit, Hawkes pushed back. "I truly must be going. My first lieutenant will worry I've been taken prisoner." Everyone smiled, and he suddenly became serious. "Do you truly have a letter of protection?" he asked.

Cooper and Dagan both responded, "Aye."

"I'll not ask to see it, but if you didn't I'd write one for you," Hawkes replied.

"Thank you, Richard," Maddy was quick to reply.

Smiling, Hawkes added, "A letter from a mere captain would not carry the weight of a vice admiral, but it'd help with some." Turning his attention to Dagan, he said, "Its bad business, this war. Some will see it as a means to promotion and wealth. I'd not like to see you troubled, old friend, so respond quickly to any warship. If Maddy can't charm your way into free passage, those letters will not have much bearing."

Maddy, who'd been sitting next to Hawkes, leaned over and kissed him on the cheek. "One more, Maddy, and I'll personally escort you to Savannah." Everyone laughed, and after saying their farewells, Hawkes went back down the battens and to his ship.

Buck was getting the ship underway, when Dagan looked at Cooper, "Another one you might have to face broadside to broadside."

"Aye," Cooper replied, not looking forward to such a day.

CHAPTER FIVE

IT HAD BEEN A week since Cooper and his new bride had arrived home. A week that had been so busy it left them exhausted. The first evening was spent dining with Eli and Debbie, and then with Maddy's brother and his wife, Josie. It was supper at Colonel and Mama Lee's house, after that, with Jonah and Moses present as well. Jonah was the Lee's son and Moses was half black and half Indian. He had been almost dead with sickness when the Lee's took him in as a child. Since then he'd been raised as Jonah's brother and a Lee. Jonah and Moses had both kept Maddy laughing so much she confessed to Cooper when they left that she had laughed so hard she almost peed in her pants. This confession caused Cooper to laugh.

In addition to the individual events, a grand celebration was given by John Will and Michael Brett. Several of the state's political figures from the Savannah area were there. One mentioned his support of the privateering venture. Cooper felt Maddy stiffen when the topic was broached. Dagan was still there with them, and he heard the exchange and caught Maddy's reaction. She then looked at Dagan and found he was looking at her…a knowing look it seemed. She managed a faint smile and gave a slight nod.

THE WEEK PASSED AND Cooper now stood next to Eli looking upon *SeaFire…* his ship. It was a damn fine ship, too. Tied up next to

SeaFire was another ship, not quite as large or heavily gunned but a fine ship...a raider.

"She was to have been Mac's," Eli said.

Cooper had told Eli the first chance he had about Mac's decision to return to the Navy. "Damn," was Eli's only response.

On board *SeaFire* were numerous men from *Raven's* crew. All of them welcomed Cooper back and most chided him for not bringing his bride to visit.

"'Fraid she'll see some real men and leave you in dry dock," Banty joked.

"In due time," was Cooper's response.

"We should have our Letter of Marque within the month," Eli informed Cooper. "We'll have the men sign the articles then."

"Articles?" Cooper asked.

"Aye," Eli responded. "Privateer ships have articles for the men to sign. It's a binding contract so each man knows what to expect and what his share will be."

"I see," Cooper said, nodding his head.

"Have you thought who you'd like as your first officer?" Eli asked.

"In truth, I haven't thought that much about it," Cooper admitted. "I've been rather busy."

Eli smiled and punched his young friend. "Aye, that you have, Coop. It's happy I am for you, son."

Eli's use of the term son caused emotions to rise in Cooper. Eli had been as good a friend as any man could expect but he'd also been a father figure to Cooper. This was something that Cooper had never known. Eli had given him an image to emulate, something more than the knowledge of a gambling fool, who not only got himself killed in a duel but left his wife and son penniless and homeless. He was not ungrateful to his Uncle Lawrence, since he had taken in Cooper and his mother. His uncle had also provided him with all the benefits as a son would benefit from. It was Cooper's cousin, Phillip, who had caused Cooper's ouster. It was Phillip who had also done his best to disgrace Cooper and have him shipped off to infamy. Cooper's mother had confided Uncle Lawrence's regrets. Phillip had even taunted the old man with his sodomite friend. Some said it was Phillip's behavior that drove Lawrence to an early death.

Since meeting Eli and becoming a pirate, Cooper had extracted every bit of revenge that he could from his cousin. If a ship was spotted flying the yellow Finylson flag, she'd be taken.

It was these raids on company ships that had allowed Cooper to buy the mortgages on his mother and father's old properties. Now as a privateer, he'd continue this vendetta. He'd see how long Phillip's friends would stay when his wealth was gone.

Eli was speaking and Cooper realized he'd missed his comment. "I'm sorry," Cooper apologized. "My mind was adrift."

Eli smiled and then repeated his comments. Mac had recommended that the ship's crew be set up similar to Navy ships. A first lieutenant would be the first officer, and so on down the crew. "You'd have a master instead of a navigator."

Cooper shook his head, not really caring either way. "Buck Jewell," he said.

Eli repeated the name and said, "What about Buck Jewell?"

"I like him," Cooper responded. "He would be a candidate as a first officer or were you thinking of him to command the other ship?"

"No, we will consider a Frenchman who I've known for years," Eli answered.

"From the sea?" Cooper inquired.

"Aye," Eli responded and then added, "A man I trust. He is in Savannah and I've sent word to him that I have a ship if he's interested."

"Who is this man?" Cooper asked.

"Henri St. Jacques"

"I've met him, I believe," Cooper said.

"You've a good memory," Eli returned. "He was a guest of LaFitte's the night that you proved your abilities with a blade."

Cooper looked at Eli and smiled. He'd been prodded into a fight by a pirate who fancied himself as a swordsman. Little did the pirate know that his foe was a man trained by the greatest master swordsman France had even known. His mistake cost him his life, but made Cooper a man that people suddenly respected. He was not just another young pirate looking for a living. It was the night the crew of the *Raven* started to look upon Cooper as one of their own.

Cooper and Eli started walking up the hill from the waterfront when he asked, "What's the name of the other ship?"

"*Thunderbolt*," Eli replied with a smile.

"Original," Cooper responded, also smiling. "Who owns her?"

"We do."

Cooper stopped and placed his hand on Eli's shoulder. "Who are we?"

"You and I own fifty percent. Colonel Lee, John, and Michael own the other fifty percent," Eli replied.

"I didn't realize that I had enough money for that kind of venture," Cooper said.

"You've forgotten about the slave money," Eli said.

On their trip to Savannah a year ago, they encountered a storm. When it was over, they came upon a floating wreck of a slave ship. They had taken control of it, saved the slaves on board, and towed the damaged ship into port. The slaves had been sold. The ship that had been built as a fast sailor was cleaned, refitted, and armed. It was now the *Thunderbolt*. Cooper had never asked about any monies related to the venture. Eli had purchased a farm next to his and given it to Cooper, so he'd considered that more than ample payment.

"We're partners," Eli said, as they continued up the hill. "Henri St. Jacques is older than you, Coop, so you should trust his judgment. Understand this though– you are the man in charge. You will have the final say so on any matters that arise."

"Will St. Jacques like that?" Cooper asked.

"He will or he'll find another ship," Eli replied matter-of-factly. "You are an owner and he is a hired captain. Don't worry, the three of us will sit down together before anything is agreed upon."

Cooper nodded his head. He had no doubt that Eli Taylor would make sure things were settled before the sails were hoisted.

Letter of Marque

James Madison, PRESIDENT OF THE UNITED STATES OF AMERICA

TO ALL WHO SHALL SEE THESE PRESENTS, GREETINGS:

Be it known, that in pursuance of an act of congress passed on the _twenty-sixth_ day of _June_ one thousand eight hundred and _twelve_

I have commissioned, and do by these presents do commission, the private armed _Brig_ called the _Prince of Neufchatel_ of the burden of

Three hundred and nineteen tons, or thereabouts, owned by _John Ordronaux & Peter E. Trevall_ of this city and

town of _New York and Joseph Bagalle of Philadelphia in the state of Pennsylvania_

mounting _eighteen_ carriage guns, and navigated by _one hundred and twenty-nine_ men, hereby authorizing

Nicholas Millin Captain, and _William Stetson_ Lieutenant of the said _Brig_ and the under officers and crew thereof to

Subdue, seize and take any armed or unarmed British bessel, public or pribate

which shall be found within the jurisdictional limits of the United States or elsewhere, on the high seas, or within the waters of the British dominion, and such captured vessel with her apparel, guns and appurtenances, and the goods or effects which shall be found on board the same, together with all the British persons and others who shall be found acting on board, to bring within some port of the United States; and also to retake any vessel, goods and effects of the people of the United States, which may have been captured by any British armed vessel, in order that proceedings may be had concerning such capture or recapture in due form of law, and as to right and justice shall appertain. The said _John Lawton_ is further

authorized to detain, seize and take all vessels and effects, to whomsoever belonging, which shall be liable thereto according to the law of Nations and the rights of the United States as a power at war, and to bring the same within some port of the United States, in order that due proceedings may be had thereon. This commission to continue in force during the pleasure of the President of the United States for the time being.

GIVEN under my hand and the seal of the United States of America at the city of Washington, the _twenty second_ day of

December in the year of our Lord, one thousand eight hundred and _fourteen_

Independence of the said states the _thirty ninth_.

By the President

JAMES MADISON

JAMES MONROE

Secretary of State

IN CONGRESS,

MAY 2, 1780.

INSTRUCTIONS

TO THE

CAPTAINS AND COMMANDERS

OF PRIVATE ARMED VESSELS

Which shall have COMMISSIONS or LETTERS

of MARQUE and REPRISAL.

I. YOU may by force of arms attack, subdue, and take all ships and other vessels belonging to the crown of Great Britain, or any of the subjects thereof, on the high seas, or between high and low water marks: (except the ships or vessels, together with their cargoes, belonging to any inhabitant or inhabitants of Bermuda, and such other ships and vessels bringing persons with intent to settle and reside within the United States; which you shall suffer to pass unmolested, the commanders thereof permitting a peaceable search, and giving satisfactory information of the contents of the ladings and destination of the voyages *). And you may also annoy the enemy, by all the means in your power, by land as well as by water, taking care not to infringe or violate the laws of nations or the laws of neutrality.

II. You are to pay a sacred regard to the rights of neutral powers, and the usage and custom of civilized nations; and, on no pretence whatever, presume to take or seize any ships or vessels belonging to the subjects of princes or powers in alliance with these United States, except they are employed in carrying contraband goods or soldiers to our enemies; and in such case, you are to conform to the stipulations contained in the treaties, subsisting between such princes or powers and these States. And you are not to capture, seize, or plunder any ships or vessels of our enemies, being under the protection of neutral coasts, nations, or princes, under the pains and penalties expressed in a proclamation, issued by Congress, the ninth day of May, Anno Domini, 1778.

III. You shall bring such ships and vessels as you shall take, with their guns, rigging, tackle, apparel, furniture, and ladings, to some convenient port or ports; that proceedings may thereupon be had, in due form of law, concerning such captures.

IV. You shall send the master or pilot, and one or more principal person or persons of the company of every ship or vessel by you taken, in such ship or vessel, as soon after the capture as may be, to be, by the judge or judges of such court as aforesaid, examined upon oath, and make answer to such interrogatories as may be propounded, touching the interest or property of the ship or vessel and her lading. And, at the same time, you shall deliver, or cause to be delivered, to the judge or judges, all passes, sea-briefs, charter-parties, bills of lading, cockets, letters, and other documents and writings found on board: proving the said papers by the affidavit of yourself, or of some other person present at the capture; to be produced as they were received, without fraud, addition, subduction, or embezzlement.

V. You shall keep and preserve every ship or vessel and cargo by you taken, until they shall by sentence of a court properly authorized, be adjudged lawful prize, or acquitted: not selling, spoiling, wasting, or diminishing the same, or breaking the bulk thereof; nor suffering any such thing to be done.

VI. If you, or any of your officers or crew, shall, in cold blood, kill or maim,—or, by torture or otherwise, cruelly, inhumanly, and contrary to common usage and the practice of civilized nations in war, treat any person or persons surprised in the ship or vessel you shall take,—the offender shall be severely punished.

This exception is taken away by an ordinance of Congress, of March the 27th, 1781, which see.

CHAPTER SIX

THE LETTER OF MARQUE made out to the frigate *SeaFire* was issued and signed by President James Madison and dated the fifteenth of June, 1812. Along with the commission was a list of instructions to captains and commanders of private armed vessels which shall have commissions or Letters of Marque and Reprisal. It gave a long list of you shalls and a few shall nots. Cooper glanced at these but turned them over and picked up what interested him the most...the ship's articles. He started reading these in earnest.

Articles for the Privateer Ship, *SeaFire*

I.   Imprimis, That the said Cooper Cain for himself, and in behalf of the owners of the privateer, shall put on board the said ship, *SeaFire*, a sufficient number of great guns, small arms, powder, shot, and all other necessary warlike stores and ammunition, as also, suitable provisions sufficient for the said *SeaFire* during the whole cruise, which cruise is to be understood to be from the time of the said *SeaFire* sailing from the Port of Savannah, until the time of her returning thither again, for which there shall be no deduction made out of the said company's shares: and in consideration thereof, the owner of the said brigantine or his substitutes, shall have and receive one-half of all prizes, goods, wares, merchandizes, monies, effects, etc. that shall be taken during the cruise, and the other half shall be divided, and paid to the said brigantine's company, by the captain aforesaid, according to the rules hereafter stated.

II.   That the captain shall have and receive, for himself, eight full shares, and shall be granted all privileges and freedoms which have been granted any captains of privateers. That the lieutenants and master, shall each of them have three full shares, that the captain's clerk, mates, steward, prize-master, gunner, boatswain, carpenter, and cooper, shall each of them have and receive two full shares. That the gunner's mate, boatswain's mate, doctor's mate, carpenter's mate, and cooper's mate, shall each of them have and receive one share and a half.

III. That the doctor of the said privateer, or whoever is at the expense of the chest of medicines, shall have and receive the sum of dollars, if well furnished. Also the doctor shall have and receive for himself three full shares, as also all medicines and instruments belonging to any doctor that shall be taken.

IV. That is any person spies a sail, and she proves to be a prize worth one hundred dollars a share, he shall receive an extra fifty dollars. And the first man who enters on boarding a prize in an engagement, and strikes her colors, shall receive half a share for his bravery.

V. That all the rest of the said *SeaFire's* company, such as shall be deemed able and sufficient seamen, shall each of them have and receive one full share, out of the effects, plunder and prizes, that shall or may be taken by the said ship during the cruise, provided, they are not found guilty of the faults or crimes hereafter named.

VI. That as to the proceedings of the vessel, and undertaking any enterprise at sea, or on shore, and into what port any prize shall be carried that shall be taken during the cruise, shall be left entirely to the captain's election.

VII. That all the small plunder, shall be brought to public sale, and be delivered to the highest bidder, for which their shares shall be accountable, excepting the captain's perquisites, which are such as did belong to the captains of prizes, and such clothing as the captain shall think proper to allow the prisoners.

VIII. That if any person belonging to the said ship, *SeaFire*, be killed in an engagement, or die on board, his shares or shares, of all prizes taken in his life-time, shall be paid to his executors, if so appointed by will; but if no will be made, then his part of what was got as aforesaid shall go to his widow, or heirs at law, if claim'd in twelve months, from the time of said ship's arrival into her commission'd port; and on failure thereof, said share or shares shall be and belong to the general interest of the whole.

IX. That if any of the company do disannul any of the officer's commands for the good of the cruise, or the general interest, he or they shall be fined and punished as the captain and officers shall direct. And if any of the company do assault, strike, or insult any male prisoner, or behave rudely or indecently to any female prisoner, he or they shall be punished as the captain and officers shall direct. And if any of the company begin an attack, either by firing a gun, or using any instrument of war, before orders be given, by the proper officers, he or they shall be punished; but if any of the said company do refuse to make an attack on the enemy, either at sea or land, at the command and in the manner ordered by the captain and proper officers, or do behave with cowardice in any engagement, he or them shall forfeit his or their share or shares for such refusal or cowardice; and if any of the company get drunk, or use blasphemous and prophane words, they shall be punished as the captain and officers shall direct: And likewise if any of the company do desert the said ship before her return to Savannah, he or they shall forfeit their whole shares to the owner and company, first paying such ship's debts as are contracted by the captain's knowledge.

X. That whoever of the company shall breed a mutiny or disturbance, or strike his fellow, or shall game with cards or dice for money, or anything of value, or shall sell any strong liquors on board, during the voyage, he or they shall be fined as the captain or officers shall direct. And if any of the company be found pilfering or stealing any money or goods of what kind soever, belonging to the said privateer or company, he or they shall forfeit his or their share or shares of the prize-money or effects then and afterwards taken by the said *SeaFire*, during the whole cruise, to the owner and company.

That if any of the company in an engagement with the enemy, or in the true service of the cruise, shall lose a leg or an arm, or be so disabled as to be deprived of the use of either, every such person shall be allowed out of the effects or prize first taken, (before any division be made) the sum of:

Loss of an eye or joint:Fifty dollars

Loss of an arm or leg: Three hundred dollars

Loss of both eyes, loss of either both arms, both legs, or an arm and a leg: Five hundred dollars

XII. at the price according to public sale: but if there be not so much taken at that time, the vessel and the company shall keep out till they have enough for the purpose; provided no extraordinary accident happens.

XII. That the division of any money or effects taken this cruise, dead shares shall be deducted out of the whole, which shall be divided by the amongst the most deserving and them that does most for the benefit of the cruise.

XII. That any prize or prizes that shall be taken during the cruise, shall be with all speed sent into the Port of Savannah in order that the same may be libeled against in the prize court for condemnation, and to no other place whatsoever, except said prize shall be so disabled that she could not proceed to said port: And any person or persons which shall be aiding or assisting, or shall give his or their consent for sending any prize or prizes, into any other port but the Harbour of Savannah aforesaid, shall forfeit his or their share to the owner and company; and that no division shall be made till they return to the Port of Savannah.

XII. That in case any neutral property, or any property whatever, be taken and sent into port, and after condemnation be had, an appeal should be entered by the claimants, then, and in such case, it shall be lawful with the full consent of the captain and company of the said privateer, for the owner, or his attorney, to compromise, compound, and settle, by giving up any sum or part of the prize, as shall seem most advisable to him for the general interest, that the captain and company may receive each and every one of them their just and lawful right and prize money, and not be kept out of their money until the appeal may be determined in America; and in case no such compromisation can be made, then a certain sum, shall be lodged out of the prizes before taken, to prosecute the said appeal. And it shall likewise be lawful for the owner or agent of the said privateer to discharge any capture that may be made during his said cruise, without the formality of a prosecution, in order that all unnecessary charges may as much as possible be avoided.

XII. That it shall not be lawful for the said officers and company, or either of them, to demand or sue for the prize money so to become due to them, or any part thereof, until fourteen days after the sale of such prize or prizes, the settlement of the accounts relating to the said cruise, and the actual receipt of the money by the agent appointed to manage the affairs of the said cruise.

XII. That if it should happen, that the said ship, SeaFire, by means of any fight, attack, or engagement, be lost, sunk or disabled, so as she may be thereby rendered unfit for any further service as a private vessel of war to cruise, that then, and in such case, the owner of said ship, shall be entitled to take to himself, and for his own sole use and property, any ship or vessel taken during the cruise, with her guns, tackle, furniture, ammunition, and apparel, not exceeding the value of the Seafire at the time of her sailing; which ship or vessel so taken shall be to the owner in lieu of the said brigantine.

XII. That in case of the death of the commander, the next in place shall strictly observe and comply with the rules, orders, restrictions and agreements, between the owner of the said brigantine and the said commander.

Cooper had finished going over the Articles for Privateers. They seemed very straightforward, and yet were not as harsh, in regards to punishment, as the articles aboard *Raven* had been. Death was not mentioned but he thought the phrase, 'punished as the captain and officers shall direct' could be death, flogging, or any other form if so directed. He'd seen one man shot dead by Eli after the rogue had shot at his back. Other than that, a few had been told that once in port their services were no longer needed.

Eli, who had been going over a ledger documenting ship's provisions, now sat back and stretched. Nodding to the articles, he asked, "Is it all to your satisfaction, Coop?"

"Yes, but I've got one question," Cooper replied. "Why do I get eight shares when St. Jacques only gets six shares?"

Eli responded, "You are in overall command. You have more responsibility, more compensation. Did you go over the section about where we have a prize agent should you not be able to make Savannah or Grand Isle?"

Cooper smiled, thinking that Eli never let go. "How could I forget? Cuba and San Juan would be my first choices, but any French or Spanish held island would work in an emergency."

Eli stretched once more and then relit his pipe. "You said you have company tonight?"

"Yes," Cooper answered. "James and Josie, and maybe Jessie."

"Does Maddy know about you and your...ahem...cousins' relationship?" Eli asked.

Smiling as if in thought for a moment, Coop finally answered, "I've felt no need to broach the subject. I could only see it causing harm for all concerned."

"Aye," Eli replied. "Josie does seem devoted to James. I'm surprised Jessie is still unattached. I think she has feelings for Jonah Lee, but I also think he has his mind on someone else.

It's too bad Mac chose to return back to the Navy. He certainly enjoyed her company."

"I believe Henri does as well," Cooper responded.

"St. Jacques?" Eli asked.

Cooper nodded as he glanced at the wall clock in Eli's office. "I better shove off."

Eli walked his young friend to the door. *Damn, I forgot to tell him that we got our commission today,* Eli thought as he watched Cooper ride off. He'd see him tomorrow, that would be time enough. Although some would feel it was too soon, with the commission in hand there'd be no reason to delay sailing. No, tomorrow would be soon enough. Bumping his pipe on the heel of his hand, Eli emptied the bowl of burnt tobacco on the ground. He put it back in his mouth and blew on the stem clearing it. As he did so his wife, Debbie, walked up behind him.

Placing her arms around his waist, she laid her head against his back. "Time is fleeting," she said. She knew her husband was torn between the privateer venture and allowing Cooper time with his new bride. His time with his previous wife had been so short. Had they done the right thing by not telling Cooper that she had been with child at her death? She would follow Eli's lead on that secret. Maddy was so different from Sophia. She was so in love with her "Sir Pirate." But who would not be? Even she, an old woman of forty, could feel her chest heave and her pulse quicken when Cooper came into the room. A young girl like Maddy could not help herself from falling in love with Cooper. He was a very handsome man even with the long white scar on his face. The scar that he'd touch at times, not realizing he was doing so.

Debbie wondered if the scar, a reminder of how cruel and unjustly he'd been treated, would ever let him be at peace. She had seen men look at the scarred face and suddenly become limp with fear. But the women…it caused a different reaction, a desire to touch, to kiss, and to hold this man, who had received a terrible wound, close to them. She'd seen Maddy kiss the scar when Cooper had lain between life and death after the fight with the pirate ship, *Cobra*. That face, the scar, made a woman weak-kneed. Cooper Cain had probably always been able to have his way with women. If he desired, they would flock to him now, yet it was Maddy who had his heart. Sophia had come along at the right time…a time when Cooper needed her. It was only for a season though. She was sure Sophia would never be forgotten, but it was Maddy now. She would take Cooper places that Sophia never could. No, God's plan was not to be questioned. Debbie knew that. She sighed as Cooper was finally lost in the dark, his shadow gone. *God, be with this man who has suffered so,* she prayed.

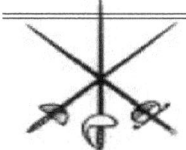

CHAPTER SEVEN

I T WAS A SOLDIER'S wind right off the beam that pushed *SeaFire* and *Thunderbolt* around the tip of Florida, through the Straits of Florida, and past the Florida Keys into the Gulf of Mexico. They had a planned stopover in New Orleans…actually Grand Terre, for a talk with Jean Lafitte, and then through the Gulf of Mexico. They would travel through the Yucatan Channel, with the island of Cuba on the larboard side and the Yucatan Peninsula to the starboard, and under the belly of Cuba to Manzanilla. After those two stops, they were to go in search of prizes.

Cooper's way of thinking was to sail the trade routes from India. He felt that these would be the best hunting grounds. Too many privateers were hitting the routes in the West Indies, and a few were even dashing out from ports in France and Spain. He didn't like the odds there. With England fighting France, the British navy would be out in force. He also wanted to pick an area where the likelihood of having to face Jake Anthony's ship or Mac's would be low. He certainly was reducing the odds by choosing the Indian Ocean.

"Sail ho." Banty was in the tops as was his wont. Cooper turned to his first mate, "Is *Thunderbolt* in sight?"

"Aye, in sight of us," Buck replied. St. Jacques had been sailing to starboard, closer to the coast.

"Can you make her out, Banty?" Cooper shouted.

There was a pause. Cooper was picking up a speaking trumpet, when Banty called down. "She be a brig, a merchant vessel, she 'pears like."

"Clamp on all sail, Buck, let's get a closer look. Ryker, Mr. Ryker," Cooper called. He was still trying to get the formality down.

"Aye, Captain." The young man had his formalities down.

"Signal to *Thunderbolt*, give chase."

"Aye, Captain."

The brig hove to within the first turn of the glass. Seeing two approaching ships that were both well-armed, the captain of the brig knew it was useless to resist. He had eight four-pound cannons which would do no good, and he'd never out sail the approaching ships. He realized, at the last minute, that he'd not run up the colors and did so now.

On board *SeaFire*, Quang got Cooper's attention and pointed to the flag. "American, is she?" Cooper said. He ordered his boat out while a boarding party went down the sides, with Quang taking his place at the tiller.

Thunderbolt hove to just off the brig's stern. "The *Mary Lou*, is she?" his first mate, Spencer said.

"She better be what she claims," St. Jacques replied. "Otherwise, she'll find out what it's like to be sodomized by a broadside of nine pounders."

Cooper recognized the portly captain right away, once he gained access to the deck of the brig. "Captain Fuller," Cooper said, removing his hat and giving a slight bow. He then waved his hat, the signal all was well.

"Captain Cain," Fuller returned Cooper's greeting.

"I apologize for any inconvenience," Cooper said. "Tell me, sir, did you know that a state of war exists?"

Fuller's face grew taut with surprise...and a degree of shock. "No, Captain, I did not. Apparently, neither do the British in Mobile. I dined with the commandant at the fort last night and he didn't bring the subject up. Would you care for a glass, Captain Cain? I think I need one. You've just delivered a jolt to my fortitude."

A glass of tolerable wine was given and Fuller sat down in one of his chairs. "I had planned to stop at Georgetown, Grand Cayman, then Montego Bay, Jamaica, and then home to Savannah."

Cooper downed the glass of wine. "I think that I would bypass Grand Cayman. Unless it is pressing, I'd also forget about Jamaica. I don't know for sure, but I would expect British cruisers are patrolling those areas. They may even by off the Georgia coast by now, but I think that the sooner you head home, the better your chances are."

"Yes, yes you are right, Captain Cain." Realizing there was nothing left to say, both men headed topside. As Cooper made for the entry port, Fuller asked, "Is there any favor, any kindness I can do for you, sir?"

Cooper smiled, "It would be nice if you were able to send word to Eli Taylor that we met and all is well."

"Consider it done, Captain. If we can dodge the British, it's the least I can do," Fuller said.

Once Cooper was back aboard *SeaFire*, Buck Jewell got the ship underway. The sun was starting to set when Johannes, who was formerly the quartermaster on the pirate ship, *Raven*, but was now the master on *SeaFire*, approached his captain. "We'll likely have a shower tonight, but it should be clear when we reach Barataria tomorrow."

"What time would you say that will be?" Cooper asked.

Smiling, the German answered, "In time to enjoy our midday meal."

SEVERAL SHIPS LAY AT anchor when *SeaFire* sailed into Barataria Bay. Quang recognized one right off and pointed her out. "There's Youx's *Tigre*." Buck Jewell didn't quite comprehend the Chinaman's meaning and looked questioningly at Cooper.

Cooper pointed to the ship and said, "That's the *Tigre*. She belongs to a friend, Dominique Youx, spelled Y-O-U-X... Youx." Buck nodded his understanding. Returning to formality Cooper said, "Have the ship put in order, Mr. Jewell, and then allow the men, except for those on anchor watch, a night on Grand Terre. I will call on Mr. LaFitte, and then meet you at the Hotel Mayronne. It's a two-story building set in the middle of the business district. It's both a hotel and a restaurant. Should you care to spend the night ashore, then that's where you should stay. They have clean rooms and comfortable beds. The restaurant has the island's only chef, but that's for the evening meals. You'll not find the common sailor there so expect to pay for the room. I'll advance you the money if needed."

Buck declined the offer of money, but decided after the ship was put to his satisfaction, he'd clean up and put on a better, cleaner uniform. He'd not want to embarrass the captain.

LaFitte's house was a two-story affair made of brick and painted white. As Cooper walked up to the house, memories of his first meeting with these men came flooding back, Jean LaFitte, his brother, Pierce; Dominque Youx, Louis, No Nose Chighizola, and Vincent Gambi. Of these men, Gambi was the only one Cooper didn't like. Eli Taylor had described Gambi as the devil himself. In addition to the hotel, the brothel and stores for clothing, and a ship chandler, there were a few food stalls that had opened where sailors could grab a fast bite to eat and a tankard. The slave barracoons were still there.

At LaFitte's house, he was disappointed to learn Jean was in New Orleans having flyers printed up for a sale. He'd left that morning so he was not expected back for a few days. Retracing his steps, Cooper stopped at Hotel Mayronne.

He turned to Quang, who had accompanied his captain. "Round up a pirogue or two for us and see if Spurlock, Diamond, and Banty would like a trip to New Orleans." Cooper gave Quang a key and said, "Open my desk and bring the small chest back with you."

The chest was two feet long, eighteen inches wide and just as deep. It was full of gold coin. Cooper was to place it in Eli's bank in New Orleans if LaFitte was not at Grand Terre. Had LaFitte had been at home, he would have taken the chest, give Cooper a receipt and made the deposit. He would have been paid a token fee of one hundred dollars. Eli swore a man could always trust LaFitte, but it didn't hurt to get a receipt and pay the man for his troubles.

When Cooper asked why he wanted the money placed in the New Orleans bank, Eli replied, "Never put all your eggs in one basket, son. I thought I'd taught you that."

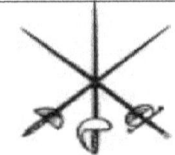

CHAPTER EIGHT

THE TRIP INTO NEW Orleans was one where you didn't rush. Gators, cottonmouth moccasins, rattlesnakes, rodents, and any number of other animals were just waiting for someone to make a mistake. There were also the undertows and quicksand hidden by the murky waters. Lying at the edge of a small island, which the locals called a chenier, a big alligator lay sunning himself.

Banty nudged Ryker and pointed it out. "Big 'un, must be fourteen feet long," Banty quipped. "Swallow you whole, I'll bet."

"No, he'd have to bite you in half first," Spurlock said.

Quang smiled, "Scare him good. Make him think careful." The big Chinaman hardly ever got his sentences right. Their meaning was fully understood, though.

"Round the next bend," Spurlock called. Cooper nodded his response.

The dark of night came quick on the bayou. The tops of trees cast huge shadows that were made worse by gray low-hanging moss. You didn't want to spend the night on the bayou in a narrow pirogue if you could help it. Around the long bend up ahead was the first of the cheniers used as a campsite. Another chenier was further up at the halfway point to New Orleans. Getting a late start on the trip made it necessary for them to take the first campsite.

THE ARRIVAL IN NEW Orleans had the same effect on young Ryker as it had made on Cooper and Mac their first time visiting the city. Thinking about it, Cooper felt his chest heave as he realized how much he missed his Scottish friend. Tying up at the wharf, Banty ran ahead to get a Negro with a wheelbarrow. Cooper took the lead once the chest had been placed in the wheelbarrow. The men stood on each side while one followed behind, forming a guarded escort.

The Bank of New Orleans was a tall three-story building on Saint Phillip Street. As Spurlock and Diamond lifted the chest, Cooper gave the Negro porter five dollars. The porter had only expected fifty cents or a dollar at most. With five dollars, the boy yanked the wheelbarrow and ran down the street, possibly thinking that Cooper hadn't realized how much he'd given him and would want some back.

Once in the bank, followed by Spurlock and Diamond, Cooper asked a clerk to see if Mr. Latrobe was in. The clerk seemed about to ask a question, maybe if Cooper had an appointment, when his eyes fell on the chest. "May I ask who's calling, sir?" He thought the man in front of him didn't look as old as he was.

"Captain Cooper Cain, with some business on behalf of Captain Eli Taylor," Cooper replied. The clerk knew that name.

Mr. Latrobe came at once. "Nice to see you again, Mr…er… Captain Cain."

Once in Latrobe's office, Spurlock and Diamond stepped outside and blocked the door from further entry. Walking to a side door, Latrobe called to a lady and asked her to have the senior teller present to his office. When the man entered, he was quickly ordered to open the chest and count its contents. This took the better part of an hour to do as the banker made him count it twice. The total came to twenty-five thousand dollars. Once the figure was given, Cooper opened his coat and took out an envelope, opened it and took out a single sheet of paper with a figure written on it…twenty-five thousand dollars.

"It seems that we are in agreement," Latrobe said. He then wrote a receipt made out to Eli Taylor. As the business was finished, Latrobe coughed. "While you are here, Captain Cain, may I speak to you on a personal matter?"

"Certainly, sir," Cooper responded.

"The sum of ten thousand dollars has been placed on deposit for you, sir."

"By whom?" Cooper asked.

Pausing for a moment, Latrobe searched for the right words. "Ahem…M'sieur Henri d'Arcy, Captain. His words were, forgive me, sir," Latrobe paused again and then swallowed, "M'sieur d'Arcy said it was for payment for your property which his son destroyed."

Cooper's face turned red and his knuckles white as they grasped the hilt of his sword. "Please sir," Latrobe whined as he backed into his desk.

Seeing the frightened man, Cooper got a hold on his emotions, "Forgive me, sir. I realize you are only the messenger." He turned and opened the door to leave, then stopped. Looking back at Latrobe, he growled, "Sophia was not my property, sir, she was my wife." With that, Cooper headed out of the bank, followed by his men. He gave each of them a twenty dollar gold piece telling them to meet him at the Hotel Provincial later. Cooper still had to go to lawyer Meek's office before the end of day. "Don't get Mr. Ryker drunk," Cooper warned.

THE SUN ROSE FROM the far distant edge of the sea. A mist hung over Barataria Bay as *Thunderbolt* and *SeaFire* made their way out of the harbor, making for the open sea. While the crews of the two ships went about their duties in a professional manner, more than one suffered from their last night on shore. There were more than a few nursed headaches and dyspepsia related to strong spirits and Creole food, most of which carried a spicy wallop. Ryker Hall was the officer of the watch on board *SeaFire*. Johannes had taken a liking to the young third officer. He stood close by dropping whispered hints as *SeaFire* got underway. Johannes could remember when not too long ago it was the captain benefiting from hints as he took *Raven* to sea.

As the ship glided out and over the gentle swells, running down the occasional white cap, the sea turned to a darker blue. A porpoise surfaced along the larboard side amidship. Several other porpoises soon surfaced until an entire school of the creatures seemed to be guiding the ship out into the Gulf of Mexico.

The captain was in conversation with Mr. Jewell, the first officer. Johannes thought that it was most likely about the poque game where Mr. Jewell met the beautiful young widow, Mary Esther. He had heard the captain say, "Buck, your attention to the game was lost from the moment you met that woman. You bid poorly, folded when you should have stayed and played very poorly."

"How do you know, Captain?" Jewell asked.

"I was standing behind you most of the last few hands," Cooper retorted. "Mrs. Meeks was also."

In fact, Carolyn Meeks, who had hosted the poque game and invited Cooper and his first officer, had said much the same thing. "I'm afraid, Coop, your Mr. Jewell has lost all interest in cards and has all his attention on Edward's niece."

Cooper and Carolyn Meeks had met when he first arrived in New Orleans and had realized that they were each very good at the cards. Being partners, they had lightened the purses of several of the city's most prominent men and a few of the wealthy plantation owners. Cooper had visited the lawyer, Edward Meeks, after leaving the bank. He had setup a charity with the ten thousand dollars D'Arcy had returned for the purchase of Sophia. The charity was for orphans, regardless of color, so that they could obtain funds to get an education.

He had been pleasantly surprised when Carolyn had been at her husband's office. He could not turn down her invitation for whist and poque when she related they could add their winnings to the charity fund. There was no thought of losing, perhaps a hand or two, but not the entire game. Carolyn had sweetened the offer by encouraging some of the players to donate their winnings once a month.

Cooper had stayed at the Hotel Provincial. Mademoiselle Renee greeted him with true delight, while he was sipping on rum punch in the courtyard with Otis. Otis was a former slave, who with Cooper joined the pirate ship, *Raven*, rather than continue life as a servant. Recognizing the black man's education and ability, he had been placed under Debbie Russell to help run the hotel. Since Debbie had married Captain Taylor and moved, Otis had run the hotel. It appeared he was doing a very good job.

Cooper had also run up with Jean LaFitte while in New Orleans. A deal had been struck where LaFitte would act as agent for any prize ship that made it to Grand Terre. However, LaFitte warned about an ever-increasing number of British warships.

Young Ryker had been taken under Spurlock and Diamond's wing and had been shown the Crescent City. He'd dined on a muffaletta, and eaten the finest meals Hotel Provincial could prepare. He had accompanied Cooper when they visited Cindy Veigh at her plantation one afternoon. They were stuffed by Cindy's cook, Belle. The noon meal had consisted of soup, fried catfish, sweet potatoes sliced thin and fried, cold lemonade, and to Ryker's delight, beignets. After a few hours, Cooper made ready to leave. In doing so, he realized that it saddened him. He loved these people. As they departed, Gus gave him a box of cigars that had been soaked in cognac. Placing the cigars on sticks to dry, they developed a crook; therefore, Gus had named them cognac crooks. The cigar factory in New Orleans bought and sold every cigar Gus could make.

Young Ryker confided, as they headed back to the ship, that he'd had the time of his life and couldn't wait to return to New Orleans and see the rest of the sights. *Just what sights does he mean,* Cooper wondered as he passed a vibrant looking mulatto.

CHAPTER NINE

S*EA*F*IRE* AND *THUNDERBOLT* LAY at anchor just off Praia Santiago, Cape Verde. Santiago was the largest of the Cape Verde islands. It was the first of the Verde islands to be settled; though legend has it that Captain Kidd buried treasure on its neighboring island Maio. Johannes said Maio looked like a beached whale. Cooper had never seen a beached whale so he took the master's word for it. However, Santiago had been an important slave trading post and while drought was always a concern, the island had everything the two ships needed.

The Verde Islands lay west to the northern portion of Africa. They were in a position where the British convoys had to pass, both outward bound and on the return voyage. The convoys would be laden with rich cargoes going or coming, but the returning ships would carry the richer loads. The dozen or so shacks that made up the village were huddled up close together. Fishing nets were often stretched between the shacks. A drunken sailor had to pay close attention or find himself arsehole over tea kettle in the nets. Several boats sat in the shallows. If they had been pulled ashore the sun would dry them out and render them useless.

The men on board *SeaFire* and *Thunderbolt* lounged about trying to find shade where they could. Lookouts in the mainmast tops were changed every two hours. One outbound convoy had been spotted the day after they dropped anchor, but they had let it pass. The ships were small and the take would have been minimal. That had gotten the men's spirits up, but that had been a week ago.

Since leaving Barataria Bay and New Orleans, Buck Jewell had done nothing but talk of the beautiful widow woman, Mary Esther. She was indeed beautiful as was her little girl Ava Katelyn. You didn't get far in a conversation with Buck without something reminding him of something that had been said or what they'd seen together. After meeting Mary, Buck had spent as much time as possible with her. Cooper had even delayed sailing for a couple of days so that they could ride out to her plantation for a visit. It was a beautiful place but one that was showing signs of neglect. There were things a man would think about repairing but a woman might overlook them. As tactfully as he could, Cooper mentioned Gus at Cindy Veigh's place. He felt Gus could surely recommend someone trustworthy to act as overseer for Mary. She seemed most appreciative for this infor-mation. When they could delay no longer, Buck promised they'd be back. This seemed to please Mary. Little Ava Katelyn even gave Buck a big hug. Cooper hoped luck would be on their side and that Buck would see Mary sooner, rather than later.

"Sail ho! Sail ho, to the east." The cry brought the ship to life immediately. After a moment, the lookout called down again, "Several sails, Cap'n. It be a convoy."

Cooper grabbed a glass and hurried up the shrouds. Yes, by the saints, it was a convoy. Taking the glass from his eye, Cooper called up to the lookout, "Do you see any escorts?"

The lookout scanned the convoy for several seconds, before he replied, knowing that his captain preferred an accurate report over a hurried one "Aye, Cap'n. Reckon there's two bombay buccaneers." He followed that with, "Small they be."

Cooper couldn't help but smile. The term bombay buccaneer was a term the British navy bestowed on the East Indiamen's navy. Officially, the bombay marines. It was the company's private navy. The company owned a few heavy frigates of fifty guns or more but most of its force was made up of a few small frigates, brigs, sloops, and smaller. A small frigate of twenty-two guns or more would prove to be an able opponent and was to be avoided if at all possible. He wasn't in the business to fight if he could help it. There would be little profit in that. Profit…that was what it was all about. Profit and helping the Americans win the war. The ships should be even with the island in the next hour. The sea breeze that had died down, around the noon hour, was picking up now. The flag now stood out with the breeze blowing. The yellow rattlesnake flag with the words, 'don't tread on me' was first used in the American Revolutionary War. Due to the British Navy's impressing sailors of American ships, Eli Taylor had resurrected the flag for his group of privateers. It was also to be used in ways to conduct a private code between ships.

Reaching the deck, Cooper placed his glass in a rack on the binnacle. "Mr. Jewell," Cooper called. "Up anchor, prepare to make sail."

"Aye," Jewell acknowledged, and then shouted, "Hands to the capstan."

Diamond was quick to get his men in place. "Ready there," he yelled through cupped hands, "heave away. Damnation Patrick, heave. You couldn't pull a sick whore off a piss pot." This caused several men to laugh at their friend's expense.

The stomping of feet on the deck planking and the steady clicking of the capstan pawls was now almost drowned out by Leon as he took up his fiddle and played a chanty. Leon, the new fiddler, was a mulatto whose plantation father had died and his wife had sent the boy packing as a freed slave. She didn't want to be reminded of her husband's infidelities with a slave woman, Otis had said. He then added, "He's not much good at anything but playing his fiddle. I thought I could dress him up and let him play soothing tunes while the guests dined in the evening but that didn't work out." Cooper had taken the fourteen-year-old boy to sea with him. Leon had been a hit with the crew. He'd done much to keep the men entertained. Banty had taken him under his wing, which caused Cooper to wonder if that was a good thing. It had worked out so far, however.

"One more pawl," Cooper heard Diamond bellow, followed by "anchors aweigh."

Mr. Jewell cupped his hand and ordered, "Make sail, aloft with you sail handlers. Lie out and loosen, stand by. Let fall!" The topsail fell and immediately caught the wind. The orders came like fluid off the first officer's tongue at just the right moment as he watched the sail handlers. He'd gotten the ship underway enough to know the evolutions and orders but Coop realized he would never be like Buck Jewell, a real seaman.

"Up forward," Diamond, the bosun, shouted. "Cat the anchor, pass the ring stopper." *He was another professional seaman,* Cooper thought.

The movement of the ship broke Cooper's reverie. He turned to Johannes Ewers, the big German master. "Set a course to intercept that convoy please, Mr. Ewers."

Johannes removed the huge smoking pipe from his mouth and spoke to his helmsman. Mr. Jewell continued getting more sail aloft and *SeaFire* picked up speed so that you could hear water sloshing down each side of the hull as the bow pushed through the waters.

"Any sign the convoy has spotted us yet?" Cooper called up to the lookout.

"No sir," the reply came back.

Hopefully, the larger of the escorts would be past them before they were noted. Across the way, Henri St. Jacques had

Thunderbolt moving along in *SeaFire's* wake. St. Jacques had met with Cooper and Eli at the River Inn in Savannah. Eli had assured Cooper that the Frenchman was a most capable captain and Cooper had no reason to doubt Eli's word. St. Jacques had stood when Eli and Cooper had entered the room and gave them a firm handshake. It didn't take Cooper long to realize he liked the man. When he mentioned his mother was married to Jean Paul dé Giraud, St. Jacques stood with his glass in salute, "To the finest swordsman in all of France, perhaps in the entire world."

When discussing tactics and private signals, the man was readily agreeable and made a few suggestions of his own that made sense and eased things in regards to signals. Now those signals might be put to the test.

CHAPTER TEN

The lookout kept his telescope trained on the convoy, looking for any signs that they'd been spotted as *SeaFire* and *Thunderbolt* left the anchorage. Cooper had used the anchorage in the past when looting slave ships out of Africa.

Johannes took a step toward his captain. "She's a lady, Captain, a fine lady." Leave it to the master to think of something positive to say about the ship.

She was a fine ship and so was the woman who came up with the name. Would he ever forget Sophia, probably not? She had been his first love…real love. A man didn't forget his first love. She was gone, but now there was Maddy; two women from two totally different worlds. He loved them both. He wondered how Maddy was handling his being away. She had James, her brother, and Josie and Jessie. They would be friends with Maddy. Debbie, Eli's wife, would be a mother figure.

"Course set, Captain," this came from Johannes.

Damn, my mind has been adrift, Cooper realized. He looked at the first mate. Buck was still giving orders. If his mind was on the beautiful Mary Esther, he wasn't letting it interfere with his ship handling. "Mr. Spurlock."

"Aye."

"Clear for action please, and load the guns on both sides but don't run them out. Put your best men on the bow chasers."

"Aye, Captain, that'll be me and Skeeter."

Skeeter was another new hand. He was obviously a deserter from the British navy. The smallish man had tattoos all over his body and was said to even have one on the head of his manhood. Cooper took his word for that. The gunner had proved himself in gun drill and had bested everyone except Spurlock, after whom he was a close second.

Glancing about, Cooper saw Beau Cannington going below deck. He had picked out two helpers in Savannah. Surgeon's mates were how they were listed on the books. One of the mates had an old sailcloth bundled under his arm while the other was carrying some lanterns. They might need the extra light if anyone was wounded but Cooper hoped that they'd not be needed.

Buck Jewell had some of the ship's boys scattering sand across the deck so men would not slip should blood be spilled. The other two ship's boys were bringing powder from the magazine. Spurlock termed them powder monkeys. On the old *Raven*, pirates had been given the task. Tubs had been placed between the guns and filled with a mixture of water and vinegar so that wet blankets could be used for sponging out the guns after being shot. Cooper hoped that they'd not need to fire anything other than the bow chasers and maybe a swivel.

"'Pears we got the weather gage on the Honest John's," Jewell volunteered as he approached Cooper.

At the same time, the lookout called down, "They've spotted us, Cap'n. Signal flags are going up and down."

"Took 'em long enough," Johannes said. "I'd flog the whoreson they got aloft."

The first officer, Jewell, approached and advised, "Ship is clear for action." Jewell, not unlike Cooper, was having some initial problems getting the formalities of a fighting ship down. In fact, Cooper had seen Spurlock whisper to him before he reported.

Cooper knew that Jewell would learn his duties as a privateer's first officer in time, but he was already one fine seaman.

Taking a glass from its rack, Cooper climbed up the shrouds several feet. Standing on the ratline, he looped his arm around the shroud to steady himself. It now appeared the convoy was stretched out nearly a mile and the two escorts had shown no action in regards to coming about to meet any threat.

Speaking so that those around the quarterdeck could hear, Cooper said, "I think we can intercept the last quarter of the convoy. We will cross the big Indiaman's bows. He'll veer, causing confusion and we'll be among them. Mr. Ryker!"

"Aye, Captain."

"Signal *Thunderbolt* to fall in line. I also want you to send up the signal for 'independent action' when I give the word."

"Yes sir." The young third officer bounded away. A single flag meaning 'independent action' had been one of Henri St. Jacques' ideas. It was simple and to the point.

SeaFire and *Thunderbolt* were now overreaching the tail end of the convoy. "Wonder what those sods are thinking," Banty said to Ox.

Ox took a step toward the ship's rail and spit what appeared to be a quart of tobacco juice over the side. Wiping his mouth with the back of his hand and then wiping it on his britches, Ox answered, "Reckon it don't matter what they be thinking now. It's later when we's board 'em is what matters. Hope we don't have to kill more'n a few."

They were now approaching the big Indiaman that Cooper planned to cross over her bow. He had counted twelve gunports, but she'd carry twenty-four guns plus swivels and smaller arms. Eli had taught him while these big ships often carried enough guns and crew to produce 'one more horrendous broadside' they frequently sailed *en flute*. With the guns dismounted more cargo could be carried. "How can you tell?" Cooper had asked. "Watch the gunports," Eli had advised. "If they bang open get down, if not the ship will likely be your prize."

Cooper watched the big ship through his glass. "Take the glass," Cooper said as he stepped toward the helm. Banty took the glass and replaced it in its rack. "Get ready," Cooper hissed to Johannes. "Mr. Spurlock, run out and be ready with the larboard side guns."

"Aye, Cap'n."

Cooper watched. They were directly alongside the Indiaman. Her gunports still remained closed, but seeing *SeaFire's* gunports open there was increased activity. *SeaFire* now surged ahead, moving like a racehorse compared to the Indiaman. Cooper watched, if he cut it too close the big ship would crash into *SeaFire*; too late and she'd not try to avoid collision.

"*Thunderbolt* is upon her now, Cap'n," the lookout called down.

"Any movement on the escort?" Cooper shouted.

"Nay, Cap'n, they still be on course."

"Too late now," Johannes volunteered.

Cooper noticed a shadow over him; it was Quang. The big Chinaman seemed to always be at hand at time like this. Cooper watched aft as *Thunderbolt* was now past the Indiaman. He looked and counted in his head. "Now, Mr. Ewers, cross her."

Johannes spoke to his helmsman and suddenly the wheel spun.

"Fire a bow chaser, Mr. Spurlock."

The big gunner raised his arm and then dropped it. The larboard bow chaser banged out just before the rudder bit and the deck canted as *SeaFire* made its turn. The crew was expecting the maneuver, but someone dropped a marlinspike and it banged to the deck and rattled its way across and into the scuppers. Directly aft, *Thunderbolt* followed her leader.

"Mr. Ryker, as soon as you are able, send up the signal," Cooper bellowed.

The young man was holding on but turned loose with one arm and gave a quick wave.

"She's doing it, Captain," Jewell swore. "She's veering to larboard."

The Indiaman's action caused mass confusion for the ships behind her. Ryker sent up his signal as *SeaFire* made its turn and the deck was steady. *Thunderbolt* came about and went along the next ship behind the Indiaman. A bow chaser barked and then grapnel hooks flew through the air and a dozen men went aboard. The British flag came down and cheering rang out.

"Lay us alongside that big girl," Cooper ordered Johannes. "Mr. Jewell," Cooper called, "take your boarding party and take possession of yonder ship. You know the signal for treachery."

"Aye, Captain, a fist pump," Mr. Jewell replied. Cooper nodded.

Johannes quickly brought *SeaFire* alongside the Indiaman and immediately Jewell was boarding their prize. McKemie and Ox went with the first officer's boarding party, providing the experience that Jewell was lacking.

Lamar Turner, who was the grandson to *Raven's* old quartermaster, was the second officer. "Get your party ready, Mr. Turner," Cooper ordered. "We are approaching our next prize." The second officer acknowledged his captain and called for his men. Johnson, one of *Raven's* old crew, would be going over with Turner. Weber, an old hand, was also at the rail. It was Johnson who shouted, "Now," as *SeaFire's* hull came close to her new foe. The men went over quickly. A pistol shot was heard and then another.

Cooper was about to board the ship when Turner ran to the rail and saluted, the signal that all was well. The next in line was a smaller ship. "Mr. Ryker, you may board this one," Cooper said, looking at Diamond. The bosun would actually be in charge of the party, but giving the young third officer the experience was essential.

"*Thunderbolt* has come about," the lookout called down. That meant he had taken all the prizes he had men to safely take.

Cooper would take the one he was coming alongside of and hopefully one more. Taking a glance, the convoy continued to sail along. Their captains were glad that they'd not been as unfortunate as the ones taken.

"Ready," Diamond shouted to his men. "Away," the bosun shouted as he and young Ryker took a party of eight men across to their prize.

"Look, Captain," Johannes called in an excited voice.

The last ship in line was nearly as big as the lead ship. The gunports opened up and out rumbled her guns.

"Nine pounders, they look," Spurlock advised.

"Fire the bow chasers, Mr. Spurlock."

The big gunner repeated his earlier maneuver and first one and then the other bow chasers went off. The sails came off their foe but instead of heaving to, the ship presented her broadside and let go with a ragged broadside. Cooper had shouted 'down' and men hit the deck. Ragged the broadside may have been and several shot were ill aimed but several did find their target. *SeaFire* shuddered as the balls struck. One tore the railing away by the entry port. One ball hit the top of the bulwark forward, gouged the deck planking and struck into the forward mast. Most of the energy was gone, but it still made an indention.

"Give her a broadside, Mr. Spurlock."

"Aye, Captain."

Without being told, Johannes ordered his helmsmen, "Put the wheel down."

As *SeaFire* swung around, Spurlock had his guns aimed and fired each gun, as it came to bear, with the gunners quickly reloading. The guns aimed at the enemies' gunports, blasting their cannons and crews to hell. On deck, the swivel guns were loaded with grape and the enemies' decks were blasted clean of everyone that they could see. The British flag came down and a white flag went up after a second broadside.

"We got the wench," Skeeter said to his mates at the bow chasers.

"Aye," Darby replied, "the Cap'n don't take kindly to being fired on."

CHAPTER ELEVEN

THE CAPTAIN OF THE prize stood by the quarterdeck. He had a bloody bandage on his arm. As the boarders filed onto the deck, they could see numerous bodies lay strewn about. One of the ship's crew spat at Darby, one of *SeaFire's* boarding party. Darby responded by slamming the hilt of his cutlass into the man's jaw, knocking him to the deck.

Cooper called out to the captain, "Have your men lay down their arms. One more stupid act like what just happened and I may not be able to control my men." The captain nodded and called for the men to put down all their weapons.

One of the passengers rang out, "Be damned if I will give up my pistol."

Using one of Eli Taylor's phrases, Cooper snarled, "I'd be obliged to you, Captain, if you'd keep your passengers under control, sir. There's been enough death already."

The captain took a deep breath and let go a sigh. "Alas, Captain, I'm only the ship's captain. That man is the owner's son." The words were spoken in a manner to let Cooper know the captain had no authority over the passengers. He had spoken in a low tone so that his words would not carry.

Cooper gave a slight nod and then spoke to the ship's captain and those gathered around in a loud voice, "There exists between our countries a state of war. I am Captain of the United States privateer ship, *SeaFire*. My name is Captain Cooper Cain.

I have a lawful commission from our government, a Letter of Marque. This ship and its cargoes are now my prize."

"Humph...still a bloody pirate in my book," the young man, who'd spoken out earlier, snarled.

Spurlock took a step toward the man but Cooper lifted his hand and walked over to the mouthy sod. The man took a step back as Cooper advanced, almost to a point where he was standing behind a mature gentleman, who was graying at the temples. Fear gripped the young man and beads of sweat broke out on his forehead and face.

Cooper reached out grabbed the front of the sod's lacy shirt and jerked him toward himself with one hand and with his other hand he roughly jerked a pistol from the sod's sash. Cooper tossed the weapon to Spurlock. He then shocked those gathered around him as he gave a backhanded slap, bursting mouthy's lips and knocking the man to the deck.

"I'm Jonathan's father," the graying man volunteered as he took a step forward. "You've no reason to treat my son so."

"I have every reason," Cooper retorted. "It's my job to prevent any harm to your people and he was jeopardizing control. If you will give your word to keep Jonathan under control, I'll not put him in shackles. Otherwise..."

The man nodded. "I'm Merriweather Woodham. We have ladies aboard this ship." The name Woodham was not unknown to Cooper.

A lady...a 'young lady' the twins' age, stepped out of the group. "It's been awhile, Coop!"

"Kate!" Cooper called and embraced the girl as she did him.

"It's been a long time since London," the girl said. "Josie and Jessie told me how you'd been abused by Sir Lawrence and Phillip. I have missed you."

Memories flooded back to when Cooper, Josie, and Jessie had partied away with Kathleen (Kate). She was as much a looker as the twins, and had tempted Cooper many times but never letting it go any further than touching and kissing. Cooper remembered telling Kate, "You bring a man's humors to a boil and then will not allow them to be doused in a proper manner." The twinkle in the girl's eyes and the stance let him know that she remembered those days as well.

"My God, sir," Kate's father spoke out. "Are you an Englishman?"

Kate answered her father's question for Cooper. She stepped forward and touched the scar on his face. "He was until he was abused so wrongly."

"Humph..." Woodham snarled, demonstrating his lack of concern as to Cooper's treatment. "A man has a duty to his country."

"I agree," Cooper said. "The United States is my country."

"Humph..." this time it was the son, Jonathan, snarling. "Englishman! He's nothing but a rogue...a pirate." Cooper's glare made the boy take a step back again, cowed by Cooper's menacing look.

"Be damn glad that I'm not a pirate, boy. If I were, your innards would be spilled across the deck for you insolence." Cooper then turned back to the father. "Because of Kate, I'd thought that I would let you keep your ship. Don't tempt me to change my mind." He then addressed the passengers as a group. "Ladies, I will let you go down one at a time and pack any personal belongings you have in your cabin. One of my men will accompany you and he will bring your chest on deck. This chest will not be touched." He then called, "Mr. Spurlock."

"Aye, Captain."

"Deploy your experienced men to search the ship except for the ladies cabins. Darby can escort each lady down one at a time. You have control of the deck until I return, Mr. Spurlock."

Cooper then turned to Kate, "I will escort you myself, dear lady." Kate gave a curtsey and turned to go down the companionway.

Cooper was headed down when he heard Spurlock say, "Turn yourself around, mate. Nobody told you to move…and I'll warn you, I'm not such a gentleman as my captain."

Once in Kate's cabin, Cooper sat on her cot. "Tell me how you have been doing." The next half hour was like old times, two friends reminiscing about significant events. He told Kate about Sophia, how he lost her to an old suitor. He was careful not to mention her background. He also told her of his marriage to Maddy.

"The daughter of a British admiral and granddaughter to a British lord, I'll bet you're the proverbial black sheep of the family," Kate responded.

Cooper had just told Kate about the twins, when there was a knock on the cabin door. "Winds are getting up, Captain."

"Very well," Cooper replied.

"I guess that I should pack up something," Kate said.

"No," Cooper answered. "You will stay aboard the ship and nothing will be touched."

Kate smiled and then reached into a box and brought out a necklace of diamonds and sapphires. "You don't even want these?"

Cooper swatted Kate on the rump, "No, you little vixen."

Smiling, Kate kissed Cooper and said, "Wait a minute." She quickly took a piece of paper and dipping a quill in an ink bottle, she wrote a hasty note. She blew the ink dry and gave it a wave through the air to make sure it was completely dry and would not smear. She folded the necklace and laid it in a small box. She folded the note several times and then placed it in the box with the necklace. "A wedding present for your wife."

"I couldn't, Kate," Cooper protested.

"Relax, Coop. It is insured. Father will just claim some rogue stole it."

Cooper smiled and kissed Kate on the forehead. She looked up at her friend, wiped a tear from her eye and whispered, "I'd always planned on you being the first man I gave myself to, Coop. That damnable Phillip messed that up."

Cooper smiled, "I've found myself thinking 'what if' a few times also."

"Go with God, Cooper," Kate said.

"You as well, Kate," Cooper responded.

When they arrived back on deck, Woodham snorted, "Damn you, sir, taking my daughter below without the decency of even her maid."

Cooper was about to blast the man but Kate spoke up first, "Relax, Father, Cooper was the perfect gentleman. My honor is intact." Woodham was still flustered but his daughter's words kept him quiet.

"Captain," Cooper called to the ship's captain.

"Aye, Captain Cain."

"Do I have your word that you will follow us to our rendezvous where upon the morrow you shall be given your ship?" For Woodham's sake then, Cooper added, "If this is not acceptable, I will put a prize crew aboard her and cast you adrift in long boats."

A wry little smile came across when Cooper winked at the captain, "Aye, Captain Cain, I'm sure that neither the owners nor the other passengers would care to find themselves in such.

We all give our word, don't we?" This the captain said, looking directly at Woodham.

"Aye, you have my word. But, were it not for the passengers…," Woodham said.

Cooper smiled now; he'd allow the man a little bravado to save face with his son, daughter, and other passengers.

Spurlock had not been idle. He had not missed what the Captain said in regards to allowing the Brits to keep the ship. He had kept *SeaFire's* boats busy, taking off plunder.

Once they got back on their ship, Cooper called, "Spurlock, Mr. Jewell, and Mr. Ewers, I want you to see this so you can be my witnesses. This necklace was given to my wife by Lady Katherine Woodham as a wedding present. Here is her note to go with it."

The note said, 'to Maddy Anthony Cain, a wedding gift. Be glad you got him before I got the chance. You are a lucky woman.' The men all acknowledged the gift. "You going to let Maddy see the note, Captain?" Johannes asked, with a smile on his face.

"Of course," Cooper answered. "Let her know that others think I am a prime catch." This caused the group to laugh.

Skeeter was nearby and witnessed the events. "Mr. Spurlock, why's the Cap'n wanting yew to see 'is wife's gift?"

Spurlock looked at the little gunner, "You read the articles, didn't you?"

"No, I made my mark, but I can't read."

"There's a rule against theft. If you takes something for personal use and don't report it, you could be shot."

"I see," Skeeter said. "Cap'n, 'e don't want to be shot."

"No, he don't," Spurlock replied. "Best you go see, Mr. Jewell and get a copy of the articles so's I can have someone read them to you."

"Banty maybe?" Skeeter asked.

"No, you idiot. I'm not sure he can read any better than you. Probably will be McKemie. He's a good hand with the words and figures." Skeeter thanked the big gunner and hurried off. *I'm glad that he's a good gunner, because he doesn't have a lot else going for him,* Spurlock thought.

CHAPTER TWELVE

THE SUN WAS SETTING and the wind had backed almost due north. The passengers from all the prizes had been placed on the *Lady Katherine* that morning. The ship had been named after Kate's mother. Cooper felt a bit melancholy watching the ship sail away; one of his happier recollections of England. Seven ships had been taken and now Cooper's convoy of prizes would sail to New Orleans. He would anchor in Barataria Bay and go to New Orleans from there. He'd see their agent and have him and his clerks come to Grand Terre to carry out the inspection and inventory. He'd allow Buck Jewell to accompany him, along with either Second Officer Turner or Third Officer Ryker. Quang, Banty, and McKemie would go along also. Regardless of which officer stayed, Johannes Ewers, Spurlock, and Diamond would really be the ones in charge of *SeaFire's* prizes. St. Jacques would have his own men selected.

St. Jacques related that he had no desire to go to New Orleans. Hotel Mayronne would fit his needs well enough with clean sheets and good food, so he saw no need to make the trip. He didn't say it, but Cooper imagined that he'd enjoy a little female companionship as well.

COOPER STAYED AT HOTEL Provincial as usual. He was greeted by the ever present and most pleasant Mademoiselle Renee, and Otis, who was cheerful as always. He was shown to Eli and Debbie's suite. His presence was always greeted with the employees going out of their way. A knock at the door and a smartly dressed young black man entered when the door was opened. "You missed the noon meal but perhaps this will tide you over, suh. Will you be staying for dinner tonight?"

"I think so," Cooper said after a pause. "I may have two more of my men here this evening but I'm not sure if they will be in time for dinner."

"Yes, suh. Will you take your meal in the dining room or in your suite?"

Cooper replied, "In the dining room, I think." He didn't want to cause any extra work for the staff by eating in his room.

"Very good, suh. I will be back later to pick up the tray," the young man volunteered.

The servant turned to leave the room, but Cooper called him back. "My cox'n and seaman, have they been settled in?"

"Yes, suh, in their usual quarters, but I believe they are in the kitchen eating now." This brought a smile to Cooper's face. The men knew when to eat.

Cooper found writing materials in Debbie's writing desk and penned two letters. One was to Eli telling him of their captures and that they had already taken the ships to Grand Terre. He also wrote that he had that afternoon met with their New Orleans agents and, of course, Edward Meeks. The next letter was to Maddy and took much longer to write. He was interrupted halfway through by Otis. The two men chatted for awhile and Otis remarked that the letters would get to Savannah faster and safer if they were sent by courier. Several ships had been stopped and seized by the British since Cooper had last visited. However, thus far there'd not been that much land force. Not so much that a courier who had a fast horse and knew the route couldn't slip past. The fee though was not cheap; it was five dollars for each letter. Cooper gave Otis the ten dollars to cover the fee. When Otis excused himself, Cooper finished his letter. He felt heaviness in his chest as he sealed the letter. He missed Maddy so much.

Breakfast the next morning caused Cooper to loosen his belt. He'd eaten too much but it had been awhile since he'd had food this appetizing. He had eaten three eggs, fried over easy, grits with butter, salt, and pepper. He ate both sugar-cured fried ham and link sausage seasoned with a touch of Cajun spice; a glass of orange juice, and two cups of coffee. All of this was topped off with golden brown buttered biscuits smeared with local honey. He looked at the platter of beignets, covered in white powdered sugar. They seemed to be calling him, tempting him…just one wouldn't hurt. Cooper's belly was so tight that he passed up on the beignets, but not without asking Otis to have the cook bag him up a dozen of them. He'd already asked Otis to get him a box of Gus' cognac soaked cigars. Crooks, Gus called them.

Cooper was barely able to walk when he and his men made their way to Lawyer Meeks' office. Eli's agents would meet him there. They'd take the pirogues back to Barataria Bay together. Buck Jewell had asked if he could remain in New Orleans. His relationship with the beautiful widow, Mary Esther, was apparently progressing well. The agents had alluded to it taking the better part of a week to put things in order, with so many ships and each loaded with valuable cargo. They had not expected so much cargo and so many ships at one time.

Cooper gave his friend nine days to be back, since it was taking longer than expected for the agents to complete the inventory of the prizes. "If you can't talk her into marrying you by that time, it's a lost cause," Cooper japed. This caused SeaFire's men to laugh.

THE MOONLIGHT WAS ALMOST as bright as the day. The moon was so big and low it seemed to be sitting on the ocean, right off the bow. It seemed like a beacon, calling to them; a force drawing the ship onward yet seemingly never getting any closer. Cooper sat on the rail enjoying a crook. He'd learned when it got down to about two inches from the end to get rid of it. The cigar became very strong and heady, otherwise. He'd given one of the cigars to Buck Jewell, who swore the damn thing had such a kick at the end it made him drunk. Ryker asked for one and was soon casting his stomach contents over the side. The men smiled but looked away, not wanting to embarrass the young officer.

Josiah, an old seaman who had a lame leg, had signed on while the ship was at Grand Terre. He had approached Cooper stating that he'd been the cook on board the *Lady Katherine* and was looking for a billet.

"Why didn't you go with the *Lady Katherine* when she sailed?" Cooper asked.

"I'd had me fill o' Woodman's pup. Kate was a fine lady but much more o' her brother and I'd have cast him over the side."

"So you can cook?" Cooper inquired.

"Aye, Cap'n. Had me own tavern 'til I borrowed from 'is Lordship. It seemed I could never get the balance paid off for all the bloody interest, so I took back to the sea. I can write and do sums as well, Cap'n. I just can't move 'bout like I did since me timber received a load of grape."

"Where did that happen?"

The man was silent for a long second and then decided he could trust Cooper. "It be from a revenoor gun, it did." Cooper nodded. The man had just admitted to being a smuggler at one time.

"If you can cook, that's all that matters," Cooper said.

"You won't be sorry," the man said.

Josiah now had young Ryker in tow and was giving him some concoction to settle his innards. The relief came quickly, and as Josiah passed heading back to Cooper's cabin, he spoke, "Young Ryker 'as sworn off cigars, Cap'n." Both men had to smile at this.

Cooper tossed and turned that night. Sleep was fleeting and only in twenty to thirty minute intervals. *SeaFire's* crew was up and ready to tackle anything the dawn happened to offer, not unlike the Navy. While not actually at quarters, the men lounged about close enough to their battle stations as made no difference. Banty was in the tops this morning. He was considered to have the best peepers of the entire crew. Johannes stood by the ship's wheel, ready to order his helmsman any changes in course. Buck Jewell was toward the stern making a systematic search of the horizon. He trusted his lookout, but still liked to look for himself. Quang stood by Cooper, while Diamond lounged near the mainmast. Spurlock was forward near the bow chaser in hushed conversation with Skeeter. *I wonder what that's about,* Cooper thought to himself, but knew if he needed to know Spurlock or Quang would inform him. It came to him that it had gotten much lighter on deck as he looked about. When he'd first walked out he'd not been able to see the bow, but now he could see it plainly. He was about ready to send down for coffee when Banty called out, his high voice breaking the morning's silence. "Deck thar, sails off the larboard beam." Sails…that meant several ships.

"Inbound or outbound?" Cooper shouted.

"They're headed home," Banty replied.

Jewell crossed the quarterdeck to where Cooper stood. "Still not visible from the deck, Captain."

Cooper thought for a minute. If they were not yet visible, that meant it might take anywhere from an hour to half a day to get up with the convoy. "Let's clamp on all sail, Mr. Jewell, and then feed the men."

"Aye, Captain."

"Mr. Ewers, plot a course to intercept the convoy. Mr. Ryker, signal *Thunderbolt* of our sighting."

Jewell was talking to the Second Mate Turner and the two of them had men climbing the shrouds.

Cooper called up to Banty once more, "Do you see any escorts, Banty?"

"Nay, Captain, but I believe that I can make out that yellow flag you hate."

CHAPTER THIRTEEN

THE SUN EMERGED FROM the horizon, burning through the haze of dawn. *SeaFire* and *Thunderbolt* were bearing down on the convoy. Two escorts had been identified. One, an old fifty-gun ship, was at the head of the convoy and a ten-gun sloop of war brought up the rear. The fifty-gun ship looked as if it might have been an old Dutch made ship.

"We'll be in and out before that old lady can come about," Turner volunteered. He had the watch and the excitement of more prize money had him more talkative than usual.

"Aye," Johannes replied. "But she's likely carrying twenty-four pounders and we could never stand up to a broadside."

Cooper heard the conversation but made no comment. His eyes were on the large merchant ship flying the yellow banner with a black "F" on it. A rage built inside of him while he wanted to extract vengeance on the Finylson flag, and on Phillip, his sodomite cousin. He had already hurt his lying cousin but that was not enough. He wanted to ruin him. He wanted Phillip to feel the despair his lies had brought to Cooper Cain. But he'd not endanger his men or his ship to wreak vengeance on Phillip. No, he would go about his duties in a professional manner.

The convoy was twenty-eight ships. It stretched out over a mile. *SeaFire* would deal with the sloop of war and let *Thunderbolt* take as many prizes as they could. *SeaFire* would then pluck her chickens.

"Mr. Ryker."

"Aye, Captain."

"Signal *Thunderbolt* to close within hailing distance."

"Yes sir," Ryker replied.

"Mr. Spurlock."

"Aye, Captain."

"I want to disable yonder sloop but not destroy it."

"Aye, Captain. A mast or a rudder should do it."

Smiling, Cooper called out, "Ten dollars to the gunner that brings down the sloop's mast." A shout went up from the men. "Er…that excludes you, Mr. Spurlock."

The gunner smiled now, "Aw, Captain, you know I'd not be taking your money but I might give some pointers just to clip Skeeter's wings, so to speak."

"Give all the pointers you like, Mr. Spurlock." Cooper then turned to his second mate, "Once we dispatch the sloop, Mr. Turner, I intend to take us a prize. Today, you will have the honor of boarding our first capture."

"Thank you, Captain," Turner replied.

Johannes ordered a course change after *Thunderbolt* had come alongside. "The ship flying the yellow flag is mine, Henri," Cooper called out. "Take independent action while I deal with the escort."

St. Jacques threw up his hand and waved indicating he understood. Cooper then ordered the change in course. The captain of the sloop of war bravely, or as Cooper thought, stupidly sailed toward her foe. Gunports were open and the black snouts of six pounders peeked out.

"He'll do his duty," Buck Jewell volunteered as he approached his captain.

"Aye," Cooper acknowledged. "He won't like it and neither will his men but he'll make every effort. If we put a mast over the side, it will probably take a while to repair. We shall have taken our prizes and be gone by then."

"Aye, Captain. I don't see him getting in any hurry to effect repair." Both men smiled.

"I hope you are right, Buck."

The distance was now in range for *SeaFire*, but not close enough for the sloop's six pounders. Cooper called to his gunners, "I want the mainmast toppled. No broadside you understand, each gun will fire as you bear. If the mast is not down by the time the aft gun has fired, you'll owe me ten dollars and Mr. Spurlock will demonstrate how a true gunner performs." This brought good-natured jabs at Spurlock.

"We're in range, Captain," Mr. Jewell called.

"I will leave it in your capable hands, Mr. Spurlock."

"Thank you, Captain."

"Banty!"

"Aye, Cap'n," the lookout called down.

"Mark the shots," Cooper said.

"Aye, aye, Cap'n."

The squeak of gunport hinges filled the air, followed by the grating sound as gun carriage wheels were pulled along the deck. The first cannon roared. A pock mark in the sail about a balls width from the mast showed. The next cannon fired and the ball was wide. The third cannon ball hit the mast and splinters spewed out where the ball impacted the oak mast.

"A hit," Banty called out, but still the mast stood.

Skeeter was at the fourth cannon. He looked at Spurlock with his snaggletooth grin. Spurlock was a bit disgusted. His pointers had been to the third gun captain. "Keeps yer eyes trained," Skeeter called to his fellow gun crews.

BOOM...

"A hit," Banty shouted down, but still the mast stood.

83

Skeeter looked through the gunport in disbelief. A smiled started on Spurlock's face, only to end abruptly, when Skeeter shouted, "There she goes." True to his words, the mast went over the side. "Hard English oak it were. Took 'er a bit," Skeeter snorted.

Cooper called to the third officer, smiling, "Dip the ensign in salute, Mr. Ryker. Mr. Ewers, bring us about and lay us alongside the Finylson ship."

"Aye, Captain."

"Mr. Spurlock, when we get close, put a ball across yonder ship's bow. Close to the bow, mind you."

Spurlock smiled, "As close as a clean shave."

"Quang," Cooper called to his cox'n. "Put us a boarding party together and include McKemie. He can look over the ship's documents while the others search the ship. Mr. Jewell, the ship is yours while I go across to our prize."

"*Thunderbolt*'as took another prize," the lookout called down, causing the crew to give a cheer for their sister ship.

SeaFire drew alongside of the Finylson ship and grapples flew across as men heaved, drawing the hulls close together. Spurlock had the swivel guns in the tops loaded with grape just in case their foe offered any resistance. Cooper glanced down at the men who would board the prize with him. McKemie, who was more educated than most, and Banty, who was a scrapper. Johnson, who had been at sea longer than Cooper had been alive. Leon... what was the fiddler doing going over, well he might be used as a runner if needed. Ox, the man was huge and had muscles that bulged out. He had won a bet hauling in an anchor with him alone at the capstan. He beat the time in a contest where he was pitted against three men at the capstan. The remaining crew going over with Cooper were Goose and Martin, brothers who did everything together.

"Ready, Cap'n," Quang said.

Cooper nodded and then adjusted the pistols in his sash and also in a belt that crossed his chest. He hefted his sword, liking the sound of the fine Damascus steel as it slid easily in and out of its sheath. Finally, he slid the dagger in and out of its sheath. The dagger was made in China out of razor sharp steel with its ornate horses head handle. It had been a gift from Quang soon after they had met. It was always on his belt.

"Ready, Cap'n?"

"Aye, Quang."

Having broken his captain's train of thought, Quang looked at the man. *What were his demons,* the big Chinaman wondered. His captain was three men, depending on the need. He was a warrior. He could easily have been a Samurai. There had been a few white men who had obtained that honor. He was a compassionate and loving man who enjoyed merriment. Quang had seen that side as well. He was also a man with a deep hatred that blackened his soul. That was the man Quang worried about and did his best to watch over him. Quang knew that was the dangerous man who could be so bent on revenge that he would forget to watch his back. *I'll be there,* Quang thought.

A groan was heard as the two ships' hulls ground together. Quang shook his head. He had been doing the same thing his captain had been guilty of. *It must be the white blood in my veins,* Quang decided.

SeaFire's boarders swarmed across the deck of the Finylson ship. No resistance was offered. The ship's captain, unlike most of his uncle's merchant captains, was fairly young and dressed like a dandy. This was most unusual dress for being at sea. Cooper often wore seaman's slops. This dandy here stood with a white powdered wig, a frilly silk shirt with tight nankeen britches, and polished boots. He took a pinch of snuff from a silver snuff box offered by a fair-haired servant boy, as he waited for Cooper to walk up. The servant boy had blond curls hanging down from his head and was almost identically attired. Cooper heard some of his men snigger.

"I'm Cooper Cain, Captain of the United Stated privateer ship, *SeaFire*. As our countries are at…"

The dandy interrupted Cooper, "Yes, yes, please talk with my mate as we simply must be on our way."

"You are not going anywhere," Cooper hissed, not liking the way he was interrupted.

"Now see here, my good man…"

It was Cooper who interrupted the man this time. "Ox," Cooper called, "Please secure this… this captain."

The burly seaman took hold of the captain's arm. When he did the blonde curly headed youth attacked Ox. He bit the man's leg and pulled a dirk out to stab Ox. Not seeming at all alarmed, Ox backhanded the boy, knocking him to the deck. His head thudded on the planking and the boy was out cold.

"Oh, such a brute," Captain Dandy said, sizing Ox up.

"Shut yer trap," Ox growled, grabbing a fist full of silky shirt.

A man came forward, "I'm the first mate," he volunteered.

He looks like a seaman, Cooper thought. "Do you understand why I've boarded your ship?"

"Yes, Coop."

Coop…he used my name. "Do I know you?" Cooper asked.

"Aye, but it's been awhile. I was second mate on the ship when we brought you and your mom from Antigua. I showed you the ship and took you up to the crow's nest."

Cooper smiled, "Stevens. You are Mr. Stevens."

The first mate smiled, glad he'd been recognized. Cooper looked at Stevens and then darted his eyes toward Captain Dandy and back. "You're his first mate?"

"Aye, I was the ship's captain and then the day before we sailed from Portsmouth, your cousin…" The word cousin was spat out. "Your cousin came aboard and said he was making a change. Wilham was to be the captain," Stevens said with a nod toward the dandy. "I could stay on as first mate but retain my captain's pay. It seems our new captain has contacts in the east and so we are carrying a cargo I would never have consented to." Stevens leaned in then and whispered, "Opium."

Cooper knew the drug would bring a huge profit if sold at Grand Terre or New Orleans. It would also be turned into the pain reliever, laudanum and used for wounded men if handled appropriately. Cooper would throw it over the side before he would sell it on the black market. No, he'd talk to Dr. Cannington and if he agreed they would take the ship and cargo to Savannah.

"Captain Stevens," Cooper said, using the man's appropriate title. "If you give me your parole, I will allow you and your men to remain on board this ship until we reach our home. I will, of course, leave my prize crew on board. I will remove your passenger and his servant."

"Captain Cain, I say, Captain Cain. You are mistaken, sir, I'm the ship's captain."

Ox shook the dandy and snarled, "Shut yer mouth. You ain't shat lessens the cap'n says so and right now he ain't said."

McKemie, who'd been searching the captain's cabin, came on deck. "Here's the manifest, Cap'n. They's carrying teakwood, silk, spices, tea, china, and a case of Oriental swords, some statues and such. That's all that's on the manifest, but I found this, Cap'n. It's a receipt for…"

"Opium," Cooper said before McKemie could finish his sentence. McKemie smiled, "Somebody talked." Cooper smiled.

"Ray," Cooper spoke again. "I'm leaving the mate Stevens aboard as captain but you are in charge. I met him when I was a boy so I trust the man. But don't you be too trusting. He gave me his parole so…"

McKemie understood. He had been a prize captain more than once. He had a crew of twelve men. They'd collect all the weapons, and then do a search of the ship. If they found anymore, that man who didn't come forth would find himself in chains. He'd rig a swivel with grape forward and aft. He'd have two men on them at all times. McKemie would trust the captain's parole until he had reason not too…then God help 'em.

They took a ship's boat and rowed back to *SeaFire*. The dandy was protesting until Ox clapped him a good one. "Shut up, you're hurting my ears."

Once aboard *SeaFire*, several men got what few things the boarding party needed and went back aboard the prize.

Mr. Jewell greeted his captain, "Four prizes for us, Captain, with the three by Thunderbolt."

"Good, have Mr. Ryker signal to St. Jacques to come aboard," Cooper replied. "When St. Jacques leaves to return to *Thunderbolt*, have Mr. Ewers set a course for home, and pass the word for Dr. Cannington to report to my cabin."

"Aye!" Buck paused and then asked, "Home, Captain?"

"Aye, Buck, you'll have to put off seeing Mary Esther for awhile. I'll explain later when St. Jacques comes aboard." Buck Jewell looked down and Cooper knew the man's feelings. He'd experienced them himself. "Relax, Mr. Buck. You can tell your lady you're a rich man when you next see her."

"Aye, Captain, but there are a few in that category already who'd like to have her as his bride," Buck replied.

"With your charms?" Cooper asked.

"Nay, Captain, not a charm one." As Buck walked off, Cooper truly wished him luck. The young widow was certainly a charming lady. She and Maddy would be friends, he was sure of that.

CHAPTER FOURTEEN

S HE'S BRITISH, NO DOUBT," Banty called down. The ship had been sighted just as the sun burned away the dawn's mist. "Looks to be a frigate," Banty had said when he first spotted the ship. They were not far from the Georgia coast. She was alone but were there more? A frigate could very well mean a squadron or even a fleet was just over the horizon. What was that Maddy's brother, Jake, had said, "A frigate is the eyes and ears of the fleet. If you're on a frigate you can get away from the admiral's grasp." Jake's dad was an admiral so he'd learned early on that the most sought after command for a young officer was a frigate.

"She's got her signal flags fluttering," Banty called down again. He knew what the next question would be, so he added, "No other sails spotted, Cap'n." He'd learned from both Eli and David MacArthur that it was not uncommon for a captain on a smaller ship to signal 'enemy in sight,' as a ruse to escape a larger enemy.

Buck Jewell had been standing on a ratline, arm wrapped around a shroud, "She's gaining on us, Captain."

"Aye," Cooper answered.

They could only go as fast as their slowest prize. The frigate would be on them before they reached the mouth of the Savannah River and the protective guns of Fort Pulaski.

Cooper made up his mind and called to his third officer, "Mr. Ryker, signal *Thunderbolt* to come about and close with *SeaFire*, and then signal Mr. Diamond's prize to head on into Savannah. After that, signal Mr. Turner to hurry along any stragglers."

"Mr. Ryker," Cooper called the young man who'd turned to carry out signals. "Aye, Captain," Ryker answered.

"When you make Mr. Turner's signal, add with cannon if needed."

Young Ryker was not certain if he had the signals for the last, but he'd spell out gun. Mr. Turner would understand that.

"Mr. Jewell," Cooper called to his first officer, who was climbing down the shroud.

"Aye, Captain."

"You may put the hands to quarters as soon as convenient."

"Aye, Captain," Jewell replied.

Cooper felt his heart pounding, to get this close to home and meet up with an enemy. They had seen a squadron off Mobile at dusk several nights ago but had got away in the dark. Seven prizes, *SeaFire*, and *Thunderbolt*…they may have been mistaken for a British convoy or another British squadron. Whatever the reason, they'd escaped. Now this!

Quang walked up with Cooper's weapons. Nerves getting the best of him, Cooper put two pistols in his sash and, cupping his hands, he called up to the lookout, "See any more ships, Banty?"

"Nay, Cap'n, me eyes be peeled." This was his way of letting Cooper know he was watching.

"The odds suit you, Captain?" This came from Ryker, who'd carried out his signaling task.

"What in thunder nation," Cooper bellowed, using one of Eli's phrases. "What do you mean, Mr. Ryker?"

"We'll be two to one, Captain."

"You could be dead too, sir," Cooper said. "What comfort do you think it'll give your mother when I tell her, but the odds were in our favor, Madame?"

"She'll not care, sir."

"You'll be just as dead."

"Ugh!" Ryker swallowed. "I didn't think of it that way."

"*Thunderbolt* is alongside," Buck Jewell said. He felt sorry for the young officer. He was still young enough to feel invincible. Hopefully, the captain had changed his notion.

Taking the speaking trumpet, Cooper called across to St. Jacques "Henri, it seems we have a meddlesome ship. I intend to disable her if possible. She's a twenty-eight, Banty says, but I doubt she can fight both sides at once."

St. Jacques knew the drill. "She'll be carrying nine pounders, I bet," he shouted back, meaning the weight of their shot would be equal.

Cooper looked toward the enemy ship. The frigate continued to gain. Looking over at St. Jacques he saluted, "See you at the warehouse." St. Jacques saluted back. "Two points to starboard," Cooper called to the helmsman.

"Aye, aye sir." When *SeaFire* swung, *Thunderbolt* did the same to larboard. This put the frigate between the two ships.

"Will she fight both sides, Mr. Spurlock?"

"I doubt it, Captain, but St. Jacques is right. She'll be carrying nine pounders. I hope she's not carrying carronades. If not, we should make up for the difference in guns with those big bruisers." He was referring to *SeaFire's* carronades.

"I'll let you see too it then, Mr. Spurlock," Cooper said.

The big gunner nodded and moved off. *Manning the guns on SeaFire and Thunderbolt would not be so easy either*, Cooper thought. His crew and that of their sister ship had so many men off as prize crews it could prove their undoing. The frigate was a larger ship so the privateers would have to be watchful and maneuver enough to get her between them. Cooper was expecting the frigate to fire at anytime but he still jumped when she finally did.

"Ranging shot," Johannes commented, as he calmly stood by the wheel. A ball landed not twenty yards off.

"Damn close if you ask me," Buck Jewell exclaimed.

"Larboard guns run out," Cooper called.

"Like a chess game right, Captain?"

"Aye, Mr. Ewers, a damnable one if you ask me."

Thunderbolt was now within firing range and fired her forward guns.

"Missed, but right alongside," Banty yelled down.

BOOM…the frigate fired again and a ball plowed across the raised poop deck. "Diamond won't like that," a helmsman commented to his mate.

"Mr. Spurlock, fire as you bear," Cooper yelled.

The enemy was now no more than five hundred yards away. Cooper would allow Spurlock a broadside at this distance, and then change course to throw off the enemy gunners.

BOOM…BOOM…BOOM *SeaFire's* guns thundered out her lethal answer to the frigate. After the last gun fired, Cooper ordered the change in course. While *SeaFire* was maneuvering, *Thunderbolt* fired another broadside but the frigate made her weight felt as she destroyed the starboard bulwark and a gun went flying aboard *Thunderbolt*.

Banty called down that he could now see, since the smoke was drifting past. "We hit her, hard, Cap'n. Our gunners be hitting her."

Cooper called to the helmsman, "Back now. Two points to starboard. Be ready, Mr. Spurlock. Fire as you bear."

The boom of the frigate's cannons was drowned out this time, with the roar of *SeaFire's* carronades. Huge parts of the frigate's rail were gone, the mizzenmast was leaning but not yet down. The frigate still fought.

"She's hit *Thunderbolt* again," Banty yelled.

"Damn," Cooper shouted. "Come about, Mr. Ewers. Mr. Spurlock, finish her this time."

"Aye, Captain. Stop yer vent, worm the guns, sponge out, reload." Cooper could hear the big gunner ordering his gun crews. He had seen the powder monkeys hurrying along with their deadly baskets. Cooper could feel *SeaFire* turn as the ship came back on course to do battle one more time. *To end it this time*, he decided. Taking a quick glance toward *Thunderbolt*, he could see she had been hit hard, but St. Jacques could still do battle.

Cooper wanted every ball to tell as they approached the enemy. He looked down at the men standing back from their guns. They were ready, fist raised, each gun loaded and run out. The frigate's bow began to swing just to larboard. He had her, "Luff, Mr. Ewers. Fire, Mr. Spurlock."

As the carronades roared, Cooper had his glass to his eye. "Cease fire, cease fire," he yelled louder than he'd ever done in his life. One gun, two guns went off but the others remained silent. "Signal *Thunderbolt* to break off action."

"Why Captain, we have her."

"Do it," Cooper snapped. He put the glass back to his eye. The figure, the man he'd seen was up and moving. *Thank God*, Cooper thought. "Secure from quarters," Cooper ordered. Seeing his first officer's questioning look, he spoke, "My brother-in-law, Buck. Yonder captain is my brother-in-law."

"My God, Captain. I'm sorry."

"So am I, Buck, so am I. Raise a white flag, Mr. Ryker. Raise it where it will be spotted. Mr. Spurlock, please make sure the guns are secured and the gunports closed."

"Aye, Captain." The gunner did not understand the sudden change in his captain. Ready to sink the enemy one minute, and then send up the white flag the next.

Buck Jewell sidled up to the gunner. "We've been fighting Maddy's brother."

"Damnation," the gunner swore and walked off.

"Mr. Ewers, if you will bring us within hailing distance."

"Aye, Captain," the master answered and gave instructions to the helmsman.

As the gap closed between the two ships, the British still had not closed her gunports. Cooper could see officers making gestures and running back and forth. Jake then stood next to a section of rail that was still intact. Cooper put down his glass and waved. A pause, like maybe Jake was checking again, and then he put down his glass and waved. The ships were soon close to each other.

"Captain Anthony," Cooper spoke first. "Are you in need of a surgeon, sir? Dr. Cannington is aboard."

Jake remembered the American doctor who had saved his life. "We have a fine surgeon, Captain Cain. We are expecting our squadron soon and they will have others to help."

He's telling me to get the hell out of here, Cooper thought. But what would happen when his commander heard of his defeat. Cooper made a quick decision, "My compliments, Captain. You are a brave leader and fought off our two ships when we had you beat in number and weight of guns. I'm glad that we didn't meet you ship to ship."

"Thank you, Captain Cain. Your comments have been most gracious."

"We will be hauling our wind, Captain. I will give your best to Maddy and James. By the way, Captain, it's my understanding that you will be an uncle soon, James and his wife."

"Thank you again, Captain Cain. I can assure you the grand-mother will do what she can to resolve this conflict soon."

As Cooper waved good-by, Buck Jewell was by his side. "Banty didn't want to shout out, Captain, but we got sails headed this way."

"Aye, Mr. Jewell, I know."

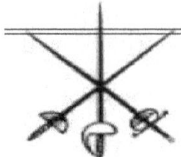

CHAPTER FIFTEEN

BY THE TIME THE ships had made their way into Savannah Harbor, word had spread. Excitement filled the street. Seven prizes…Captain Cooper Cain and Captain Henri St. Jacques had captured seven British ships. From the beginning, a messenger had been sent by John Will to inform both Eli Taylor and Maddy of the privateers. Michael Brett was off doing business with Colonel Lee and Colonel Sidney Bledsoe. Timber business… tall straight timbers that could be used as the mast for ships. Colonel Bledsoe's daughter, Suzanne, had become good friends with Maddy over the last few months. They had met at Maddy's brother, James' house. It seemed that the Bledsoe farm backed up to part of the Lee's farm and James' farm. James and Josie Anthony had benefited from the motherly tutelage of Colonel Bledsoe's wife, Mrs. Emma. With Josie starting to show, Mrs. Emma and Suzanne had been a big help in getting things ready for the baby.

Mama Lee had also put them in touch with an elderly black woman, who was a midwife. "She's as good as our sawbones," Mama Lee said with conviction. "I guess he's good enough if he ain't got his snoot in a jug of corn squeezing. But Lulu, I'd trust her any day." Mrs. Emma agreed, so now it was a matter of time.

Maddy, Jessie, Suzanne, and Josie, when she wasn't sick, had been shopping and fixing up a room for the baby.

When the messenger notified Eli Taylor of Cooper's return, he sent a rider to tell Maddy. Suzanne was walking out to her rig, saying good-by to Maddy when the rider rode up.

Upon hearing the news, Suzanne took charge. "Don't just stand there, girl, get in. Let's go, I want to meet this man anyway."

Smiling, Maddy climbed aboard. "What will he say? Just look at me."

"He'll say I love you or I'll run him through," Suzanne said smiling. "Hang on, Maddy," she said, as she used the buggy whip. "Get up, you nag."

COOPER SPOKE WITH THE second mate, Turner, who was getting a crew ready for a longboat. Buck Jewell would stay aboard *SeaFire* with half of what was left of the crew. Turner would go to each of the prizes to make certain they had no immediate needs. Most of *SeaFire's* crew knew the process for bringing in a prize. It made little difference, be they pirate or privateer.

Quang had Banty, Johnson, and Ox in Cooper's gig. They would row over to *Thunderbolt* so that Cooper could get a close up look and some ideas of the repairs the ship would need before they sailed again.

Jacob Anthony had gunners that knew their trade. *Thunderbolt* had been hit hard in several places while others were no more than superficial. Still, even the superficial repairs would take time and money…and men. Cooper figured from the hits he saw score that they had lost eight to ten men, and that didn't count the wounded. Would new men be as easily signed after seeing the dead and wounded come off the ship? What was that Buck had said, "Young men never think they'll die." One had certainly changed his way of thinking, and that was young Mr. Ryker. Feeling the hot hell of battle has a tendency to sober one up, Johannes had sworn. I'd say Mr. Ryker aged years in just a few minutes. What about Jake...Jacob Anthony? What if Cooper had not recognized him and broken off the action? Would he have fallen, would Jake have broken off the action? So many questions, Cooper thought...and Maddy. What would he tell Maddy? He would not lie. He would have to tell her. She'd hear about the battle, even if he didn't say anything, someone would. No, good, bad, or indifferent, he'd tell her. He would not jeopardize the trust the two of them shared by lying. No, he'd tell the truth. Hopefully, it would be when they were alone. He'd not dodge the situation if it came up regardless of when or where.

THEY WERE ALONE...FINALLY. ELI Taylor had been at the warehouse office almost as soon as Cooper got there. Cooper had met with St. Jacques, and gotten a thorough summary of the damage that had been done to *Thunderbolt*. The bad thing was a main brace span line had been hit and parted when Jacques had ordered to come about. The line fouled a tackle when it snapped. Hands went aloft to fix it but it was too late. The British ship got in her licks. "Lucky, we didn't suffer more damage," St. Jacques said, sounding relieved. He and Cooper both knew it could have been much worse.

Cooper had quickly given Eli a rundown on the prizes, their cargo and the battle when the sound of a rig outside was heard. Maddy flung the door open a moment later. She rushed to Cooper, as Suzanne Bledsoe entered the room. *So that's Cooper Cain,* she thought to herself. *No wonder Maddy is so in love with the brute. He's a man.*

The rig was crowded. Suzanne drove while Cooper held Maddy in his lap. Cooper had been introduced to Suzanne. "She's one of 'me mates'," Maddy said, using one of Uncle Bart's phrases. This got a smile from her man, like she knew it would.

The rig had pulled up in front of Maddy and Cooper's home. Maddy had thanked her friend for the ride and then added, "Will you tell James and Josie that Coop is home, so I won't be coming over."

Suzanne gave a wink and nodded she would as she clicked for her tired horse and drove off at little more than a walk.

Maddy spoke to the cook as they went in the house, "Finish what you are doing and then you can be off. Coop's back and we have some catching up to do." *That wasn't so subtle*, Cooper thought.

"The breads are about done...," the cook started to say but stopped as the bedroom door closed.

The windows in the bedroom had been opened and a zephyr came in one window and eased out the other, and as it passed through some of Maddy's hair wisped up a bit. Cooper pushed it down with his hand as he bent down and met her lips rising to meet his. Maddy felt his hand on her cheek as he pushed back the hair and drew her to him.

Tears started to fall and Maddy whispered, "I'm so glad you are home."

He held her so close he could feel her heartbeat; her chest rose and fell as he kissed her long and passionately. Maddy could smell the sea, the ship, tar, and something else on her man. Gunpowder...the distinct smell of gunpowder was strong on him. He'd been in a battle not long ago. She unbuttoned his shirt and slid her arms inside his open shirt and pulled it off his shoulders. Another scent...the strong sharp scent of a man...her man. She felt Cooper touch the string that tied her dress in the back. Loosened, it fell to the floor. Her undergarments fell away and she was naked...naked and longing. Maddy met Cooper's gaze. She could feel the gentle breeze against her back. Was he feasting his eyes on her body as he'd told her before he left?

99

Cooper bent down and touched her firm breasts with his calloused hand and then he kissed one hardened nipple followed by the other nipple.

"Sit down," she said.

Cooper sat on the side of the bed and she took off one boot and then the other one. Looking up, she saw her man looking at her. Eyes fixed on her breasts. "Do you like what you see, Sir Pirate?"

"Aye."

"Would you still fight off a hundred men?"

"More," he said.

"Are you just going to look?"

"No."

"Get out of those britches then."

Cooper shed the rest of his clothes, and then he lifted her up to him, his hand around her slim, flat waist. Maddy's legs entwined around him and he sat back down on the bed. She buried her face against his chest and when he lay back he entered her. Hours later they still lay together. He stirred around and she asked, "Are you hungry?"

"For what?" he responded.

Maddy smiled and started to laugh, causing Cooper to laugh. They laughed together, their hearts full of joy.

CHAPTER SIXTEEN

GRAY CLOUDS COVERED THE eastern sky. Rain was pouring down and there was just enough wind to make it slant. When the wind would pick up momentarily, the rain came down in sheets. Cooper watched a jagged bolt of white light up the sky and then another bolt of lightning followed by a low long increasing rumble of thunder. The last few years of rising this early at sea had turned Cooper's internal body clock to a precise awakening. It was not cheerful but it was precise. It would not be a day for the hands to be working in the fields.

Luke, the overseer, who was the son of James Anthony's trusted man, would probably put the men to work repairing and sharpening farm tools in the big new barn that had been built in his absence. James had made that recommendation, since the old barn had been standing and that's about all one could say about it. Maddy, at James' recommendation, had hired Luke. Luke had surveyed the barn and had it pulled down using a brace of mules. Once down, he supervised salvaging the good wood that would come in handy later. The ground was cleared so that the new barn could be built, and was half again larger in size.

Several blacksmith lean-to's were added to house everything from a blacksmith's forge to a place to park the wagons to keep them out of the weather. Thinking of the wagons, Cooper realized that he needed to purchase a carriage. They'd dined with James and the very pregnant Josie earlier. Cooper was not use to the sight of a pregnant woman, and it made him nervous.

He was not sure that he wanted see Maddy's belly so big. Josie, though she looked ready to pop, was in a cheerful mood. Her movements were all wrong, though. James had said for her to waddle on over here and sit down…that was it. Josie didn't walk with her same grace as before, she waddled. The supper had been just the four of them. Jessie and Maddy's friend, Suzanne, was off visiting. It had been a nice cozy evening with just the two couples.

Hearing the bed creak and the rustle of the covers, Cooper turned around. Maddy was sitting up and stretching her arms up over her head. Her mouth was stretched wide with a mighty yawn. *Nude…damn*, thought Cooper. *She hasn't even woken up good yet, and she stirs the humors most savagely.*

"Morning, Sir Pirate."

"Will you never cease with that?" he asked.

"You deserve the title, you blackguard. You stole my heart."

Knowing that he'd never win an argument with Maddy, Cooper smiled and said, "It's raining," as he crossed to the bed.

Glancing at the dawn light coming through the window, Maddy could see and hear the big drops hit the glass. "Will it last?"

Cooper replied, "The clouds are moving fast, but I don't think it's a quick squall."

Maddy reached out and took Cooper's hand and pulled him closer to her. "Would you love me if I had a fat belly like Josie?"

"Of course, I would." He had wondered when that would come up in the conversation.

"Did you enjoy Josie before she and James got together?" Cooper was stunned. How the hell did Maddy find out about that?

Seeing the shocked look on Cooper's face and also his stunned silence, Maddy continued, "We talked about the night you got your scar…and how she and Jessie tried to make you feel better." Before Cooper could respond, Maddy added, "I wouldn't have done that. I wouldn't have shared you with my sister or anybody."

Cooper whispered, not knowing where it came from, "You won't ever have to worry about that."

Maddy could sense the sincerity and tenderness in Cooper. She held the covers up and said, "Come back to bed, Sir Pirate, your wench awaits you."

When Cooper woke up again, it was not the rain that aroused his senses, but the aroma of coffee. Rosa was in the kitchen and had the coffee on to boil. Looking over at Maddy, she was deep in her slumber. Cooper eased out of bed and got dressed. So Josie and Maddy had talked. *Damned if women are not as bad as men*, he thought. His stomach growled then. His early morning exercise had created an appetite. He would find out if Rosa was as good as Belle.

"Hogs! Yes sir, down by the river. A full acre or more rooted up by those damnable creatures." Luke was propped against the corner post on the front porch, talking to Cooper. "Mr. James, Colonel Lee, and Colonel Bledsoe have already sent word for the hog man."

"What about Captain Taylor?" Cooper asked.

"He's agreed to pay his share, but so far he hasn't had any damage to his crops."

"Who do the hogs belong to?" Cooper asked, not sure if he was showing his ignorance or not but truly wanted to know.

Taking a straw that seemed to constantly be in his mouth out, Luke took a breath and then replied, "Nobody and everybody, I'd say. Everybody has a pig get loose now and then. Soon they're all running together, and the next thing you know you got more hogs than hairs on your head. They are worse than rabbits at breeding and suddenly they are destroying crops."

Cooper knew nothing about rabbits, but figured they must be very active at reproducing. "You can't just shoot them?" Cooper asked.

"We do, but killing a hog here and there is about as good as spitting in the wind." Cooper got that. "It takes a man that knows what he's doing," Luke went on. "A man with trained dogs, mean dogs. One of Jonah and Moses' coonhounds got caught up in a pack of hogs and they tore it to pieces. No, you got to have a man and dogs that know what they're doing."

"Who are they bringing in?" Cooper asked.

"A man named Spurlin. Kinda backwoods types who don't take lip from them know it alls." Cooper smiled; he'd known a few of those. "They's to be a meeting at Colonel Lee's house tomorrow bout noon. Thought we might ride over if you was a mind to."

"Sure, we'll go," Cooper replied.

Luke took out a worn looking pipe and leather pouch of pipe tobacco from his back pocket. As he filled his pipe, he said, "You might want to take Miz Maddy. Wimmin folks generally get together when the men folks meet. Before the day's over, there's usually a heap of good food to be had."

Cooper nodded, "Where can we find a nice rig for Maddy, Luke? She needs something besides a farm wagon to travel around in."

"Yes, sir, that she does. Oxford left one that could be fixed up and it wouldn't take much. It needs a new roof, too many pigeons have roosted on it and now it's ruined. There's a black-smith in town that is a fair hand with carriages. He has a black man who ain't quite right in the head that works with him."

"What do you mean, not right in the head?" Cooper asked.

Luke fired up his pipe before he answered, "He's...simple-minded, almost childlike. He does everything that Zeke, that's the blacksmith, tells him to do, but he has to be told everything. He sleeps in a room at the back of Zeke's shop. He don't truck with no wimmin or other blacks, though I bet he's in his thirties. I have never seen him far from the shop. Everybody likes him, and treats him nice. Never seen a soul act ugly to him. Zeke would bust their head if they did. He ain't got a name that I've heard, but he seems to know when you're speaking to him. I mention him because he likes to mess with leather. People have him make knife scabbards all the time. I've seen him repairing saddles as well. Zeke has to stop him when he gets going and remind him to eat."

"I see," Coop said.

"He's a good hand with deer hide as well as cowhide," Luke added. "I mention this as I bet he could fix a nice new roof for Miz Maddy. You can't be in no hurry however. He don't work fast."

"When can you talk with the blacksmith?" Cooper asked.

"Oh, I can do that today. I will have one of the hands hook it up and drive it over."

"So, it's serviceable?" Cooper inquired.

"I wouldn't go that far, but we got a hand or two that I trust to see it gets there," Luke replied. Both men laughed at Luke's attempt at humor.

Quang, who had been standing over to the side, volunteered, "I'll go along." He didn't have a lot to do when not at sea. Unlike the rest of the two crews who spent most of their time down at the waterfront gambling, drinking, and in sporting houses, he stayed close to Cooper. He was never underfoot but always close by. He ate in the kitchen or over in the overseer's cottage with Luke and his wife. Cooper had seen Luke and Quang sparring, much as the two of them had done when they first met. Unlike most of the other men, Quang seemed to enjoy the livestock. He particularly liked one little colt.

Seeing the Chinaman petting the colt, Cooper asked, "You like horses, Quang?"

"Yes. We had horses. I always liked to ride."

"Which one is your favorite?" Cooper inquired, pointing to the dozen or so in the corral.

Quang smiled, "This one."

"He's yours," Cooper said. Quang nodded, but didn't speak.

Luke said later, "That was a nice thing you did, boss. That little colt comes to the fence every time Quang walks up."

Cooper smiled, "Guess who has to care for it when we go back to sea?"

"I'll see that he's taken care of. Quang has already named the little fellow. He said he was white like a ghost so he calls him Gweilo. In Chinese, it means ghost man. He says that in Cantonese it's used to describe a white man."

Had he heard that before? Cooper wondered.

CHAPTER SEVENTEEN

SUZANNE BLEDSOE CAME BY and picked up Maddy for the ride to Colonel Lee's to meet with the hog man, Mr. Jimmy Spurlin. Cooper rode a horse so the small rig wouldn't be overcrowded. Luke and Quang followed along on horses as well. The Lee's yard was crowded when they got there. Maddy and Suzanne went on up the steps while Cooper, Luke, and Quang walked over to where a group of men were gathered around two wagons. One was covered and the other wagon was open. Inside the open wagon were numerous dogs. Some looked like everyday dogs but others were brutes. The brutes were on chains and though none were acting unfriendly, everyone walked out a ways to avoid getting to close to the menacing looking rascals.

Jimmy Spurlin was a tall man. His buckskins were worn but clean. His face and hands were leathery. His whiskers were gray and he sported a long drooping mustache. His thinning hair was gray streaked as well.

A young woman dressed much like a man still sat on the wagon seat. Though dressed in a man's attire, she'd never be mistaken for one. She was absolutely beautiful. Jimmy explained that she was his daughter and was good help at handling the dogs.

Somebody rang a bell which indicated it was time to eat. Colonel Lee indicated that tables had been set up at the back of the house for everyone. "We all want to hear from Mr. Spurlin, but we'll do that after we eat. So everybody find you a spot and have a seat."

Cooper found Eli Taylor close by so he walked up to him. They were quickly joined by Jonah and Moses. "Smell that fried chicken?" Jonah asked. "My mouth is already watering."

"Your mouth is always watering," Moses joked. "I believe your stomach controls your every thought."

"Not all of them," Jonah answered. "Look at that girl. I heard Mr. Spurlin calling her Shanna."

"You had better be on your best behavior," Moses chided. "See those dogs. They'd tear you apart. You heard her daddy say she's good at handling them."

Cooper smiled. "I think Moses is right, Jonah. You don't want to lose a hand."

LUNCH HAD BEEN A grand affair. Chicken fried to a crisp. Mashed potatoes with homemade gravy. Collard greens, which Cooper was still trying to convince himself wasn't animal food. He was told that the chunks of meat called ham hocks in the collard greens were there to flavor them. "Why not just eat the ham hocks then?" he asked, only to get an elbow in the ribs by Maddy. The corn that had been creamed was good and had a bit of a sweet taste to it. Cornbread and golden brown biscuits with fresh butter were also available. The biscuits were something he could get addicted too. Both honey and syrup were available if wanted.

A table, set down the way, was loaded with cakes and pies. Cooper had heard one of the cakes was a thirteen layer chocolate cake. He intended to get a piece of that, even if he had to trip Jonah to get it.

Once the meal was over, the men loosened their belts, lighted up pipes or cigars and found a place to relax. Mr. Spurlin was patiently describing how the hog hunting would progress. As Cooper walked up, he noticed Colonel Lee, Colonel Bledsoe, James, and Luke were listening intently. Next to Eli, his overseer, David Gill was giving Mr. Spurlin his full attention as well.

"My daughter, Shanna, is a better riser than me. She will have the dogs loaded in the wagons and ready to go by first light. Each of my dogs has a double thickness leather collar to put around their neck and a thick leather vest or cover to go around their body to protect them. The collar has studs worked in to cut down on a big hog biting through the leather. Once we get to an area known to hold hogs, like down close to the river, I'll cast Hondo, Bama, Dixie, and Bob out to try and find them. Bama and Hondo are my lead dogs. If they go to baying, we know they got the hogs stopped. Once the hogs are bayed up or stopped, we close in but no closer than about two hundred yards. That's when I unchain Gator, BoBo, and Rocky. They will have four-inch thick collars on for protection. These are my catch dogs. We walk them in pretty close. My helpers, Dan and Cody, who will be here tonight, and Shanna will release these dogs. The dogs go in and catch the hog. Shanna will go in and stab the hog behind the front shoulder once one of us gets a good hold onto the critters back legs. Those big dogs, especially Gator and Rocky, once they get a hog caught I sumtimes have to get a stick and pry their mouths open."

"Bet they'd put a hurting on your arm," Luke volunteered.

"They'd likely break it," Spurlin replied matter-of-factly. "It's then on to the next hog."

"Why don't you just shoot the hog, Jimmy?" David Gill asked.

"Likely as not to shoot one of my dogs as the hogs," Spurlin replied. "They ain't always being real still. Good hog dogs don't come too easy. It takes a heap of training."

Moses whispered to Jonah and Cooper, "Hear that, the girl ain't afraid to tackle a big boar and stick it. Think what she'd do to you, Jonah."

Jonah swallowed hard and managed a grin. "My intentions are most honorable." Moses and Cooper smiled.

"They'd better be," Moses said, and then continued, "If one of the catch dogs like Gator could snap your arm into with one bite, think what he'd do with something else…something a lot smaller."

"Shut up, Moses."

No one noticed the newcomer when he rode up as they were so engrossed in listening to Jimmy Spurlin. It was only when one of Jimmy's big brutes growled that heads turned. Seeing the man, dressed in a blue officer's uniform of the United States Army, Colonel Lee stepped forward. "How can I be of service, Captain?"

"My pardon for the interruption, sir. I have an urgent dispatch here for Mr. Jonah Lee."

Hearing his name, Jonah stepped forward. Moses was a half step behind. Seeing Moses, the captain said, "This is a private correspondence, sir."

"There are no secrets from my brother, Captain. I'd tell him anyway, so it'd save time if we went over this just once."

The captain was obviously confused. He'd not been the first one. For a white man to call a man of mixed breed, part of which was obviously Negro, his brother; was very uncommon. "Is there a place we can speak?" the captain said, still trying to digest the term brother.

It was at that moment that Cooper looked up on the porch and saw Maddy. Until that moment, the war had seemed like a far off thing. It had not touched the community. The war now had suddenly come home. Cooper saw Colonel Lee put his arm around Mama Lee, concern written all over their faces. For these two it was very real. The possibility, probability actually, that their sons, yes their sons; would be leaving soon, to take part in the war. With that, many questions arose. When would they be back…would they be back? Quang appeared at his side. The festive event was gone, chased away by events they had no control over. Colonel Lee knew and recognized that. Mama Lee never would. Like the Anthony's, James and Maddy. Their mother was on Antigua with her husband. She was torn with trying to support her British naval officer husband and son, yet loving her American son and daughter.

Cooper could sense a change in Maddy as she walked toward him. Had not he and her brother just battled? A very real battle with men dying. Had Cooper not recognized Jacob…Jake, he would have sunk his ship. Would Jacob have discontinued the action as Cooper had done? Yes…if it had been left up to him. A man's actions were not always in his control.

"I'll get a wagon ready," Quang volunteered in his chopped English.

"Yes, you and Luke can…" Cooper paused. They had not brought a wagon. Maddy had ridden with Suzanne.

"Bring wagon back," Quang said. Obviously, he'd already worked it out.

Cooper could see the tears start to emerge, as Maddy held out her hand to him. "Damn this war," she said. "Damm it."

THE HUNT STARTED AT about seven in the morning after a satisfying breakfast at Colonel Lee's. A fair number of men were there, including Colonel Bledsoe, Eli Taylor, and his man David Gill, Cooper and Luke, as well as Colonel Lee. Cooper noted right off the heavy leggings that Spurlin's men wore, including Shanna.

"Helps us keep from getting bit by a hog or snake," Spurlin replied when asked by Colonel Bledsoe. *Snakes...now he tells me*, Cooper thought. "Lost the best hog dog I ever had to a rattler," Spurlin swore.

After deciding where to start the hunt, Colonel Lee led off to a field that bordered the swamp close to the river.

"Hog signs everywhere, Colonel," Spurlin shouted to be heard above the baying hounds. They were already excited, having gained the scent. Chains were put on the catch dogs and his trail dogs were turned loose.

Spurlin had, as he called it, cast Hondo, Bama, and Dixie out to find the hogs. They'd already had their protective gear put on that morning. The dogs sniffed around a bit and then took off.

"I don't think that you will get far on the horses," Shanna told the men. "Keep your weapons uncocked and don't shoot one of my dogs," she said, emphasizing her point with a cold stare.

The men quickly found Shanna's words to be true. The trees were thick and the undergrowth was such that Cooper was amazed at how the dogs got through it. However, once they got on to the path the hogs actually traveled it got easier. You still had to duck down but it was better than fighting the briars and 'gotcha vines' with sharp thorns. Up ahead a loud squeal was heard.

Dan, one of Spurlin's helpers, looked at the group and said, "Pig." The squeal ended abruptly.

Cody, another of Spurlin's helpers, spoke, "Made short work of that one."

"Probably Hondo," Dan replied.

The catch dogs were almost dragging Spurlin and Cody now. The ground began to get soggy and squishy under the men's feet as they got deeper in the swamp. All the dogs were baying now.

"They got 'em," Shanna said, making her father give a brief smile.

Wiping the sweat from his eyes, Cooper looked down just in time to keep from stepping on the dead pig. It had been killed quickly by the lead dogs. *If the lead dogs did that, what would the catch dogs do,* Cooper wondered.

The men ran stumbling through the swamp until they almost collided with Spurlin, who had lifted his hand for everyone to stop. Looking at Colonel Lee and Colonel Bledsoe, they didn't seem to be as out of breath as Cooper was. Eli was gasping but David Gill and Luke were both in good shape. Cooper realized his face was stinging, and he touched it to find blood. Eli reached over and pulled out a thorn.

"We've spent too much time on a confined ship's deck," he said as he looked at the size and length of the thorn.

The baying dogs up ahead of them were high pitched and you could hear grunts and squeals from the hogs.

"That deep grunt is probably a big boar," Shanna advised the group.

Spurlin had eased into a small clearing where the dogs had the hogs. The dogs were running back and forth trying to hold the hog.

"It's no more than one hundred and fifty yards," Spurlin said. He then spoke to Dan and Cody, "Let Bobo and Rocky loose." He unchained Gator as he said this. With a bound the dogs were off. Cooper watched in awe as the catch dogs did their work keeping the boar hemmed up at the edge of the clearing. The dogs were dodging and darting as the boar would charge. However, if he went after one dog, the other two were nipping at it. It ended quickly once the catch dogs bounded in. Gator, showing no fear, charged right into the hog grabbing part of its neck and ear. Bobo was like a flash then, diving into the melee and grabbing the other ear while Rocky jumped in, winding up on the boar's back as he closed his powerful jaws down on the hogs neck.

Jimmy Spurlin's dogs put on a show. When the hog was subdued, Cody grabbed the hog's back legs and Shanna plunged a hunting knife deep into the hog's side, killing it. With the hog dead, the rest of the group walked up.

Spurlin looked at Cooper, "Ever seen such as this in England, Coop?"

Shaking his head, Cooper replied, "I won't say it doesn't happen but I've never seen anything like it. They know their business," Cooper said of the dogs, and then he asked, "What do you do with the meat?"

"If it's one hundred pounds or there abouts you can eat it. When they are as big as that one, we leave it for the varmints, as it ain't fit to eat."

They killed four more boars that day. A sow and a couple of pigs also fell prey to the dogs.

"Every day is not as productive as this one," Shanna said as the group gathered up at Colonel Lee's.

"I wish it were," the colonel interjected. "They are ruining my crops."

"They're getting braver, as well," Colonel Bledsoe added. "A hog went right in the settler's store last week, and scared Mrs. Hatfield right out of her bloomers." Everyone laughed at this. "I think it was actually after her potatoes," the colonel added. The men laughed again.

"I've had as much of this as I can stand," Eli said. "I think I'll call it a day."

As they broke up the group, Cooper nodded to Spurlin, "I'll never forget this day, Jimmy. If you ever decide that you want to go sailing let me know. All of your group can come. Shanna, if you desire to come along, I'll let you be captain."

Smiling, she replied, "I'll think on it, Coop, I'll think on it."

CHAPTER EIGHTEEN

THE SKY WAS A deep blue, so blue it bordered on black to the north-northwest. The wind seemed fickle at best, never quite gone, but the sails would grow lax and then pop right back out with a snap. The next time they'd flutter a time or two before growing taut.

"It's an eerie look," Buck Jewel volunteered.

Johannes nodded. "They call that a Prussian blue," he said.

Astern of *SeaFire*, the freshly repaired and painted *Thunderbolt* followed. This time they sailed north toward Nova Scotia and the shipping lanes that supplied the British possessions of Nova Scotia, Prince Edward Island, New Brunswick, and even Canada. The supply routes varied little outbound from England or inbound. The outbound ships were more likely to carry goods that would contribute to America's war needs. According to Eli's notes, the route from Falmouth to Barbados was four thousand two hundred miles. The ships would then sail northerly from Barbados to Antigua, west to Jamaica, and then northerly to Bermuda and north to Nova Scotia.

Cooper's charts were vague for the most northern aspect of Nova Scotia, as well as the western aspect. Cooper's thoughts returned to the meeting that he, Johannes, and Buck had had in his cabin when they'd decided to try their luck to the north.

Johannes had pointed out areas that were not identified on the chart. "This is the Bay of Fundy off the western coast of Nova Scotia. This land mass here is New Brunswick and down here is Maine. The Bay of Fundy separates Nova Scotia and New Brunswick." He went on filling in blank spots. "To the north of Nova Scotia is Newfoundland. Between the two is the Cabot Straits which leads to the Gulf of Saint Lawrence. There's only one way in and out of the Bay of Fundy, and only one good way out of the Gulf of Saint Lawrence."

"We don't want to get hemmed up in either of those places," Buck volunteered.

"We don't want to even get close," Johannes returned. "There's bound to be British warships patrolling the area."

Cooper agreed, "We'll stay well out and patrol. We'll replenish in one of Maine's coastal towns as we discussed, if need be."

The cry of 'sail ho' broke Cooper's reverie. His mind was going over the thoughts and conversations regarding Nova Scotia. In what seemed an eternity but in reality was only a couple of minutes, the lookout called down, "Fishing boat by the looks o' her."

"Why wouldn't it be?" Buck snorted. "We're off the Maine coast. Most of those Yankees fish." Cooper had to smile. Buck's mind was clearly on prizes…prize money to set himself up for a run at the New Orleans beauty, Mary Esther.

"Shall we close with the fishing boat," Johannes asked.

"Aye, we may gain some information," Cooper replied.

"Go to quarters?" young Ryker asked.

"I think not, Mr. Ryker. I believe you could sink yonder vessel with a swivel."

"Aye, Captain. He'll learn," Buck said. "He'll be a good officer, if he survives."

"Aye, if he survives," Cooper replied. "There is always that."

George Jewett was the captain of the fishing yawl, *Lazy Susan*. When he pulled alongside of *SeaFire*, Cooper called down, "Care to come aboard for a bit of refreshment."

Jewett was about to grab onto the man rope but paused, "The flag says you're American, but you sound English."

Cooper smiled down at the man, "Captain, you would definitely sound out of place in Savannah." Jewett smiled and got a firm grip on his pipe and climbed on board.

"Cooper Cain, born in England, now of Savannah," Cooper said, introducing himself. "This is my first officer, Mr. Buck Jewell; my second officer, Mr. Lamar Turner; and my third officer, Mr. Ryker Hall...all from Georgia." The officers exchanged handshakes and greetings.

Quang went down to make Josiah aware that the captain was bringing a guest down. Before they went below, Cooper ordered a signal be sent for St. Jacques to join them.

"Aye, Captain," Ryker replied and then went to signal *Thunderbolt's* captain.

JEWETT PROVED TO BE an affable sort who was loaded with information. "Portland and Freeport would be good places to drop anchor to rest your crew or make repairs. We have a few raiders who are at home there. Ye be too big for Harpswell or Cundy Harbor, I live there. I'd stay away from Eden, sometimes known as Bar Harbor also, seems that a few Redcoat raiders claim that place for themselves."

"Have the Freeport or Portland privateers had any luck?" St Jacques asked.

"I'd say several have," Jewett replied. "The brig, *Rapid*; and schooners, *Partridge*, *Parrot*, and *Rover* have done middling. But *Dash*, she was built to be a raider, much like this ship but not as big. She's been lucky at evading the Royal Navy leaving Freeport and returning with her prizes. She's fast - some say the fastest topsail schooner to ever put water under her keel. She doesn't patrol hereabout as I know of. She cruises the West Indies."

"We've had a couple of cruises in that direction ourselves," Buck admitted. "We felt it was time to change our pattern a mite."

"Ye may do well if you get out of Casco Bay," Jewett said with a grin. "I can't catch a New York fish, otherwise." This had everyone laughing and Josiah refilled their glasses.

Josiah appeared to pause after the glasses were filled. Noticing this, Cooper inquired. "Just wondering, Captain, what type of fresh fish or possibly lobster the good captain may have to sell."

"I've enough to fill your pots," Jewett happily replied. "May I make a suggestion, Captain Cooper?"

"Certainly sir," Cooper said.

"Would you like to follow me into Freeport? Folks seeing two strange ships might cause a panic. Were you to follow me in, it would cause less of a fuss, I believe."

"A splendid idea, M'sieur," St. Jacques replied instantly.

"I guess it's decided then," Cooper said.

"Ah…my pardon," St. Jacques started but Cooper waved it away.

George Jewett said his goodbyes a much happier and a bit wealthier man. He and his mate sailed the *Lazy Susan* to Cundy Harbor. Before he left Freeport, he went ashore with Cooper and St. Jacques and introduced them to Mr. Jameson, the owner of Jameson Tavern, and a man named Isley, who owned a ship's chandlery.

"We deal mostly in goods for fishing boats, but I will do my best to help out when you need anything," Isley promised. He was a jolly man, whose buttons strained to keep his shirt pulled together over an enormous belly.

St. Jacques whispered as Isley was leaving, "M'sieur misses few meals, I'd say." Cooper smiled.

The men drew straws to see who would keep an anchor watch and who would spend a night ashore. Cooper decided to sleep aboard ship. Surprisingly, over half of the ship's company had returned before Cooper went down to his cabin. He, Johannes, and Buck had gone over charts and developed a plan based more on known shipping routes and guesses than anything.

When Cooper put out his pipe and brushed his teeth, he lay down but couldn't sleep. He thought of Maddy's look of surprise when Luke, good as his word, pulled up in front of the house in a newly rebuilt carriage. The carriage, and even the spokes on the wheels, were painted white. The leather seats were a deep maroon color. The top, which was also white, could be let up or pushed down, depending on the day. The springs had been cleaned up and blackened.

Maddy had been ecstatic. "Oh, Coop, it's so big."

The trip to the house from the warehouse came to mind when Maddy said that. Hopefully, Maddy wouldn't have to sit in his lap now, although it hadn't been an unpleasant ride at that.

CHAPTER NINETEEN

I 'M NOT SAYING IT was a bad idea, Johannes," Buck explained. "I'm just saying it hasn't turned out to be a good idea so far."

SeaFire and *Thunderbolt* had sailed back and forth for three weeks straight without sighting anything other than a few fishing boats. St. Jacques was in the captain's cabin aboard *SeaFire*. He and Cooper were having a discussion as to whether one and then the other would sail back to Freeport and replenish supplies or wait another week. They also discussed maybe even heading more easterly.

"The Azores," St. Jacques volunteered.

Cooper traced circles on the table made by the bottom of his glass. "Let's give it three more days, Henri," he said, addressing St. Jacques by his first name. "After three days, we'll both head for Freeport to replenish and then head to the Azores as you recommend."

"Salute," St. Jacques said raising his glass to clink against Cooper's. "We have a plan, do we not?"

"We do," Cooper replied.

Once St. Jacques shoved off from *SeaFire*, Cooper called Johannes, the master, and his three officers together. Everyone had a glass of cool hard apple cider, something that everyone aboard the ship had acquired a taste for since arriving in Freeport. The owner of the Jameson Tavern had offered a free round to the ship's crew the first night they had gone ashore. The small gesture had paid the owner dividends.

The tavern owner gave Cooper and St. Jacques an abbreviated history on apples in the state of Maine. "A fellow named Ephraim Goodale started planting apple trees in Orrington, Maine about 1804. Hard apple cider has become an everyday choice of libation in Maine, since then. A man in Boston tells it that they had it before we did, but he has no proof." Cooper couldn't remember it being in Georgia or New Orleans, but maybe it was.

Josiah found something that proved to fit Cooper's appetite even better than the beverage. The cook at the Sloop Tavern made a sweet pastry, not unlike those made in New Orleans, but flavored with regular, not hard, apple cider. It was then sprinkled with sugar. Josiah bought a sack full and they lasted three days. Cooper swore that he'd have Josiah keelhauled if he gave any of the pastries to anyone other than the two of them. Cooper's conscience got the better of him and he invited the three officers down along with the master for refreshments. He gave each of them a pastry along with a glass of lemon juice. When everyone left, he had two pastries left.

"Josiah."

"Aye, Captain," Josiah replied.

"I think you and I shall enjoy these last two pastries," Cooper said.

At that moment, Quang knocked and came in, watching as Josiah took a bite of his pastry. Seeing where his cox'n's eyes were focused, Cooper handed the last one to him. "Try one of these, Quang," Cooper offered, feeling his last taste of culinary pleasure slip away.

Quang downed the pastry in two bites, whereas Cooper would have taken several small bites savoring each morsel. "Good," Quang said, and then reported, "Mr. Ewers thinks it might rain."

"Thank you," Cooper replied. "I'll be right up."

The pastries were long gone now, so Cooper decided that when they returned to Freeport he'd have Josiah buy as many as he could…and if possible, get the recipe.

THREE DAYS CAME AND went and still no sign of a convoy. The day was overcast and the master promised fog by tomorrow. *SeaFire* made its way toward Freeport with *Thunderbolt* to starboard. The men were restless so a day or so in Freeport wouldn't be amiss. They had just entered Casco Bay when Banty, who was the lookout, called down, "Sail Ho! To larboard."

The men rushed to the larboard rail to get a look but it was still too far away to see from the deck. Buck was at the wheel next to the master when the call came down.

"Not surprising to spot a sail in the bay," Johannes volunteered.

"I agree." The two men turned. The captain had made his way on deck, having heard the call through his open skylight.

"She be a fishing yawl," Banty called down, and then after a few minutes, he followed it up with, "She's the *Lazy Susan*. Captain Jewett." Another minute went by and Banty yelled again, "Jewett is waving his arms back and forth, Cap'n. I thinks he wants us to heave to."

"Aye! Mr. Buck, make it happen. Mr. Ryker, signal *Thunderbolt* to heave to and captain repair on board."

Orders were barked out and Johannes brought *SeaFire* into the wind as the sails were taken down. In a matter of a quarter hour, *Lazy Susan* had pulled alongside.

"I saw a British frigate," Jewett explained in an excited manner. "I think she must be scouting ahead of a convoy."

"What makes you say that?" Turner, the second officer inquired. A look from Cooper made him swallow and murmur, "Sorry, Captain."

"I'll tell you why," Jewett explained. "The last time I saw a frigate in this close to shore, an entire by Gawd convoy followed the next morning."

Cooper looked at Henri St. Jacques, a smile on his face. Using another of Eli Taylor's phrases, Cooper said, "Maybe we haven't been skunked after all."

St. Jacques smiled, "Aye, and if the fog comes as the master promises..."

Plans were made and signals worked out but each captain knew attacking a convoy was always fraught with hazard. It could be worse in a fog. It would have to be independent action with a rendezvous at Freeport.

After accompanying St. Jacques to the entry port, Cooper shook his friend's hand. "God's speed, Henri."

Smiling, St. Jacques came to attention and gave a smart salute and replied, "You as well, Coop, you as well."

THE FOG MOVED IN as predicted by Johannes. It was a miserable eerie feeling. The wind was faint, and the moisture from the fog soon soaked through the crew's clothes. Banty, in the tops, constantly wiped his eyes and the lens of his scope with a rag that was now soaked. The ship was, other than an occasional slap of a wave against the hull, silent.

Josiah handed Cooper a tarpaulin, at dawn, before he went on deck. "You'll need this sooner than later, I'm thinking." It was a little warm, but at least he wasn't wet.

Thunderbolt lay to larboard but she may as well have been in Freeport or Savannah as far as it mattered. Cooper couldn't see the ship. *Hell, I can barely see SeaFire's bow*, he thought. The plan was to let the convoy pass and then approach from astern and take what they could, doing it as silently as possible.

Three boarding parties had already been planned, with each party ready when their captain signaled. There would be no shouting, pistols or muskets. Blades, spikes, and belaying pins would be their weapons...that and surprise. The leader of each party would have a brace of pistols. Hopefully, they'd not be needed.

"I hear something," Buck whispered. After a pause, he said, "There it is again."

"A ship's bell," Johannes said. "It's a ship bell!"

After what seemed an eternity of floating along in a sea of fog, Banty suddenly slid down a backstay and rushed to the quarter-deck. "There they be, Cap'n," he hissed, pointing into the fog.

All eyes watched in the general direction Banty had pointed to. There it was. Out of the early morning, a ghostly ship emerged out of the heavy fog, moving slowly. As it sailed past, two lanterns could be seen giving of a reddish glow. Shortly after it passed, another ship with its sails partially visible could be seen more distant and to larboard than the first ship. *She would be closer to Thunderbolt,* Cooper thought.

"That was a good size merchant man," Turner whispered. The men on the quarterdeck nodded but didn't speak.

Closer and right off the larboard bow, sails appeared with glimpses of the hulls, smaller ships, but whose holds would be full of merchandise and possibly war materials. Other than the twin lanterns and the clanging ship's bells at intervals, the ships sailed almost blindly, at the mercy of the fog.

Cooper glanced through his telescope but it was useless. Patiently they waited. When it had been ten minutes since the last ship had passed by, *SeaFire* got underway. Unlike the usual noise associated with the evolution, it was done very quietly. As wind filled the sails, waves broke against the bow and timbers creaked and groaned. *SeaFire* cut across the water, causing a chilled, salty sea spray to come in board. Cooper, leaving the ship handling to his professional men, took the opportunity to take off his tarpaulin. It would be a hindrance if he were called into battle.

The glow of stern lanterns could be seen in the distance. Cooper thought to himself, *that's one ship that will not be taking supplies to Nova Scotia.* Sailing along at a steady clip, they were now directly astern of the merchant ship. Men had gathered forward. Mr. Ryker with the gunner, Spurlock, was ready to board. Johannes had the wheel himself. He had watched the ship as they approached. She sailed along in good fashion, not wallowing or veering. They were alongside the merchant ship now, and the boarding party went over without a word. All eyes had been to forward so that it was only at the last minute that a shout was heard.

"Veer off, veer off." They'd obviously mistaken *SeaFire* for another ship in the convoy. *They'd soon learn their mistake*, Cooper thought. A few more shouts were heard, followed by a thud.

As previously arranged, Ryker came to the rail quickly and shouted, "Secured." Had any other word been said, *SeaFire* would have sent another party over, enough to overwhelm the merchant ship. As *SeaFire* pulled away, the merchant ship could be seen as it come about and headed for the rendezvous point.

"That went well," Buck volunteered energetically. The ship was silent again as the men returned to their duties.

"Wind is picking up," Johannes informed Cooper.

"How long?" Cooper asked.

"Long enough if we don't get greedy," Johannes replied bluntly.

It was not long before Buck broke the silence, "It appears that we have two ships sailing almost parallel, Captain."

The two men walked forward. There were four sets of stern lights. One set was higher and wider apart to the others which were lower and closer together.

"What do you think, Captain?"

Cooper shook his head. "I don't know, Buck. Another merchant ship would not overtake and pass in this fog. The larger ship could be an escort ship. Maybe the smaller ship has some clue that we just took one of theirs and is sailing forth with a warning."

Cooper, Buck, and Johannes watched as the smaller ship closed with the larger one. "Steady as she goes, but be ready to come about," Cooper hissed to Johannes.

Things looked out of place. It came to Cooper as he watched, "We have another raider in our midst, gentlemen."

"David has picked Goliath it appears," Buck said.

Cooper was thinking along Buck's lines when gunfire broke out. Bright flashes followed by the report of guns as pistols were fired.

"Damnation," Buck was frustrated and slapped his leg with his hat.

Do we go forward or what, Cooper thought to himself. *Would the gunfire alert the escort ships? Which side of the formation was the escort ship on? Was there one on each side? Would St. Jacques think they were the ones having a go of it? What to do?*

Shouting could now be heard on the larger ship. 'Cheers, cheers' that sounded like it came from the British..

"I don't think that's a grocery ship," Cooper said. "I bet that is a troop ship."

"I believe you are right," Buck replied.

Moving back toward the quarterdeck, Cooper spoke just above a whisper, "Two points to starboard if you will, Mr. Johannes."

No sooner had Cooper spoke, than a flash was noted to larboard. The flash continued up but the visibility in the fog was lacking for any distance. "A flare," Johannes guessed. He then added, "Though little good it will do in this fog."

CHAPTER TWENTY

THE SHIPS IN THE convoy continued on their course. It was the better part of a quarter hour before the next set of stern lights could be seen. Was it another small merchant ship, a brig perhaps?

Looking for a silver lining for the disappointment he felt, Buck quipped, "Less likely to be a troop ship."

Cooper smiled. "Aye," he replied. "Send your next party over as we come alongside, if you please."

Buck smiled now. "Aye, Captain."

The boarding went smoothly. *Shall we try one more*? Cooper asked himself. They had been lucky so far, but the fog was clearing fast. The stern of the next ship was visible already. It was not a small brig, like the previous ship, but no liner either.

"Let's try this one," Cooper told Johannes and Buck. "We will make a run for it after that." Both men nodded their understanding. Luck had been on their side. No need to push it.

The sound of bare feet running on the deck planks alerted Cooper. It was a seaman named Goose. "Ship to starboard bearing down on us, Cap'n. It is coming from in front of the convoy."

"Do we have time to fall back in behind yonder ship?" Cooper asked.

"Not without some risk to our bowsprit."

"Keep on course." Cooper grabbed a speaking trumpet. He paused, and looked at Buck,

"Be ready to let go a broadside if I don't pull this off." He then rushed to the starboard rail almost as the bow of a British frigate came alongside. "Blimey, it's our escort," Cooper shouted. He paused and then continued, "Jump to it, blast ye," he yelled excitedly. "The bloody jonathans are being beastly. They've already pinched a couple of ships, I'm thinking. You need to get this sorted out."

Somebody on the frigate yelled back, "Up yer arse." It was then followed by, "Silence, take that man's name." The frigate passed by and was quickly out of sight.

Johannes and Buck were smiling as Cooper returned to the quarterdeck. "Fooled me," Buck said.

"Aye," Johannes agreed.

"Buck, let's let this ship go and get the next one. Once you have control come to starboard and stay in our wake. We are going to give the convoy a wide berth. I doubt a ruse would work a second time," Cooper said. Buck nodded and then went to round up his party.

"Quang!" The big Chinaman stepped forward. He was never far away, Cooper had come to realize. "Tell Mr. Jewell if yonder ship is bigger than the last one, he is to take ten extra men." Quang made a quick nod and then ran forward.

"She has the looks of an Indiaman," Johannes said speaking softly.

Cooper looked in the direction of the ship. The fog was dissipating rapidly as the wind seemed to wake up. Looking through his glass gave Cooper a better view now, but the moisture quickly clouded the glass. It was an Indiaman and she was pierced but other than a few old brass cannons, she was probably *en flute*. Another term that he'd learned from Eli. 'Means no guns,' Eli swore. 'They didn't teach you anything,' Eli had sworn again.

"Yes," Cooper replied. "A lot about loving and fencing, but very little about stealing other than some maiden's heart."

"Well, you've got the best teacher now," Eli had said with a grin. "Most captains and owners are such skinflints that they don't want to give up cargo space for cannons. Nor do they want to pay the men to man them, so they sail without them or *en flute*."

"Sounds French," Cooper had said.

"You got an ear for that. It is French," Eli had said.

Quang touched Cooper's shoulder, effectively bringing his attention back to the matter at hand. They were almost alongside the Indiaman. A man had walked to the rail. He saw *SeaFire* but before he could yell, a belaying pin was hurled at him. It struck the man in the head and dropped him.

"McKemie," Quang volunteered, pronouncing it 'MacIme.'

The boarding party went over, including the extra ten men. Yells and shouts could be heard as the skirmish was on going. Nervously, Cooper waited. The sounds were diminishing but there was still no Buck. Cooper had decided to send another party over, one that he'd lead, when Buck came to the rail.

"There are lots of passengers...some of them are army officers."

"Do you need more men?" Cooper asked.

Buck hesitated briefly, "Wouldn't hurt, Captain."

Seeing Skeeter and Johnson, Cooper called to them, "Get six more men and go over to help Mr. Jewell."

"Aye, Cap'n."

"Skeeter, if anything goes amiss and you need help tell me everything's perfect, and then get down."

Skeeter smiled, "Don't worry, Cap'n, we's will handle it. But if not, you blast away." With that being said, the man was gone.

After another minute, Buck called back, "Secured."

Skeeter then pumped his arm as he did back in their pirating days. Things were well.

"Mr. Ewers, bring us to starboard, if you will," Cooper said.

The master knew the plan. He changed the course with as minimal sail handling as possible. Cooper stood at the stern and watched the prize follow in their wake. They'd pulled it off...so far. Hopefully, St. Jacques and the other prize crews were safe and headed toward the rendezvous location.

Josiah came on deck, carrying a dry cloth and a cup of steaming black coffee. Cooper had been too occupied to realize how wet he was. The fog had soaked his uniform and the wind had created a bit of a chill.

"We will continue on this course for another thirty minutes," Cooper advised his master. "If there is still no sign of trouble, we will change course and head to our rendezvous with the other ships."

"Browne," Cooper called to one of the cook's helpers.

"Aye, Cap'n."

"Tell the cook to light up the galley stove and let's get some coffee or cocoa for the men. Be ready to put out the fire at a moment's notice, mind you."

"Yes sir. I'll have a bucket of sea water ready."

The cook was a fat little Mexican, who had been the old cook's helper. When *SeaFire* was commissioned, the old cook had retired. Pepe had done a good job, though he did on occasion use a few more peppers than were called for. 'Keeps their bowel flowing,' Dr. Cannington had joked. In truth, it was no spicier than a lot of the Cajun meals that Cooper had eaten. Besides, Pepe knew how to make good hot cocoa. He mixed just the right amount of sugar in to make it very pleasing to drink. In port, and when it was available, he used milk instead of water. It would be water this time. However, after a raid in such conditions, the men would appreciate the hot cocoa.

"Casco Bay," Johannes said, while closing his glass with a snap. All the ships had rendezvoused as planned, with *SeaFire* and the last prize the only stragglers. After meeting up, *SeaFire* led the prizes while *Thunderbolt* brought up the rear. Shepherding the ships to their destination was not difficult at all. Once the ships were taken, their captains started dwelling on how much they'd make on insurance after they were able to file their claims.

Cooper had not left the quarterdeck for over twenty-four hours. Trying to stifle a yawn, he decided he'd send down for another cup of coffee. He turned to speak to Quang, and noticed that Johannes was yawning also.

A smile lit up Johannes' face once the yawn went away. "Aye, Captain, it's catching they say." Both men smiled now.

"Quang, have Josiah send up two cups of coffee."

Quang gave the briefest of nods and then headed through the companionway and down to the captain's cabin. Cooper was sure he'd gone through a pot of coffee but it had helped to keep him awake. It also had chased the chill away. Touching his coat, he was surprised it no longer felt damp. His hands no longer looked white and shriveled up from being wet hours on end. Not so his boots…they squished when he walked. He'd get them off in the next hour or so.

Leon walked by, barefoot. Cooper wondered if he should try bare feet for a while…but no, he couldn't do that. Why…he didn't know but it didn't seem "captainly" to do such a thing. Looking about, the men all seemed to be of good cheer…and why not? Most of them had taken turns going below for ten to fifteen minutes at a time and drinking Pepe's hot cocoa. While that helped, what was lined up behind them like baby ducks following their mama was what cheered the men so. Prizes... prizes meant prize money. A good number of them had probably already been calculating their share. Some of the men, once they were paid off would be broke before they sailed again. Alcohol, gambling, sporting houses full of wenches ready to take a man to his own brand of paradise...for a fee. Other crew members would bank their money after taking out a bit for spending. Johannes, Spurlock, Diamond, and McKemie, they were the ones who thought of the future. Even Skeeter and Banty had started putting back a little money. Quang had given his money to Cooper for bank for him. Cooper kept a booklet with Quang's money recorded in it. He'd tried to give it to his cox'n, and said, "You keep the book so you will know how much you have."

Quang said, "Me already know."

"He might not be good with English," Eli had said and laughed, "but he knows his sums though."

"Fishing boats, Captain."

Who was that in the lookout, Cooper wondered. It wasn't Banty. Shielding his eyes with his hand to look into the sun, Cooper still couldn't see who spoke.

"It's Leon, Captain. He went up with Browne." It was one of the helmsmen, Lopez, who spoke. He and Pepe were the only two Mexicans on board. "Banty has been taking him up." Cooper nodded. Lopez didn't have the distinct accent that Pepe had.

Quang was back with the coffee. He spoke one word as he handed a cup to Cooper and then Johannes, "Hot."

The fishing boats were headed out for the morning. One of the boats came within hailing distance. "Morning to you, Captain."

"To you as well," Cooper called back.

"Is the schooner, *Mary E.*, in company?"

"No, just *Thunderbolt* and our prizes," Cooper replied.

"Thank you, Captain," the man shouted as his boat sailed out of the bay.

Could that have been the ship attacking the troop ship, Cooper wondered. He turned to Johannes, who spoke before Cooper could ask, "I don't think that was a schooner, Captain. It seemed more like a brig, though in truth, I didn't get a good look at her." Cooper nodded but didn't reply.

The next fishing boat was Jewett in the *Lazy Susan*. "It looks like you made a nice catch," Jewett said.

"Thanks to you," Cooper shouted back. "How would you like to rent me your boat today, Captain Jewett?"

"How much?"

"More than you'd make fishing," Cooper responded.

"Done, Captain Cain," Jewett replied.

Cooper smiled, and turning to Johannes, he said, "Lets anchor off Chebeague Island."

"Aye," Johannes replied. "Do you want Darby to send up a signal?"

"Aye, I'd not want Mr. Jewell to put a bowsprit through the stern windows." The helmsman laughed, and then so did Cooper and Johannes.

CHAPTER TWENTY ONE

QUANG HAD JUST HELPED Cooper out of his wet boots. A blister was forming on his heel. Quang looked at the blister and said, "Wait," and then he left the room.

While Cooper was waiting, Dr. Beau Cannington knocked and came in. "Mr. Jewell and several of his boarding party were knocked about. They have a few contusions and lacerations. Mr. Jewell is one that needs ligatures.

"Why are you waiting then?" Cooper asked.

"He says that he has a present for you, Captain. After which, he will come down to be attended to. I know how likely it is for our Mr. Jewell to be called upon, so I decided to wait here if you don't mind."

"Of course not," Cooper replied.

"My captain! Let me see your foot, that's a large blister you have there," Dr. Carrington exclaimed.

"Yes, I've noticed. Quang told me not to put on anything until he returned. Would you like a refreshment, Doctor?"

"I don't mind. I'm curious as to what our heathen friend prescribes for your foot."

Josiah got Dr. Cannington a glass of sweetened lime juice and had just given it to him when Quang entered the room. He carried a small roll of cloth, a plant in a small pot, and what appeared to be a pair of cloth shoes. Cannington looked on with interest as Quang broke open a leaf from the plant and squeezed a greenish gel from it. The gel made the blister feel cool immediately. He

135

covered the entire blister with a bit of cloth. After tying the cloth, he put a pair of Chinese slippers on Cooper's feet.

"No hurt," Quang said.

Cooper smiled and said, "Feels good, Quang."

Quang picked up his plant and cloth and left the room.

"Well, damme," Beau Cannington swore. "That's aloe he put on your blister. It's been around since biblical days, but I didn't know that it helped blisters."

Buck Jewell knocked and then came in, "Present for you, Captain." With that said, Buck pulled out a cloth that was tucked in the waist of his britches. He unfolded the yellow cloth to show a large black "F". You got yourself another one of the buggers," Buck swore smiling. "It was the last ship that we boarded. The captain was a cheeky little man who's been terribly inconvenienced."

Cooper was now smiling, "Josiah!"

"Aye, Captain."

"Whiskey man, we've a toast to make…and go ahead and get yourself a glass. You will, anyway." When the whiskey was poured, Cooper stood, "To Buck Jewell, the best mate a captain could have."

Once the toast was made, Cooper sat back, more pleased than he'd been earlier. Doctor Cannington prescribed one more round of whiskey for Buck, as a medicinal, and then led him to his sick bay.

COOPER STOOD AFT LOOKING as the last of the sun settled over the horizon. They were headed home, back to Savannah. *Thunderbolt* led the small convoy of six prizes. Between *SeaFire* and *Thunderbolt*, they had picked up twenty volunteers to help with the prizes in Freeport. The military items carried on the prizes were taken to the military receiving officer in Portland and receipts were given. The colonel at the Portland office was glad to get the munitions, tents, boots, and even a few winter coats, but related the 'damnable Redcoat's uniforms' were worthless. He did include them in his inventory of received goods. He also took charge of the military prisoners, which consisted of four officers. There was one colonel, one major, and two captains. Each officer had a servant and there was one quartermaster sergeant. The officers gave their parole and would be used in a prisoner exchange. The colonel gave his word for the sergeant, which Cooper thought was odd until being told only officers were considered gentlemen, whose honor entitled them to give parole. Cooper thought, *I'd rather trust the sergeant than a slew of officers I've met.*

The *Lazy Suzanne* was used to transport the war supplies and prisoners ashore. Jewett made two trips after that to Eden, taking the captains and crews. Cooper had taken another tip from his mentor, Eli Taylor, and in addition to personal goods, each captain was given, in front of the ship's crew, sufficient funds to last them until passage could be made home. The one exception was for the Finylson ships. He allowed the crew everything as on the other ships. However, when it came to the cheeky Captain Ross, Cooper took pleasure in telling the fellow that he'd have to use his own funds for his passage home. He also explained that his cousin would likely want a receipt for every schilling spent, so he cautioned Ross to keep good records.

The crew of *SeaFire* was headed home, back to some rest and down time. It was a time to relax. Cooper wanted to see how the hog hunt went, and to sit with Eli. Most of all, he was excited to back with Maddy, his wife and lover. His mind was on their last parting and lovemaking before he left when Quang called, "Captain!"

"Yes, Quang, what is it?"

"Josiah has meal ready."

"Thank you, Quang." Cooper wondered if his cox'n would ever make a complete sentence but decided it didn't matter. They could communicate with each other. Besides, when he was handling Cooper's boat and ...more importantly, when he needed his blade, those things were done exceedingly well. The thought then came to Cooper, *what would he do with Quang when the war was over and he didn't need him as a cox'n or his blade in battle?* Cooper smiled to himself. Quang could do what he wanted. He'd always be welcome with Cooper.

Cooper got to his cabin just minutes before Beau Cannington and young Ryker Hall. They were both his guests for the evening meal. Josiah had prepared a meal that started with lobster chowder. When they finished this, a golden fried cod was served with new potatoes, peas, and buttery carrots. Hot fresh baked bread was prepared and disappeared rather quickly. A white wine made from Maine's grapes was served with the meal. After the meal, brandy was served.

Beau tasted the brandy and announced, "Armagnac, a wonderful choice."

Cooper smiled, "A bottle from a case sent over by Jean LaFitte."

Beau smiled, "To your education, Mr. Ryker. Claret is for ladies and boys. Brandy is for men. It's like a fine cigar. It can be enjoyed alone or in company. It is without a doubt the choice of true gentlemen for an after dinner libation." Turning to Cooper, Beau continued, "Did you know, Captain, that Armagnac was introduced in France in the 1500's. In fact, it came to be seven hundred years before cognac. It came from the foothills of Pyrenees, as I recall."

"I'm glad that we were able to appeal to your taste, my good doctor. I will endeavor to obtain more."

Beau grew very serious. "For Jean LaFitte or anyone else to give you a case of this brandy, Captain, means one of two things.

Mr. LaFitte didn't realize what he had, which I doubt, knowing him as I do; or he thinks of you as a considerable friend. You may desire to offer something as nice when you next meet."

"Thank you, Beau. I will certainly do as you say," Cooper replied.

Josiah was back at the table, "Would you and your guests care for coffee with your dessert, Captain?"

"Aye, coffee for me," Cooper said.

"Me as well," Ryker answered.

"If there's another glass, I think I will stay with this," Cannington replied.

Damn, there goes me taste, Josiah thought. *Maybe the glass didn't have to be completely full.* Smiling to himself, Josiah headed to the pantry. Taking a nip, he filled the good doctor's glass half full. Seeing there was still a bit in the bottle, Josiah shrugged and turned it up. *Ah! He was right…an exceptional brandy.* Carrying the tray with the pastries and drinks back to the captain's table, Josiah did not miss the look he got. *Caught*, he thought, and hurriedly put down everything. When he turned to ask if anything else was needed, he caught the wink. Providence…yes sir, meeting young Captain Cooper Cain was providence. It was not a berth he'd want to give up anytime soon.

CHAPTER TWENTY TWO

HOMECOMING WAS EVERYTHING THAT Cooper could have asked for and more. Maddy knew how to make her man feel glad that he was home. They had eaten with James and Josie, Eli and Debbie, Colonel Bledsoe and his wife. Suzanne, the colonel's daughter, had made him laugh until he cried. They had even dined with Colonel and Mama Lee after church on a Sunday afternoon. It was good to talk and visit with the Lees, but things were not the same with Jonah and Moses gone. They were off 'to help the president', Colonel Lee volunteered. Jonah had been made a special agent to President Madison at the recommendation of the Secretary of War.

It was almost Christmas. The days had started to turn cold before they left Maine. The mornings and evenings now had a chill, but the middle of the day was nice. Eli had been most impressed with the ships and cargo that Cooper and St. Jacques had returned with.

"Coop, not only I, but also the investors, have recouped their investments and are very happy. So much so, I'm sure they will be more than willing to underwrite any further cruises." Catching the look Cooper gave him, Eli smiled, "Don't worry, son, you'll be home until after the holidays. It's storm season in the Caribbean and I doubt there will be any more convoys north for a spell; so you will have some time off. Your only problem is keeping a crew together. You'll have your usual crew, those that date back to the *Raven*. They'll hang around as long as they have money. It's the others you have to worry about. Speaking of money, our agent has monies for the first two cruises now. They can meet outside the warehouse tomorrow afternoon and collect part or all of their pay. We will set up accounts for them that desire one at the Bank of Savannah, that's our bank. I'm on the board, by the way."

Cooper looked at his mentor, "That's like putting a fox in the henhouse, I believe." He said this smiling.

"My boy, why would you say such a thing?"

Cooper found an unexpected visitor when he got home, though a most welcome one. Sitting in the kitchen drinking a cup of coffee was Dagan. "Nothing to keep me in Norfolk, so I decided to come visit my family," Dagan threw out, without being asked. "I figured you'd be home for a few months."

"Dagan, you are always welcome with us."

Dagan still had fire in his eyes but Cooper could see his age was catching up with him…and probably the loneliness. Maddy looked at Cooper with that look that melted his heart and made him give in to anything she asked.

Maddy then said, "I told Uncle Dagan that he needed to sell his old house up there where it gets cold and come stay with us."

Cooper realized that was a great idea. There was no one he'd like better to be around when he was gone than Maddy's uncle. "You are right," Cooper exclaimed.

"Your house is not that big," Dagan protested.

"We'll add on to it or build you a house or cottage," Cooper replied. "We will not take no for an answer."

Dagan smiled now, "In truth, I've already sold my house to one of Caleb and Kitty's sons. I told you about Caleb being Maddy's father's first ship surgeon, if you remember. His son is a doctor now and needed a place."

"You planned to stay with us, Uncle?" Maddy inquired.

"In truth, Maddy, I'd planned to stay for a while and then go to Antigua, but I believe it was meant for me to be here. Things are just not as clear as they once were."

Maddy was happy, Cooper could see that. It would be good to spend the holidays at home with family. Tomorrow he'd let Dagan decide on an additional room to be added on or a separate cottage and where he wanted it...close by certainly. He'd already thought about building a place for Josiah and Quang. *Things seemed to be turning out, at least for the time being*, he thought. In war, anything was possible; something he'd be well advised to remember. Things could go bad very quickly...and frequently did.

ANTIGUA...GOVERNOR SIR ROBERT BASSNIGHT sat across from Vice Admiral Sir Gabe Anthony, enjoying a brandy and discussing his recent visitor. Cooper's cousin, Phillip Finylson, had been to see Sir Robert in regards to finding out who had acted as Cooper Cain's agent. The man had essentially helped Cooper steal his property. Who was this man? The bank didn't know... or wouldn't tell.

"Sir, you must understand," Sir Robert had explained. "Those matters are most confidential. You were, in fact, delinquent on your payment. An investor stood by with cash money in hand to buy the land. Surely a businessman, such as yourself, should know the bank couldn't wait any longer for their money."

"The money was on its way. My ship was taken by my cousin who has turned pirate," Phillip said.

"A cousin, you say. Why would one steal from his relative?" Sir Robert asked.

"He has...he and my father had a falling out," Phillip replied.

"Oh, come now, man."

Phillip continued, "His mother and that Frenchman own the place now, stole it really."

Sir Robert stood up at that. "Young man, as governor of this island, I can tell you 'that Frenchman', as you say, is highly regarded. He is also a master swordsman. If word got out that you slandered him or his wife, I'm sure he'd require satisfaction. Now as we have nothing further to say, I bid you good day."

"Did he offer any further argument?" Sir Gabe asked.

"None, sir," Robert smiled. "In truth, I rather enjoyed sticking it to the sodomite."

Sir Gabe smiled, but it quickly vanished. "Unfortunately, our 'Sir Pirate', as Maddy calls him, has been sticking it to our convoys. He's taking our ships, seemingly at his leisure, from the Indian Ocean to Nova Scotia."

Sir Robert nodded as he puffed on his pipe. Taking the pipe in hand, he said, "I understand had he not recognized Jake and broke off the action, he could have sunk his ship."

"Aye," Sir Gabe replied. "Officially, Jake fought off two privateers. He'd all but finished the one privateer when Cooper showed up. Cooper could have sunk the ship, and would have had Jake not been recognized. Then damned if he didn't talk about Josie and James, telling Jake they were going to have a baby. He did inquire if Jake needed a surgeon or anything. He then had the sense to recommend to Jake that when he wrote up his report, to make sure he documented he'd defeated one privateer and then fought the other off until it gave up and left. Jake had the good sense to write up his report just as Coop told him to."

Knocking the burnt ash from his pipe bowl, Sir Robert looked at his friend, "I give you this, Gabe. Nobody...and I mean nobody can say they've ever seen the like as our young Cooper

Cain. Were he in the navy, he'd have given Nelson a run." Both men smiled at this.

"He's too good and too lucky, Sir Robert. Lloyds of London has spent a fortune on insurance claims. They have the Prime Minister's ear. No longer will convoys go out poorly escorted. They now will be escorted by at least one third rate and two or three frigates."

Sir Robert looked at Gabe and asked, "Jake just got command of a frigate, did he not?"

"Aye, a new thirty-six, *HMS Storm*," Gabe responded.

"A step up for Jake, is it not?"

Gabe closed his eyes momentarily. "Yes, but one expected to go in harm's way, to do what's necessary to protect the convoy. That's not all," Gabe continued, "Mac, Cooper's friend David MacArthur, has now been given command of a sloop of war."

Sir Robert could see the lines of worry on his friend's face. Faith would not make matters any easier. How could she, with a husband, and children on each side? He wondered what kept Gabe from hauling down his flag. He thought then, *how could he?*

JIMMY SPURLIN AND HIS crew had finally put a dent in the damages that the hogs were doing to crops and started to focus on the swamps.

"Swim they do, I seen 'em," Luke was telling a group of men at the local tavern. "They didn't get far though, as they came out of the ditch, Spurlin's dogs was there. They had that ole hog caught up in no time at all."

"How many you reckon he'd done kilt?" one man asked.

"I don't know, but hundreds I expect."

"Is that pork fittin' to eat?" someone else asked.

"I ain't sure bout that neither. You don't see any of Spurlin's crowd eating it."

"How long you 'spect he'll stay around?"

"I think as scarce as the hogs have been lately, he'll go back to Alabama soon."

"Think the hog problem be over, does he?"

"No, he said they'd be shy for a while and then they'd be back," Luke said, as he tipped a glass of ale.

The men muttered amongst themselves for a bit, and then the turkey shoot came up. "Hear they's going to give out a whole side of beef to the winner." The shoot was to be on Christmas Eve, two days from then.

"I wonder what it will be like," Luke said.

A number of the local marksmen were off with the war. Luke finished his ale and said good bye to the loafers, who always seemed to be gathered at the small tavern outside Thunderbolt.

THE WAGON WAS LOADED down with cedar shakes to roof Dagan's cottage. The sawmill had done a wonderful job sawing them. The chimney had been just about finished when Luke had left. Colonel Bledsoe had a man who turned out to be a better than average stone mason. He, with Quang's help, had the fireplace and chimney butted up to the cottage with little visible cracks. Chinking would seal it perfectly.

Dagan, Maddy's uncle, was a strange but likeable fellow. His being around seemed to make Cooper feel more at ease in regards to being away from Maddy. He was not someone to mess with, Luke decided. Even as old as he was, he had the look and demeanor that said 'don't take me for granted'. No, anyone with a brain could see the old sailor could still be a formidable opponent.

CHAPTER TWENTY THREE

I T WAS CHRISTMAS EVE 1812, the day of the turkey shoot. The prize was sponsored by Colonel and Mrs. Lee. The Lee boys, Jonah and Moses, had been winning for the past few years, and the side of beef had been given to the orphanage. A crowd always gathered for the turkey shoot. Tables were set up and covered plates were brought to the shoot. Kegs of cider and beer were put out. Men arm wrestled, Indian wrestled, threw knives and tomahawks at targets, and then shot for the side of beef.

"Are you going to enter any of the contests?" Eli asked Cooper.

"No, my expertise is with the blade," Cooper said smiling. "Besides, Eli, I've been chosen to be the judge of the pie contest."

"Better pick Maddy's then."

Cooper smiled again, "She didn't enter one."

The number of people shooting in the turkey shoot was more than usual. The judge was Reverend Goodin. The preliminaries started at ten a.m. Each man was allowed three shots at the target, which was a large V. The shooters that got the closest to the bottom of the V, without going outside of the lines, moved to the next round. By noon, the shooters had been pared down to four people. They'd break for lunch now, and start again after everyone had eaten.

Cooper, meanwhile, had narrowed the pie contest down to the final three...an apple pie, a blackberry pie, and a cherry pie. In truth, the contest was between the apple and blackberry pie. He knew that there would be a first, second and third place winner.

The cherry pie was good so it would be the third place winner, but trying to choose between the apple and blackberry pies was difficult. He asked for a cup of coffee, and as it was being fetched he stood up and put the third place ribbon on the cherry pie. A girl shouted, danced in a little circle, and then snatched the ribbon off of the pie. She gave Cooper a kiss on the cheek and danced off squealing, happy that she'd taken third place.

When the coffee arrived, Cooper took a sip after blowing on the hot liquid. He then took a bite of the apple pie and took another sip of coffee. He waited a full minute, building suspense in the contestants. He then repeated his steps with the blackberry pie. He stood up, after taking another sip of coffee, "Second place to the apple pie and first place to the blackberry pie."

"I won, I won!" It was Suzanne Bledsoe. The apple pie was made by David Gill's wife, and both women seemed happy that they had won, but Maddy was ecstatic.

"You won, Suzanne, you won!" Maddy said. "Coop."

"Yes, Maddy," Cooper replied.

"How did you decide which pie was the best?"

"I chose the one that went down the best with coffee. If it went down easy, you could eat more." The women were all laughing at Cooper's logic now.

Once lunch was over, the shooting started again. One of the shooters was a young man named Buster Reynolds. The other shooter was Spurlock, Cooper's gunner. The two men had just beaten out their rivals.

"Captain, I'd sure like to have Reynolds with us as a sharpshooter. The kid can shoot," Buck said. Cooper nodded his acknowledgement.

Reverend Goodin was looking at the targets. "Tie as near as I can tell," he said.

Reynolds looked at the targets. "Put a nail in the center and back up to one hundred yards, and the closest wins," he said. The two targets were put up and the men stepped off the distance.

"I can't even see the target," Cooper said. "I can barely see the V."

Spurlock wiped the front site, and lifted the gun and fired, almost without aiming. "He hit the nail," a voice shouted.

The men moved back and gave Reynolds room. His motion was fluid as he raised his gun and fired. "A hit," was shouted, followed by, "Dead center."

The targets were brought to the firing line where the reverend examined them. Spurlock's nail was hit just to the right, bending it slightly. Reynolds' was dead center and drove the nail into the target.

Cooper leaned in and whispered, "Come see me sometime, son," as the reverend announced the winner. Reynolds gave a slight nod but didn't speak.

"What are you going to do with all that meat, Buster?" someone asked.

"Give it to my ma," he replied. "I'm tired of greens and peas." Everyone laughed at his comment.

Cooper called Quang over, "Give this to the boy. Tell him it was a special bonus that we didn't announce." Quang hefted the bag, nodded and went to catch up with the boy.

"That was generous." Cooper turned to see Dagan standing there.

"They can use it," Cooper replied. Placing his arm on Dagan's shoulder, they walked back to the crowd.

It was starting to cloud up, and Dagan volunteered, "It will be a wet Christmas and then turn cold."

"We will be warm and dry," Cooper responded.

Dagan paused in his stride, after a few steps and said, "Tell me, Cooper, do you ever miss our British meals?"

Cooper stopped, his head canted skyward as if in deep thought. "Kidney pie, pickled salmon, suckling pig, cold mutton, and mincemeat pies, mmm…I could go on." Lowering his head and opening his eyes, Cooper looked at his friend a moment and they both started laughing.

Maddy, seeing her husband and uncle walking shoulder to shoulder and laughing so, felt all was right in this world full of chaos and war. Tomorrow was Christmas. She'd have Cooper, Uncle Dagan, and James…*but what of mother and father?* It would be her first without them. She then had another thought; *it might be the first of many Christmases without my parents.* Tearing, she rushed to Cooper, burying her face in his chest.

"I'll get the carriage," Dagan volunteered. As he walked off, he half-turned and mouthed to Cooper, "Christmas without mother and father."

Cooper gave a slight nod to indicate he understood, while at the same time pulling Maddy to him and holding her closely. His wife was having the same type of emotions that he'd experienced when he'd been banned and sent away from his uncle's house and his mother. He'd even cried, vowing to wreak havoc on the man that had caused this separation…more determined in his desire for revenge than ever.

Maddy sniffled, trying to stop her crying. Cooper bent over and kissed her on top of her head. He'd been alone and idle when he'd been overcome with emotions. He'd not let Maddy stay idle. James and Josie were coming to eat after church service. Jessie would come as well and probably Suzanne Bledsoe. She was one of the funniest people that Cooper had ever been around. It was no wonder Maddy liked her. He had realized that having young friends around was certainly good for his wife, especially at times like Christmas, when she was separated from her parents.

DAGAN WOKE UP IN his cottage, his newly built and so far sparsely furnished cottage. The cottage had been quickly built by men experienced in their craftsmanship…carpenters who knew their business.

Dagan's left shoulder and hand ached where he'd laid on them in his sleep. He stretched out, turning onto his back, his hand moving to his chest. He felt the scars that covered his body from countless sea battles. The one on his shoulder felt tight and uncomfortable as it usually did in cold or rainy weather. It would rain…and then turn cold, he decided. Old injuries proved good at predicting the weather.

The cottage was chilled this morning; undoubtedly the coals in the fireplace would be all but out. Rising up and sitting on the side of the bed, Dagan could see himself. His once thick black hair now hung in loose silver gray strands. His knees popped and cracked as he started to stand; another old injury from boarding an enemy ship. These injuries tended to rise up when he did each morning. Some felt like they'd never healed, and sometimes he felt like he'd been in pain most of his life. More so, since Betsy had gone to heaven. He missed his wife. She had added a spark to his life. He was not ready to die. He knew that, and for the first time in a long time he felt a calling…he felt needed. His presence would help Maddy while her husband was off at war… raiding ships. Be it pirate or privateer, there was little difference, in truth. Once it got in your blood it was hard to turn loose of, this Dagan knew. Would Cooper be satisfied to give up the life as a raider once the war was over? Some wouldn't, they'd pick back up being pirates. But not Cooper, Dagan felt this. His knee popped again as Dagan walked to the kitchen.

Decades spent out on the open sea, battling enemy cannons or enduring the forces of nature crept into a man's soul…his very being. You were always glad to come home, but also always ready to get back to sea. Something a landsman wouldn't understand. But to a seaman, it would always be there, always a yearning, even if you put out your anchor like he and Eli Taylor had done. Looking back, Dagan had decided that there was little he'd change even if given the opportunity. The future…he didn't see things as well as he once did. Was it because he was not at sea? Not one with the elements. Regardless, 'the gift' was not at the forefront as it had once been.

The gift that caused people to whisper when they thought he was out of earshot. "E's a soothsayer, 'e is. Aye! 'E sees the future 'e does and can make ye do things to yer self. 'E can call down the forces. Aye! I seen it, me 'as!"

His mother had told him it was a special gift. One that was not to be abused, but used carefully and wisely. He had done his best to make good on that promise. Others in his family shared it, but it was rarely mentioned.

A crack and groan were heard as the front door of the cottage opened. "It's me, Mr. Dagan," a voice called. It was Priscilla, the girl that had been assigned as his housekeeper. Dagan could hear her stirring the coals, trying to find some hot embers. The loud snap as the fat lighter caught fire let him know she'd been successful. The sound of a dipper bumping the coffee pot was a comforting sound. The aroma of fresh coffee would soon fill the cottage as the fire chased the chill out. The cottage only had two rooms. A single wall with a doorway separated the bedroom from the front of the house.

"You sho' need some mo' furniture," Priscilla called out. "You ain't got much for folks to sit on." Dagan smiled. Priscilla would always find something to cluck away about.

The cottage was sparse. Dagan's bedroom had a bed, a side table with a chair. His trunk sat at the foot of his bed, and a mirror hung on one wall. A painting of Betsy hung on another wall in the bedroom. There was a large dining table with two benches and chairs at each end, in the other room. Cabinets had been built along one wall for food, coffee, and cooking utensils. A few pots and pans hung on a wall. The coffee pot sat on the hearth of the fireplace. There were nails behind the door to hang hats and coats on. Above the door was a place for his rifle. More would come later, but for now, he had all he needed. Dagan knew this would be his final home. He'd travel occasionally and would see little Cain's come into this world. He'd move no more.

"It's getting dark and cloudy," Priscilla said. "My mama done said we'd have a wet Christmas."

"She's right," Dagan replied. He'd dressed and come into the room. He would put his boots on by the fireplace.

The coffee was starting to boil and smelled good. Priscilla poured a cup for Dagan. "Like you like it, black as midnight and strong as a ox be." Dagan smiled, that hadn't been his exact words but it was close enough.

The carpenters had put one window in Dagan's bedroom and three in the front of the cottage. Light was starting to enter through the windows and little dust balls were visible in the air.

"Ought to be brighter by now," Priscilla mused, looking outside. "Ain't you glad they had enough glass fo' yo' windows, Mr. Dagan?" Before he could answer, the girl added, "Mama say Mr. Luke gonna get some glass for our quarters." Turning back, Priscilla continued, "You want me to fix you sumthin to eat? Mama said Maddy don't get up early when the Capum be home." She took a deep breath and gave a sigh when she said this. Dagan couldn't help but smile. Priscilla saw him smiling and smiled as well.

"They'll be up early today," Dagan said, taking another sip of his coffee. "It's Christmas."

"I 'spect you right bout that." Seeing he'd drained his cup of coffee, Priscilla took it from his calloused hand. "I'll get you another cup." Handing the freshly filled cup back to Dagan, she said, "You navy men like yo' coffee."

Dagan gave a 'mmmm' after taking a timid sip of the hot black liquid. "We especially like it when it's made good like you make it, girl." This compliment pleased Priscilla. "You go on and take the rest of the day off now," Dagan instructed as he took a coin from his pocket. "The next time you go to the store, you buy yourself something."

"Thank you, Mister Dagan." Priscilla said, and then fled from the cottage, already thinking of what she might buy.

The skies to the west crackled with lightning. Thunder rumbled for a few seconds and then boomed. The light in the windows dimmed as dark clouds scudded eastward. Watching, Dagan thought, *today we'll see how good they did roofing the cottage.* The cedar shakes had not been cheap. They'd cost nearly as much as the board and batten exterior walls. The wood came from Colonel Bledsoe's sawmill. Dagan knew buying cedar, barring some storm, ought to last his lifetime. If the shingles had been laid right, his cabin should remain dry. Finishing his second cup of coffee, Dagan sat the cup in a wash pan sitting on the hearth. He pulled the coffee pot back. It was still half full. He wouldn't pour it out for now. Banking the fire, he gathered up his hat and tarpaulin and made a dash for the main house.

The first of the huge raindrops hit his back as he entered the door. He thought to himself, *timed that about right.* A burst of thunder and the sound of lightning striking close by seemed to shake the walls.

"Lawd," Rosa shrieked. She was Maddy's cook and house-keeper. "Gives me the she be's," Rosa declared as she saw Dagan.

He wasn't sure what 'she be's' were, but he guessed it to be an unpleasant feeling. It seemed like the sky opened up as rain came pouring down in hard, driving sheets. Lightning flashed and the sky popped here and there.

"Glad I'm not at sea today."

Dagan turned to see Cooper entering the kitchen. Agreeing, Dagan said, "Aye, that's two of us."

"It's going to be a gully washer," Rosa swore as she sat two cups of coffee on the table. Cooper and Dagan both smiled, hearing the phrase gully washer. They enjoyed the local phrases and descriptions by the southern Americans.

"What's a gully washer?" Maddy asked as she walked in, still rubbing the sleep from her eyes.

Before Rosa could answer Maddy, Cooper said, "I see you decided to get up."

Maddy eyed her husband. "Who can sleep in this, Coop?"

Dagan decided not being a good riser was one trait that Maddy had taken from her father. He was never an easy riser.

"You were sleeping a few minutes ago," Coop said, picking at his wife.

"That was before you started stomping your feet into your boots. And then when I doze off, thunder rattles every window." Maddy walked over and gave Dagan a warm hug. "Morning, Uncle."

"Morning to you, Maddy, its Christmas."

"I know. I'm so glad you're here," Maddy said as she worked her way into Cooper's lap, causing him to push his chair back from the table a bit.

Rosa brought Maddy a cup of hot cocoa. "Would you like a good breakfast, or just some biscuits and honey or preserves to hold you over?"

"I like the honey and biscuits," Maddy replied.

Rosa looked at Cooper, "They's some of that ham you like, as well, Captain."

Cooper winked at Rosa, "That's my woman."

Dagan smiled, another southern tradition he'd learned to enjoy. Ham biscuit followed by honey on a hot buttered biscuit... *mmmm.*

CHAPTER TWENTY FOUR

A NEW FALL OF SNOW had settled upon the old. The dirt was covered by the new snow, hiding the grime that had spread over the previous snow. It would freeze also. Vice Admiral Sir Gabriel Anthony knew this, adding another layer to the ice that had already blanketed London and the countryside. The snow swirled as a breeze picked up. The ride to London from Portsmouth had been cold, reminding him of the first trip he'd made to the Admiralty with his brother, Gil, all those years ago…a lifetime, it seemed.

The halls of the Admiralty were chilled, as always, during the winter. He was escorted past a room full of captains and lieutenants waiting to be deployed. He doubted many would be kept on the beach with another war with the Colonies starting. It seemed England had been at war since he was a middy and now he was a vice admiral. The last war with France had no sooner ended, than this new war with England's Yankee cousins started. A war that should not have been. One that should have and could have been avoided.

He had arrived at the Admiralty just as the evening shadows turned the day to dusk. The Port Admiral had said he was expected at the Admiralty as soon as convenient. That was pleasant wording that really meant right away, vice admiral or not.

Faith had been escorted to his mother, Maria's house by Captain Davy's first lieutenant. He had not expected to be called to the Admiralty but the trip allowed him time to visit his mother who was now up in age.

When the escort presented Gabe to the First Secretary the usual greetings took place. The First Secretary then said, "Viscount Melville is expecting you. The Port Admiral sent a message via the semaphore." Gabe nodded.

A system of semaphore towers carried the news far faster than a messenger on horseback and certainly faster than a coach.

As Gabe entered the First Lord's office, he was greeted warmly by Robert Dundas, Second Viscount Melville. A brandy was offered and accepted. Once the servant had poured the brandy and departed, Dundas got right to the point.

"Wellington is raising hell because we can't get supply ships through to Spain. This has become increasingly difficult after the outbreak of hostilities with the United States." Gabe noticed that Dundas didn't say Colonies as many still addressed the Americas. "It appears this second war with our former Colonies has unleashed hordes of American privateers on the Atlantic." Dundas stopped his pacing and continued, "Word has even gotten back to me that your daughter has married one of the privateer captains." He waved away Gabe's reply. "No need to respond. I know the poppycock from whence the news came. If all I hear is correct, he and his sodomite companions deserve all they get from Cain."

Gabe spoke, after taking a deep breath, "Would you like me to lower my flag, sir?"

Dundas paused, brandy glass in hand, "Never, Gabe. Neither I, nor this nation could ever doubt where your loyalties lie or your sense of duty. It would be a lot bloody worse if I didn't have a few commanders in critical positions, such as yourself. What I'm doing, Gabe, is giving you what you've asked for in your reports. Frigates...every commander's dream. More frigates, a thirty-eight, thirty-six, and the rest will be thirty-twos. They are not to stand in a line of battle. They are to search out and destroy these American raiders. I want the privateers destroyed. A list of the ships and their captains will be in your orders."

The meeting was over. Gabe drained his brandy and picked up his hat. Dundas offered Gabe his hand. "God go with you, Gabe...and I truly hope young Cain survives."

Gabe managed a half-hearted smile. "Thank you, sir that was very kind of you."

He found a clerk waiting outside the door with a sealed Admiralty pouch. Inside would be the names of the ships and their captains. Men he'd send out to end the problems with the privateers. Capture or destroy...if captured, they would be brought to Antigua. God help the man who didn't follow his orders.

THE RAIN SLOWED TO a soft patter, dripping down from the yards and riggings. A slow drip was also coming in around the skylight. It would need to be caulked. The rain made Captain Cooper Cain think of Christmas. The rain had been a deluge that day as well. Maddy's brother, James, and his family had come over and later in the day Suzanne Bledsoe had arrived. There had been good fellowship, singing, and one of the finest dinners Cooper could recall. Rosa had called upon Priscilla and Rosa's daughter, Bess, to help with the meal. Luke and his wife had been invited, and just before the meal Eli Taylor and Debbie had arrived.

Rosa had cooked a huge turkey and a ham. There had been potatoes, green peas, and a fruit salad. Some of the fruit Cooper hadn't even known was available. They also had sweet yams, fresh bread, egg custard, pies, and chocolate cake. Cooper remembered Eli loosening his belt after the meal.

After a meal fit for kings, the men gathered in a group and played cards, while Eli lit up his pipe. Cooper remembered hearing the women in another room, laughing at times. It had truly been a good Christmas. But Christmas had come and gone, as had the New Year.

They had put to sea on March 18, 1813. Maddy had been quiet the week leading up to the sailing date. She never once mentioned it. She'd seen her mother go through her father putting to sea a number of times, no doubt. Cooper knew she worried about his return, just as Faith had done with Gabe...Sir Gabe.

Sir Gabe had politely told Cooper that between the two of them there could be no formalities. When other naval officers had been around, Cooper showed the respect his father-in-law deserved and addressed him as Sir Gabe.

The bang of a musket was heard. Buck Jewell had been so impressed with Buster Reynolds' marksmanship, that he had the young man put on a demonstration. Would Buster have won the turkey shoot had Jonah and Moses been there? No one knew. It was Buster's first time at the competition. It would have been close...too close to chance anything but a token gentlemanly wager on. Buck and Spurlock both had wanted Reynolds and so did Cooper.

When the young man had knocked on Cooper's door a few days after Christmas, he bluntly said, "What do I have to do to join up." No good morning, it's nice to see you; it was straight to the point.

Cooper had given him a brief overview and then sent him to see Buck to review the articles and if they were to his liking—he'd be signed on as a sharpshooter. He would report to the gunner, Spurlock, who he'd shot against at the competition. Cooper had also sent a private note for Buck to give Reynolds one hundred dollars in advance. The money would be deducted from his shares but that would help his family until they returned...when and if they returned.

Cooper had explained to Reynolds that theirs was a risky business. They must go in harm's way to obtain prizes. Men had been and would be killed. One of his jobs, as a sharpshooter, was to recognize any threat and stop it immediately. By doing this, he'd be bringing attention to himself and thereby become a target himself. This discussion did not seem to faze Reynolds. Cooper wondered if at that age, he'd felt ten feet tall and indestructible.

It had been fun watching the crew initiate young Reynolds. Banty filled his head with so many sailor superstitions, Cooper wouldn't doubt it if he asked to be put ashore. Everything from why it was an ill omen to set sail on Friday, supposedly the day Christ was crucified, to whistling takes away the wind , and even selkies and the difference between mermaids and sirens.

A cry from above interrupted Cooper's thoughts. "Sail ho!" That was Banty in the tops. What would the sighting bring? A prime merchant ship ready to become a prize, or a British war-ship just waiting for the chance to take *SeaFire* or *Thunderbolt* as a prize. It would be a feather in their hat when reporting to the admiral.

Cooper went on deck. They were still a good half day's sail from Barataria Bay. By the look of the sky it'd be dark within the hour. What was the likelihood of a merchant ship or convoy being this close to shore? Waiting for Banty to call down more information tested Cooper's nerves. Buck nodded to Cooper but kept his eyes on Banty. The men knew Banty would let them know more when he was sure.

Young Ryker grabbed a glass from its rack on the binnacle. He hoped that he'd be sent aloft. Seeing the glass in Ryker's hand, Cooper reached for it. "Thank you, Mr. Ryker."

Ryker smiled and managed a weak, "My pleasure, Captain." He knew his hope of going aloft had just been dashed.

"She be a warship, Captain. A frigate with a smaller set of sails behind her. She's wearing ship now and making signals, Captain."

"Damnation," Cooper swore. "Let's clamp on all sails, Buck, she'll not catch us before dark. Mr. Turner, have Mr. Spurlock man the stern guns. Mr. Ryker!"

"Aye, Cap'n."

"Make signal to *Thunderbolt*, 'enemy in sight'." Cooper returned the glass, and as an afterthought, he said, "Thank you for the use of your glass." Before Ryker could speak, Cooper turned to the master, "Will she catch up before dark, Mr. Ewers?"

"It will be close, Captain, but I believe we have the wind advantage."

Cooper smiled, "I trust we will keep it, Mr. Ewers."

"Aye, Captain, so do I."

CHAPTER TWENTY FIVE

THE BRITISH SHIP PROVED a good sailor. There was only a quarter moon but by the time it came up the frigate had been firing her bow chasers regularly. *Thunderbolt* had split off on a different course but the frigate captain seemed to have his mind set on *SeaFire*. The other ship with the frigate, the one Banty felt certain was a brig had long been left behind, unable to keep up the speed necessary for the chase.

"She's a fine ship," Buck had commented, paying respect to the enemy frigate.

"A bit too fine for my liking," Ewers snarled.

Cooper had complied with every suggestion Buck and Ewers had come up with. Most of the suggestions coming from the old pirate, Ewers. He'd spent the better part of his life avoiding capture.

Mr. Turner, the second officer, approached. "Should I tell Mr. Spurlock to secure the stern guns, sir?

"Aye, Mr. Turner. They've not been able to fire a shot so I see no need to keep them at the guns."

"Or your wine cabinet," Buck threw in with a grin.

Turner, usually a very stoic individual, smiled at this. "I hardly think it will be more than a temptation with both Josiah and Spurlock in the cabin."

"No, Mr. Turner, I think your assumption is correct." Cooper was once more all business, "Mr. Jewell, let's make sure the ship is completely darkened. I don't want so much as the ember from a pipe bowl to show. With the clouds overhead, we'll choose one and when the moon is completely cloud covered, we'll change our course."

"Think that will fool him?" Buck asked.

"No, I'm sure he will expect us to do just that. What I'm hoping is within the half hour when we resume our original course; I will catch him off guard. What I want to do on our second change is to do it in such a way we don't leave much in the way of a wake."

"I've known Captain Taylor to follow a prize trying to escape," Ewers admitted. "We were a bit closer, of course, and the moon was brighter."

"The wake will be gone, with any luck, before yonder ship can pick it up," Buck added.

"We can hope," Cooper agreed.

The sail handlers sat about on deck waiting to be called to change course. There was not a sound to be heard beyond the slap of a wave against the ship's hull and the groans of the ship's timbers and riggings. When a large cloud moved to cover the moon, the men jumped to action. Buck Jewell and Diamond, the bosun, had already laid out the plan so the men moved with practiced experience when the word was given.

Young Ryker stood near the aft rail looking at the wake. Having heard the comments of the captain along with the master and first officer, he was relieved to see the wake quickly dissipate. Still gazing over the stern, he saw what he thought were stern lights pass directly aft following the same course they had been on. Running toward the quarterdeck, he reached Cooper and blurted out his sighting just as a whispered report came down from aloft.

Seeing Ryker's excitement, Cooper smiled in spite of his trying not to. "Speak before you bust, Mr. Ryker."

"Thank you, Captain. I believe the enemy ship continued on course, sir. I saw what I believe were stern lights passing us on the same course we were just on."

"Thank you, young sir, that confirms the report sent down from the tops." Ryker looked crestfallen. He should have known the captain would have had someone ready to report the enemy ships' movements. Cooper patted the young officer on the shoulder, not wanting him to feel let down, "I'm glad you were paying attention, Mr. Ryker. It's always good to have confirmation on such an important sighting. Shows motivation on your part."

Ryker was now feeling sheepish. Should he admit that he'd just been skylarking and happen to glimpse the British ships' stern lights. Mr. Turner winked at him, as he turned away. *He knows*, Ryker thought. *He knows, but being a friend, he'll not tell the captain.*

THUNDERBOLT, TO COOPER'S RELIEF was anchored in Barataria Bay when *SeaFire* entered. Goose, a young seaman, was in the tops. Spying their sister ship, he called down the sighting as soon as he saw it.

Knowing the relief the sighting had on his captain, Buck Jewell approached Cooper, "All's well that ends well, Captain."

SeaFire had spotted another British frigate and instead of making the usual run for Barataria, they'd sailed further south in the Gulf of Mexico. They made a stop at Veracruz and then headed north, past Brownsville and Galveston. *SeaFire* always kept the coast in sight from the tops so that a dash could be made to it if an enemy ship was spotted. It had been clear sailing, though, after they'd lost the second frigate.

"Will we make any trips in New Orleans, sir?"

"Aye, Buck. I've correspondence and business to conduct so we'll leave first thing in the morning. I'll have you at Mary Esther's door before you know it."

"Thank you, Captain. Is there anyone special you want to take along, other than Quang, that is?"

"You can ask Josiah if he'd like to come along. Our new hand, Buster Reynolds, might find the city an enlightening experience. I'll leave the rest up to you. I'm sure Doctor Cannington would like to come along."

"Pardon me, Captain."

"Yes, Mr. Diamond."

"I think yonder boat has both Mr. LaFitte and Captain St. Jacques in it. They appear to be heading our way."

"Thank you, Mr. Diamond. If you'll see that our guests are welcomed aboard, Mr. Jewell, I'll go below and have Josiah prepare some beverage. You are most welcome to accompany them down."

"Thank you," Buck replied, as Cooper headed down the companionway.

Jean LaFitte was as trim and polished as ever. He was a man of exquisite taste, and the money made from his operations allowed him to fulfill his every desire. During the conversation, LaFitte brought Cooper up to date on the increasing number of British ships and patrols. He then admitted Governor Claiborne lived in fear that the British would invade New Orleans. He'd written letters to everyone he could think of, asking for soldiers and guns to fortify the city."

"Everyone but the one most able to help," Henri St. Jacques threw out, indicating Mr. LaFitte with a slight tilt of his brandy glass.

A slight smile tugged at the corners of LaFitte's mouth, "He has failed in every attempt to have me thrown in prison. Therefore, I think hell would freeze over before our good governor called on us. The word is he's given Commodore Patterson permission to lay waste to our little island and keep the spoils for his troubles."

"Surely you could repulse any attack by Patterson's puny gunboats?" Henri swore.

"No, my friend, I've never fired on the American flag, nor will I. I feel our nation will need us before this is over. I may be considered a smuggler…a pirate even, but never let it be said that the LaFittes were not first and foremost patriots."

Cooper found LaFitte's words very touching. Did he have the same noble feelings as LaFitte? He admitted to himself that he didn't. Had it not been for treachery on his cousin's part, he'd still be squandering away his allowance in England. That treachery had set things in motion that had given him the opportunity for the life he now lived. He had lived for revenge, and then he'd found a true friend that had nurtured him to manhood. Eli had taught him the ways of the sea and trained him to be a leader. He had found love, not once but twice. He'd found a way of life that afforded him a living beyond his wildest dreams, not only for himself but for his mother and Jean Paul as well. He thought, *I damn well better consider myself loyal to my adopted country…damn loyal.*

Cooper passed out some Havana cigars after the brandy had been served. The topic of conversation changed at different times. Finally, a slight tap was heard. It was Josiah wanting to know if he'd be required anymore that evening. Seeing the empty decanters and small plates littered with crumbs from the food that Cooper didn't even remember eating, he told Josiah that he'd be needed no more that evening.

"I think we should all call it an evening," LaFitte said. "I'd hate to call all hands to fish Henri out of the bay."

St. Jacques smiled a drunken smile and said, "With Captain Cain's permission, I shall sleep where I sit." The last of this was followed by a prolonged belch.

LaFitte took the stub of St. Jacques' cigar from between his fingers. "I fear you have a guest for the evening, Coop."

"I'll have Quang see that he's put in a cot," Cooper replied. He then saw LaFitte, who was amazingly steady on his feet for someone who'd done his part in emptying two decanters of brandy, over the side.

Cooper turned to see his master. "Johannes, have you already returned from your night on the town?"

"Aye, Captain. It doesn't hold the same lure as it once did. I don't mind enjoying a good meal but the gambling and women you can keep. I may open a place like the Captain and Debbie's, after the war. It may be on the water and cater to officers and men like Mr. John Will and Mr. Michael Brett."

"Will you call it Ewers?" Cooper asked.

"Not sure, Captain. I've even thought of going back to Germany for a visit. I may open it there."

"Well friend, and you've been both a friend and mentor, should you open an establishment near me, I will be glad to invest in your endeavor."

"Thank you, Captain. You have something about you that draws people. They say you are lucky. Opening a new business, I'll need some luck, so I may take you up on your offer."

The sound of a boat approaching had both men looking over the side. Diamond slung somebody over his shoulder and started up the battens to the entry port while Spurlock held the boat alongside *SeaFire*. Diamond set his load down and steadied him, once on deck. Young Ryker was smiling from ear to ear, even though a bit wobbly from drink.

"Johannes, from that smile, I believe our young officer got lucky."

"First night back on Grand Terre, Captain. I'd say members of our crew made sure that he got lucky."

Spurlock, hearing the master's words, nodded. "Aye, we did that, but we made sure he didn't wind up with some poxed wench. Dr. Cannington said he would not be going to New Orleans just yet, Captain. It seems that Mr. Mayroone has his family visiting, including that young lady the doctor was smitten with."

Cooper said, after a second or so, "Erin?"

"Maybe, Captain, she's a looker."

Johannes said, as Spurlock walked off, "I hope we don't lose our doctor."

"We won't," Cooper replied. "If he's planning on getting married, we won't."

CHAPTER TWENTY SIX

THE SHRILL WHISTLE ON one of the new steam powered river-boats startled Cooper, as it did others in the two pirogues. Looking at the steamer whose sign along one rail declared her to be the *New Orleans*.

"Damnation," Buck Jewell declared. "Ugly wench if I ever saw one."

"Aye," Diamond, the bosun, agreed.

"She's got no grace, no lines," young Mr. Ryker threw in.

Reynolds surprised them all when he commented, "She's made for the river trade…cargo and passengers alike. She makes the trip in half the time it used to take barges. Passengers travel in comfort. They have little staterooms like a tiny hotel room. It also has a dining room and a saloon where folks can drink, play cards, and gamble. I doubt it will be long before you see more steam powered ships at sea."

If a man had the money, it would make a good investment. Cooper quickly tucked that thought away. He would look into it while in New Orleans. With the pirogues tied up, Cooper advised the men that he'd have lodging set up at Hotel Provincial.

"Check in with me every morning for what my plans are." The group nodded. "Quang, you may want to accompany Josiah." Cooper knew Josiah would need help with the goods to replenish his pantry. He also knew it would take a brave man to interfere with a servant with the fearsome Quang in company.

Other than a militia marching down the street to the waves and cheers of the townspeople, the city looked like it had changed little. That might not be the case if the British attacked, as LaFitte was sure would happen. Saloons and gambling houses were bustling with trade Cooper noted as they made their way from the waterfront. Many of those patrons were in uniform, and they seemed to be filling the doors at the brothels as well. They might find less competition for the pretty ones back at Barataria. *Illicit pleasure,* Cooper thought. New Orleans was still as Banty had labeled it, 'the most delightfully sinful city in the United States'. The city was just as busy away from the waterfront.

Cooper was reminded of Sophie as he was making his way past the Place d'Armes. Extraordinary beautiful women were everywhere. The Creole ladies were dressed in their finest. The women were exotic and they carried themselves proudly, with their heads held high. No doubt, a number of them were under contract as mistresses to some rich planter or his son….as Sophie had been. He was suddenly saddened and feeling guilty for having his thoughts on any other woman than Maddy.

He looked at his first officer. "Buck, I know you wish to make your arrival known to Ms. Mary Esther, so feel free to go you own way. I will have a room reserved for you. However, should you not need it, just send me a note. I'm sure that we will be in the city for three days and maybe longer."

"Thank you, Captain. I will be in touch."

Buck broke off at the next corner, while Cooper headed to the hotel to let Otis know he would be using Eli and Debbie's suite for a few days.

COOPER WAS NOT SURPRISED to see the beautiful Mary Esther with Buck Jewell in tow two nights later at the home of Edward and Carolyn Meeks. He'd talked with his lawyer friend about investing in steamboats. Edward said he'd look into it and be back in touch. Cooper was then invited to Carolyn's monthly card night. It had become poque night, lately. The evening, however, started out with a cocktail hour where guests met and gossiped about the war, the latest fashion changes, horse races, and on this occasion, a duel.

On the occasion of the duel, whoever had the responsibility for the pistols forgot, though some said on purpose; to put balls in the weapons. The duelists were both so glad they'd not been shot; they shook hands and the incident provoking the duel was forgotten.

After the cocktails, the evening meal was served. Buck's place card was alongside of Mary Esther's. *Imagine that*, Cooper thought to himself.

Carolyn asked, seeing Cooper's smile, "Something amuse you, Cooper?"

Still smiling, Cooper replied, "Are you as accomplished playing matchmaker as you are at the cards?"

Carolyn smiled now, "When I've been given prior notice, I am."

Carolyn and Cooper had become good friends. When they'd first met, they had become partners by accident when Cooper had accompanied Eli to a dinner. As partners, they'd lightened the purses of some of the wealthiest planters considerably. To prevent anyone from becoming angry, they played with different partners at the tables as often as they did together. They usually won, though, when they played together.

Seeing Buck as they arrived, Cooper realized his first officer had spent some time with a tailor. He'd probably paid extra to have his suit ready for tonight. Mary Esther was dressed in a pale blue gown that, like the other ladies, was off the shoulders and came to a V at the right spot. While some of the ladies were younger and some older, none of them had commanded a man's attention like she did. Every man's head turned when she stepped in the room. She wore a necklace of emeralds that set the dress off. She also was wearing matching earrings. Cooper could only imagine Buck was the envy of most of the men at the party.

Mary proved to be easy to talk to at the dinner table. She was witty and quick to smile. He recalled a previous comment about losing their surgeon to marriage. It might also prove true for Buck.

Someone rang a bell as dessert was finished. This was the cue for ladies to go to the powder room while the men took care of nature and cigars were lit. Not everyone would stay and play cards but most of the guests would. Cooper noted five card tables had been set up. That meant Carolyn was expecting twenty people, mostly men, to stay and gamble. Buck and Mary had commented during dinner that they were going to the theater after the meal. *No wonder they are so dressed up,* Cooper thought. He'd made Buck smile when he said they'd be the loveliest couple there. Cooper watched as a hired carriage drove off with the two of them.

He was about to reenter the house when Edward Meeks walked up and offered him a cigar. Taking time to clip the end, Cooper then rolled the cigar as Edward used his striker to produce a small flame. Enjoying the taste and aroma of the cigar, Cooper looked at his host and spoke one word, "Gus!"

Nodding the affirmative, Meeks spoke, "Figured you'd be able to identify a good smoke."

Gus was a very progressive black man. He worked for Cindy Veigh and had done things to improve and advance her crops while also having time for a few profitable ventures himself.

"I checked on steamboats and steam engines. It appears steam engines were invented by Thomas Savery way back in the late

1600's, 1698 if my memory serves me right. At first, they were not very useful." Meeks drew a piece of paper from his pocket where he had jotted down some notes, and continued, "In 1712, a Thomas Newcomen perfected the steam engine and used it to pump water out of the mines. The next big use for steam engines came about fifty or so years later. A Scotsman named James Watt invented a better engine. Next a fellow…" Meeks paused. He placed his cigar in his mouth, taking a puff. He fiddled with his notes as he exhaled a large plume of smoke. He continued, once he found what he was looking for, "Here it is James…"pausing he held his note closer. "No, no John Fitch made the first success- ful steamboat on the Delaware River in 1787. It was forty-five feet long. He later made several more, larger ones built to carry passengers. However, he didn't watch his cost, and the end cost was more than the profit."

"Sounds depressing," Cooper said, brushing his coat with the back of his hand where cigar ash had fallen without him seeing it.

"It must have been depressing," Meeks said, looking at his own jacket to make sure it was clean. He continued, "In 1807, an inventor named Robert Fulton built a successful steamboat. I'm sure you know he built a ship or a boat to go underwater. A sub- marine, it's called." Cooper didn't know but he was determined to look it up.

"Fulton named his steamboat the *Clermont*," Meeks contin- ued. "He made history by making the one hundred fifty mile trip from New York City to Albany, New York in thirty-two hours. That averages five miles per hour. In 1811, he and Robert Livingston became partners and built the '*New Orleans*'."

"I saw her the day we came in," Cooper reminded his friend.

"As far as investing, I feel it would be a good investment, a bit risky perhaps. I understand they could be a fire hazard," Meeks said.

"So are houses, if they are made out of wood," Cooper replied.

"There's that," Meeks agreed. "One last thing, now most of the steamboats are paddle driven. Fulton is talking of making a ship that moves by a turning screw or propeller. It's supposed to be a better plan than paddles when steam goes from riverboats to ships on the ocean."

The door opened, at that time, and Carolyn stood there looking peeved. "Are you two playing cards or what?" Both men tossed the remainder of their cigars away and headed inside without saying another word.

CHAPTER TWENTY SEVEN

NEW ORLEANS, GRAND TERRE, and Barataria Bay all lay beyond the distant horizon. The two ships, *Thunderbolt* and *SeaFire*, sailed into the Gulf of Mexico on a night when the moon seemed to shimmer in the calm waters off the bow. There was a very light breeze, with small wavelets. The crest was almost glassy in appearance. They seemed to slide along under the bow, not breaking. Cooper had on a light shirt with the sleeves rolled up. He'd come on deck to smoke one of Gus' crooks. This one had been soaked in cognac and allowed to dry. The smoke from the cigar drifted upward due to the light breeze. Cooper could, however, still feel a slight chill on his arms and where his collar was open.

Buck was walking through the ship. One of the men, Ox, had gotten into a fight in Barataria. A likely concussion, bruised ribs, and worst of all, a fractured ulna had been Dr. Cannington's report. One of Vincent Gambi's crew had made a comment about *SeaFire* only having boys on board instead of real men. The comment had been made about Mr. Ryker, however, the loyal seaman, Ox, had intervened. Gambi's man was beaten to a pulp but he'd tried to hit Ox with a chair. The bull of a sailor blocked the chair and demonstrated what kind of men sailed on *SeaFire*. Had Nez Coupé not intervened Ox would have killed the man.

Spurlock had said, "We were waiting for more of Gambi's men to join in, Captain. But shows you what kind of weasel they be when not one of his mates offered to help."

That was something, Cooper thought, remembering his first scrape and all of *Raven's* men who were ready to join in should there have been a need. Most of those same men were now aboard *SeaFire*. It didn't say much for a man when his shipmates didn't offer to help him out of a fix, be he right or wrong...didn't speak well for the captain either.

THE PLAN FOR THIS leg of the cruise was to sail south in the Gulf of Mexico, pass through the Yucatan Strait or Channel as some called it. They would sail under Cuba toward Grand Cayman, Jamaica, and then possibly toward the Windward Islands; maybe even as far south as Tobago. It all depended on what prizes might be had.

"Look, Captain." It was Reynolds.

Cooper stood up and took a step to the larboard rail. A school of porpoises swam alongside the ship.

"I've never seen the like," Reynolds said.

"Aye, something to behold. So peaceful," Cooper agreed.

"A good omen, it is," Banty volunteered, as he walked up.

Several of the hands not on watch had come on deck. Mac had once told Cooper a crewman should never speak to the captain without seeking permission first. Cooper was glad he wasn't on a Royal Navy ship. The camaraderie enjoyed first on *Raven* and now aboard *SeaFire* would surely be missed. Forward, men gathered around the mainmast as Leon broke out his fiddle. It wasn't long before a little chantey had men dancing around. Otis had been right. Leon hadn't proved to be worth much, even as the cook's assistant, but he damn sure could play the fiddle. A good fiddler kept the crew merry. Looking at his cigar, Cooper thumped an ash about two inches long over the side.

"Rolled right?" Buck asked.

"Aye, Buck. Gus doesn't do anything that's not done right." Handing Buck a cigar and then offering the hot end of his cigar to his first officer, Cooper gave a shudder. "I believe the wind is picking up a bit."

Buck puffed away until Cooper's cigar had lit his. He looked aloft, "Aye, I believe you are right. It may rain tonight."

"Will that dampen your thoughts about the lovely widow, Buck?"

"Nay, Captain, those fires burn deep."

COOPER WAS ON DECK at first light. Mr. Turner had the watch. Seeing his captain, he mumbled a greeting and offered his glass to him. Accepting the glass, Cooper thought, *our second officer does not appear well this morning.* Putting the glass to his eye, Cooper could make out the gray silhouettes of the shore.

For some unexplained reason, Cooper had woken up feeling uneasy. Returning the glass to Mr. Turner, he asked, "Are you unwell, sir?'

"It's just my stomach, sir. I believe the Cajun food ashore, though tasty, has caused a bit of dyspepsia." Turner's comments were followed by a loud belch. He then turned and cast a load over the rail. Wiping his mouth, with the back of his hand, Turner apologized, "My apologies, sir. It's the vilest, sour, and most burning taste I can ever remember."

Cooper felt sorry for his second officer. "I had a bout of similar symptoms after a long weekend of excessive drinking and general debauchery once as a young man. I was most repentant the following day when my stomach burned like the fires of hell. The thick vile that rose in my throat also burned and had the worst taste. My fencing master said my breath smelled like the Russian army had staked their horses in it the previous evening. It was so bad my mother, who had it in mind to show me a degree of sympathy, turned away, putting her handkerchief to her nose. 'My God, Cooper,' she said, 'your breath is most distressing'. 'Not as bad as my stomach,' I replied. In a few minutes, Jean Paul, that was my fencing master's name, returned with a glass of greenish liquid. 'Drink this down', he ordered. Looking suspiciously I asked, 'What is it.' 'Drink it down,' he ordered. I did and it tasted much better than it looked. When I downed the glass, he smiled. 'Pickle juice,' he said. 'Napoleon's army never marched without it.' He then handed me some mint leaves. 'For your mother's sake,' he offered."

"Do you think the pickle juice will help me?" Turner asked.

"It certainly won't hurt," Cooper answered. "If that doesn't do it, see Dr. Cannington."

"Aye, Captain, thank you."

Johannes Ewers stood there smiling as Cooper turned away from talking to Turner. "You, Captain, a night of drinking and debauchery."

"In my younger days, Mr. Ewers, in my younger days."

"Aye, Captain. I think we all had it in our minds to deflower every young maiden we could in our youth."

"Deck thar," Johnson, in the tops, shouted down. "*Thunderbolt* is signaling gunfire to the west. Requests permission to investigate."

"Aye! Mr. Ryker."

"Aye, Captain."

"Acknowledge *Thunderbolt* and give permission to investigate."

At that moment, Buck walked up. "My apologies, Captain, nature called."

"No apologies needed, Mr. Jewell," Cooper said, all business now. "Wear ship if you will and set a course to follow *Thunderbolt*. I've had a nagging feeling all morning thus far."

"Aye," Jewell answered. "Bosun, pipe all hands to wear ship."

Cooper marveled at how fast and expertly the ship's crew went to their tasks. *Credit went to Buck Jewell and Diamond, the bosun,* he thought. He had learned to wear ship but it was not in the same fluid manner. It will come, Johannes had said. Sailing closed hauled, *SeaFire* was quickly overtaking *Thunderbolt.*

Johnson, still in the tops, called down, "I sees two ships, Captain. Smoke is coming from one like she fired her guns. She carries a British flag, she do."

How big is the British ship? Cooper wondered, knowing Johnson would say when he was sure. His eyes were not as good as young Mr. Ryker's, nor Banty's for that matter. Cooper was about to send Banty to the lookout as Ryker would be needed for signals, when Johnson called down again.

"British ship appears to be a small frigate," he said. "Too much smoke to see the other ship good."

Hell's fire, Cooper thought, *we don't need to get into a battle with a British frigate…even a small one.*

Johnson called down again, "The other ship is flying an American flag, Cap'n."

That solves that problem, Cooper thought. "Mr. Jewell, put the men at quarters, if you will."

"Aye, Captain."

Cooper half listened to the shrill of the bosun pipes and the stamp of feet on the wooden deck as his crew hurriedly went to their battle stations. To what profit some would say.

Almost like he was reading his captain's mind, Buck Jewell looked at Cooper, "You have no choice, Captain, and the men know that." The words were kindly spoken, but were they true?

Quang was suddenly there handing Cooper a brace of pistols and his sword. "Ready," Cooper asked his cox'n.

"Quang ready," the big Chinaman replied in his broken English. Cooper had no doubt his cox'n was ready. He was always ready, regardless of the task.

SeaFire's bowsprit was now even with *Thunderbolt's* stern. "She'll fly, will she not," the master, Mr. Ewers volunteered. A smile was on his lips demonstrating the pride he had in his ship. When *SeaFire* passed their sister ship, *Thunderbolt's* crew waved and cheered.

Trying to think of the right words in which to signal *Thunderbolt's* captain, Cooper called Ryker. "Mr. Ryker, make a signal to *Thunderbolt*, engage enemy."

Ryker waited, "Is that all, Captain?"

"That's all, Mr. Ryker." Cooper doubted St. Jacques would have any difficulty understanding the message. He was free to engage as he saw fit. No fighting instructions were needed. They would be worthless once the battle started. St. Jacques would engage, of that Cooper was certain.

The battling ships could now be easily seen from the ship's deck. The British ship had now spotted *SeaFire* and *Thunderbolt*.

"Think she'll run, Captain?"

Turning his head to see who spoke, Cooper answered, "What do you think, Mr. Turner?"

"I would...but then I'm not a British officer."

Cooper said a quick prayer, as he spoke to his second officer. "God, don't let it be Jake or Mac."

"She's a thirty-two gun frigate," Buck said as he approached. He then added, "Hands at their battle stations, Captain?" Cooper acknowledged his first officer with a nod.

"Wonder what they are doing this far west," the master threw out.

"I was thinking along those same lines," Cooper replied.

They'd passed through the Yucatan Channel the previous evening but hadn't expected to see any British ships for at least another day.

"She's fired her bow chaser at us, Captain." This came from Mr. Turner. "Way short," he added.

"Thank you, and Mr. Turner!"

"Yes, Captain."

"I believe we have time for you to go see the cook and get a cup of pickle juice."

"Aye, Captain, I'll make it fast."

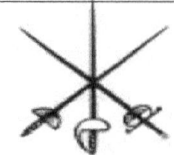

CHAPTER TWENTY EIGHT

THE BRITISH SHIP WAS visible now, heading directly at *SeaFire*, bowsprit to bowsprit. Buck stood next to Cooper, "She's a larger ship, right enough."

Cooper merely nodded he'd heard. "Mr. Spurlock!"

"Aye, Captain."

"Man the bow chaser, if you will. Mr. Turner, take charge of the main deck guns. I think we will be engaged momentarily. We can't get too close to that frigate, Mr. Buck, but I believe with *Thunderbolt's* assistance we should be able to fight her."

"Aye, Captain," Buck replied, being more formal than usual. He took the glass from his eye as he spoke, "She's got heavier timbers, being built as a war ship. She'll be able to withstand more punishment than either *SeaFire* or *Thunderbolt*. She'll carry a heavier broadside, I'm thinking."

"All noted," Cooper replied. "The time for deciding whether to engage is long past."

"Aye, there's that," Buck agreed.

"Helmsman!" Cooper barked. "Two points to starboard."

"Aye, aye, Cap'n."

Cooper watched the approaching enemy frigate. The British captain would have to make a decision soon. If he allowed the two privateers to keep their distance, they could pass both sides of the frigate, each engaging the ship and raking her larboard and starboard.

The enemy fired, with the balls landing along the larboard side, sending spray in board drenching several, including the master and Buck.

"Mr. Spurlock, you may open fire," Cooper shouted. The big gunner waved his arm in reply.

BOOM...BOOM, the forward guns spoke and the acrid smoke was quickly swept aft by the wind. *Thunderbolt* was sailing almost abreast, where she'd run down the British ship's larboard side. She looked so graceful with topsails and topgallants set kicking white spray out as she dashed through the waves.

"I believe our foe has sheeted more sails, Captain," the master informed Cooper.

"Aye," Buck acknowledged. "She's trying to gain the wind to keep from facing both of our broadsides simultaneously."

"Mr. Turner, I think we'll engage with the larboard battery." Cooper didn't know why, but he could feel the rush of excitement as he readied for battle. Turning to his cox'n, he was not surprised to see the big Chinaman grinning. "Ready, Quang?"

"Quang ready." *What a useless question*, Cooper thought. *It must be my nerves.*

Thunderbolt had inched ahead some. The frigate would have to man both batteries, and that would cut down on the number of broadsides she'd be able to fire in a three minute period.

"Mr. Ewers," Cooper spoke in his official tone. "Have the helmsman luff. Mr. Turner, run out the larboard battery."

"Starboard your helm a little more," Ewers ordered the helmsman.

Cooper's subconscious mind heard the master, Mr. Ewers, instructing the helmsman. He could feel the vibration as *SeaFire's* gun crews threw their weight on the side tackles, hauling each gun to its port. The crews on the two carronades were adjusting their screws.

"Mr. Turner, fire as you bear. I want every ball to strike home."

Ewers looked at Buck, a smile spreading across his face. How many times had they heard that? Yonder frigate is still bows on, Buck made a mental note. Forward, Cooper could see Spurlock looking down the barrel of the long nine. *He'll strike home*, Cooper thought. *No doubt in his mind.* Overhead the sails began to slap as they lost some of the wind when they luffed.

BOOM…The forward gun spat three feet of flame as it hurled itself inboard, the iron shot screaming out as it scored a hit to the frigate's bow. Cheers went up but were quickly drowned out as gun after gun flung death at the British ship.

Above the din, Cooper could hear Mr. Turner shouting, "Stop yer vents, worm out, sponge out, careful now, don't get the powder cartridge so close. Reload, run out."

The guns fired again. Thick smoke drifted back. The cry came down, from aloft, "They're firing on *Thunderbolt*." Miraculously, the smaller ship made it past the frigate and appeared to be in good shape.

"Come about, Mr. Jewell," Cooper ordered, as the last cannon had fired and *SeaFire* slid past her foe. He rushed astern and watched as the British captain brought his ship around, presenting a row of black painted snouts poking out of her gunports.

"Ready with the starboard battery," Cooper yelled.

The gun captains all stood next to their cannons, signaling they were ready. It would be close. The yards groaned as *SeaFire* came around. The sails filled with a series of loud snaps and cracks as the ship quickened its turn.

Looking at the enemy ship, Cooper could see the jib boom hanging and sections missing in its rail. The sails were pockmarked but the ship seemed to be under control. Buck had been right. Her heavy timber had taken two broadsides, larboard and starboard and she was still a fighting ship.

"Fire as you bear," Cooper ordered once more.

Spurlock's fo'c'sle gun was the first to fire. The air was suddenly rent with balls passing from each ship. Both sides were striking their enemies time and time again. Shrill sounds bellowed by. Sections of the rail leapt in the air as flames spouted from the wood and then died. Men screamed above the din of battle. A section of blasted rail slammed into Cooper's ribs. He fell to the deck stunned, his ears ringing.

"They're twelve shitten pounders," Buck cursed.

"Damnation," Johannes cursed as well. "Where the devil is *Thunderbolt*?"

Quang helped Cooper to his feet. Standing, Cooper could see one of the quarterdeck's guns was blown off its carriage and what had been a crew was now nothing but a pile of bloody gore. Everywhere he looked, Cooper saw blood splattered across his once beautiful ship. Sections of bulwark were gone and riggings and lines were hanging down almost to the deck.

The main guns were still at it, though. Gunners worked like madmen, not waiting to be told. They were not firing in a concerted broadside, but as quick as a gun could be fired, it was made ready and fired again.

BOOM...The sound of the explosion seemed to suck the air right out of Cooper's lungs. Mighty balls of searing flame filled the sky, and then smoke so black it seemed to block the sun. Fiery debris rained down creating hissing sounds. The once powerful British frigate was no more.

SeaFire's crew stood stunned, mouths agape, feeling lucky to be alive. Cooper realized, looking about, that he'd never experienced such an explosion, such a horrendous sight.

"Mr. Jewell, let's find out what the butcher's bill is. Mr. Diamond, get with the carpenter and see how the ship fared. Mr.

Ryker, signal *Thunderbolt* to close up with us. Mr. Turner, you are to be commended on such a fine job."

"Thank you, Captain. The pickle juice worked, sir. Dyspepsia's gone."

Cooper smiled. "Quang, get together a boat crew and see if there might be any survivors."

The cox'n quickly called together a crew, but nobody expected to find any survivors. Still it had to be done, and done before the sharks arrived.

CHAPTER TWENTY NINE

"D EAD."

"Aye, Captain, almost from the start."

Thunderbolt's master stood in Cooper's cabin, rain water dripping from his clothes. St. Jacques and his first mate were both killed with the British frigate's first broadside. Matthew del Rio, the master, had handled the sailing of *Thunderbolt* while the gunner, Eric Toland, fought the ship. St. Jacques had a second mate, but he was much like Mr. Ryker, not much beyond a boy.

"Our carpenter was killed as well," del Rio was saying. "Our bosun is a capable man but the loan of your carpenter would not go amiss."

Cooper looked at Buck Jewell. What would he have done had he suddenly lost Buck? He was about to. He had no one else to take command. Looking at his first mate and friend, Cooper spoke in his formal tone, "Mr. Jewell, gather your things together and go take command of *Thunderbolt.*"

"Aye, aye, Captain."

Slipping back to his usual familiarity, Cooper added, "You better take McKemie with you as they need a carpenter."

Buck nodded and said, "Thank you, Captain."

"No, you've earned it, Buck. You've commanded a ship in the past and stepped down for me. It is I who thanks you. I will be over once I see the captain of the ship the British were engaged with."

"The *Southern Cross*," del Rio injected. "We crossed her stern as we came about. They appear to have a woman captain."

A woman captain! Cooper had never met a woman who commanded a ship before. A few women had worked with their husbands on fishing boats, bumboats, and the like back in England, but he'd never seen an actual female ship's captain.

Dagan and Eli Taylor spoke of women pirates commanding their own ships, back in the heyday of piracy. Banty told a tale of a woman pirate with an all female crew. When they attacked a ship, they wore no tops. Cooper wondered if this was not one of Banty's sea stories. However, Dagan spoke of a Chinese woman, Ching Shih, who succeeded her husband when he died. She commanded over one thousand eight hundred ships, and eighty thousand men. Eli Taylor spoke of Rachel Walls who started as a privateer during America's First Revolutionary War. When the war ended, she became a pirate. They had both spoken of Ann Bonny, Mary Read, and Grace O'Malley. O'Malley was said to rule over twenty ships.

An hour later, as Cooper was still thinking about female pirates, Josiah announced, "Tina Hai, Captain of the privateer ship, *Southern Cross*."

Cooper was not sure what he expected but was not disappointed at what he saw. Captain Hai was dressed in brown britches and a tan shirt. The same as many captains wore at sea. These were not men's clothes, though; they were obviously made for her. Her face and hands were darkened by endless days at sea, under a blazing sun. Cooper suspected she spent most of her time in the Caribbean. Her hair was dark and her face was proud and angular. If she dressed in a gown in New Orleans, she'd turn some heads. Taking the outstretched hand, Cooper noticed she had a firm grip. He also noticed she wore no rings.

"I'd like to thank you, Captain Cain for coming to our assistance. I realize you've lost good men by your actions on our behalf."

Cooper thought this is a woman, nay a sea captain I like. "The frigate was as much a threat to us as he was to you, Captain Hai. It was good we could meet where we had the advantage in battle. It might not have been so at some other time. I am sorry for the loss of so many lives, British and our own men."

"We need to make some repairs," Captain Hai said, and then added, "as it appears you do as well. It's only a short sail to the island of Roatan. There are good harbors there, where the repairs can be completed much easier than at sea."

"I thought that island was controlled by the British," Cooper said.

"The island has a few Colonists but most of the British are on the mainland of Honduras. The island is mostly free of British influence. I frequently share some of my supplies and plunder with the people there and they are most appreciative."

Hmmm, Cooper thought. *Maybe we need a closer look at this island.*

COOPER WAS ROWED OVER to *Thunderbolt* after Captain Hai departed. As the gig made its way over, an eerie feeling came over Cooper and suddenly he wished Dagan was present. Looking about, Cooper realized the sea was very still. Nothing moved but a slight breeze and a few last, lingering drops of rain. There were no birds gawking about, in fact, there seemed to be no sound. Cooper turned to look to his cox'n. Quang was looking about as well.

"Death," Quang said.

Only an hour ago, death had visited this place. This empty place on the sea was now the watery grave of an entire crew.

Their lives were suddenly taken. No time to write letters, make amends where needed, or a kind word to a mate. Men took by the press gang…men at sea against their will. Gone, gone in a flash and no way for their families to know what happened to them.

Cooper was depressed as he went up the battens and through the entry port. The guns were all lined up, but several sections of the bulwark was ragged or gone. Cooper suddenly felt the urge to return to his ship, but he couldn't. He had to show he still commanded. He had to show concern and respect for *Thunderbolt's* crew.

Alive…and dead, he thought as he looked at the shrouded bodies lined up on the deck. Planks had been setup. These brave men were about to join the others consigned to the deep.

Buck came forward with a prayer book in his hand. He offered the book to Cooper, who shook his head no. "It's your ship, Captain."

Cooper stepped over by the rail and took off his hat. He felt a lump in his throat. His chest felt tight. He barely heard the words that Buck spoke. His mind was on the night in Barataria when he, St. Jacques, and LaFitte drank the night away. It had been a happy, enjoyable evening. One he'd always remember. A splash! This shook Cooper out of his reverie.

Cooper approached Buck after the service was completed. "Is the ship in any danger?" he asked.

"We've a few leaks, nothing the pumps can't handle for now."

Cooper nodded. "We will sail to the island of Roatan and complete our repairs there. Captain Hai has assured me it will offer a good place to anchor and the islanders will welcome us. She has used the harbor many times."

"She?" Buck asked. "Did you say she?"

"Aye, Captain Jewell. *Southern Cross* has a woman captain." Cooper couldn't help but smile at Buck's expression.

Cooper started down the battens, and holding onto the man-rope, he said, "We will dine together once we reach the island."

"Aye," Buck replied. "I will know the needs of the ship by then."

Cooper nodded. St. Jacques had been a good man, seaman, and captain. But he was not a man to keep his ship the cleanest. Buck Jewell would change that, Cooper was sure.

OVER A GLASS OF cool lemon juice and water, Cooper found Captain Tina Hai to be a very knowledgable person. She had told Cooper how for two centuries Roatan had been a focal point for pirates. The Bay Islands of Honduras, which included Roatan, had plenty of fresh water, wood for ship repairs, and food supplies to restock empty ships and empty bellies.

She told of a village on Roatan, Punta Gorda, that was founded by black Caribs, known as Garifuna. They had been forcibly removed from Saint Vincent by the British and left on Roatan. In 1788, the British left Roatan after years of battling with Spain. The island was, to the American's favor now, a Spanish possession.

Tina said, "Tales or legends have it that ghosts or as the islanders call them, duppies, have been seen by numerous locals. The duppies are supposed to be from pirates burying gold, and then killing a man, leaving his body with the gold to watch over the plunder. Famous pirates such as Henry Morgan, Dutchman Van Horne, and John Coxen, along with about five thousand pirates used Roatan as their haven."

Knowing what he did about Henry Morgan, Cooper didn't doubt men had been killed or buried with their loot. In regards to ghosts or duppies, Cooper would have to see one to believe.

CHAPTER THIRTY

FOLLOWING THE *SOUTHERN CROSS'* lead, *SeaFire* and *Thunderbolt* dropped anchor off the village of Coxen Hole. The village was named after the pirate of the same name. A crowd was gathering on shore and a few pushed off from there in canoes. All seemed to be headed to the *Southern Cross.* A man better dressed than others went aboard the ship but within minutes returned to his boat, along with Captain Hai.

Julio Villarreal looked to be a prosperous man, if the girth of his great belly was an indicator. He wore a shirt open to the waist. His hair was jet black and he had eyes that took in everything around him, including the still fresh signs of battle. He wore no weapon, but long machetes and various other blades were tucked into the belts, ropes, and sashes tied around his men's waists. Julio was a man with a quick smile and charm. Cooper realized he liked the short little man.

"Buenos dias," Julio greeted Cooper. "Thank you for coming to the aid of our daughter." Seeing Cooper glance at Tina, as if this was news to him, Julio explained. "Si!, she is everyone's hija."

"He means the island considers me to be their daughter. I steal from the hated British."

"Si, odiar Ingles," Julio piped in with his smiling face. He pointed at Cooper now. "Tû Americano. Tû ser Nuestro el Amigo."

"You are our friend," Tina translated quickly.

Julio alternated between his broken English and Spanish, but with Tina's help it was soon obvious everyone was invited to a huge fiesta. Cooper was trying to decide how to explain without insulting his host that he had to leave a watch on each ship to give an alarm if need be.

"You don't have to worry, Captain Cain. This is a small island. No one likes a thief and where would one go."

Thinking fast, Cooper replied, "I was thinking of the British, Captain, not the islanders."

Tina gave him that horse manure look but didn't call him on it. Instead she explained to Julio that certain men must remain behind to be on lookout for the odiar Ingles. Julio shook his head in acknowledgment but clearly thought such was a waste.

COOPER FELT A PEACEFUL calm come over him, as they rowed ashore. If Maddy and a few others were here it would be perfect, with the turquoise water, the sunny sky, and a gentle breeze. Yes, it would be a perfect day in paradise. When the boats ground into the sand, the islanders grabbed the bow of the boats and tugged them closer so that the water was only ankle deep when they got out. A man with a booming voice and body to match size of his voice held out his hand.

"William O'Grady it is, and I'm proud to meet you." O'Grady was a strapping man and like Julio wore a constant smile.

Cooper wondered how he kept his fair skin from burning, with red hair and freckles. He quickly learned O'Grady made his living building and repairing boats and doing carpentry when the villages wanted something more than a thatch house… which wasn't often.

As they walked toward the village from the beach along a shaded path, they were greeted by shy children darting about. A few friendly dogs came up and sniffed, making sure they were not duppies. They passed a hen with several little chicks behind her. One of the dogs barked at the hen only to be cuffed a good one by O'Grady.

When they neared the village, O'Grady was greeted by several islanders. After explaining that they were Americans, they all smiled and gave a slight bow, causing Cooper to realize just how polite the islanders were.

Reaching the center of the village, Julio, accompanied by Tina, approached Cooper once again. "Your men can find a place to rest. If shelter is needed, we will find it for you. O'Grady will keep you busy; I'm sure, until the fiesta but do not drink or eat too much. The heat will make you sick and spoil tonight's fiesta."

Quang, who was only a couple of steps behind Cooper, heard the exchange. When Cooper looked his way, the big Chinaman spoke, "Me tell men." *Probably with more force than I would,* Cooper thought.

Cooper addressed O'Grady, as Julio walked off with Tina, "Is there such a place where I could meet with my officers?"

"Certainly, I have a cabana under some mangrove trees that will offer shade from the sun and I'll find ye a bit of beverage to bargain."

Thinking of Julio's warning, Cooper smiled, "Not too spirited I hope." Realizing when he said it that O'Grady probably didn't have any other kind.

CHAIRS WERE PROVIDED AND Cooper realized that though he couldn't see the bay from where he sat, he could still smell the ocean's salty smell. The smell was mixed, nay overpowered when the wind changed, by the smell of food being cooked. He couldn't recognize each smell but the distinct aroma of fresh baked bread made his stomach rumble. He looked about and he could tell the others had picked up on the same smell.

"Mmmm," Buck muttered.

"Who is cooking?" Cooper asked O'Grady when he and a young island girl brought out a tray of glasses filled with beverage.

"My wife, and don't think ye can be stealing her away from me when ye sail," O'Grady answered.

"Damnation," Cooper swore. "You're a mind reader, as well."

Taking the cream colored beverage from O'Grady and taking a cautious sip, Cooper commented, "Not bad."

"Horchata," O'Grady volunteered. "It comes from the Egyptians, I'm told. On Roatan, it is generally made with ground up rice, spice, gourd or morro seeds, all mixed with milk and sugar. The O'Grady version also has a tot of rum added, but just a wee bit."

"Buenas noches, good evening. Julio and Tina Hai greeted Cooper, Buck, and their group. The two nodded at O'Grady, who smiled at Julio, but his eyes were upon Tina. She was, Cooper had already noted, an attractive woman. The smell of food being cooked had invaded Cooper's nostrils and his stomach growled.

Cooper had noted several fishing boats coming in earlier, as he walked along the waterfront with O'Grady. Red snapper was being grilled while some other variety was being fried in a pan of butter and spices. Chowder was being cooked in a large pot. Diced up conch, onions, and garlic were added as Cooper watched. Another pot was boiling and O'Grady nudged Cooper to show him the large lobsters that would go into the pot. Along with the different types of seafood, black beans, slaw, and various desserts were being prepared.

One man seemed to be overseeing the cookout. "Esteban," O'Grady called to the man.

The little man hearing his name turned. "Cómo estás," Senor O'Grady. Bien, gracias."

"Well, thanks." O'Grady introduced Cooper to Esteban. All the while that polite conversation was going on, Esteban's eyes watched as the food was being prepared.

Wonder what he'd do if someone spilt the chowder, Cooper thought.

Cutting to the business at hand, O'Grady asked, "Is that lazy drunkard still working for you?"

"Si, Senor Virgil is a fine seaman."

Cooper had confided in O'Grady his need for a good first officer. Virgil Culpepper had been a British officer who'd tired of sailing under a tyrant of a captain who lived to see the 'cat' released from its red baize bag. He'd resigned his commission at the first opportunity. That was at the British held island of Tobago. He'd wandered around since then, and about a year ago he landed on Roatan. O'Grady felt sure the seaman had conquered the entire population of single and some of the married women on Roatan. Word had gotten out that the seaman had worn out his welcome and might find life more comfortable and possibly much longer were he to up anchor and sail away. O'Grady felt sure Virgil would be at the cookout if he was not topping some willing maiden, furthering the anger and making himself more 'persona non grata.'

The evening meal went along until Cooper found himself utterly stuffed. However, when Julio's wife brought a piece of key lime pie to Cooper, he couldn't resist the temptation. It was sweet with a slightly tart flavor, a delicate flaky crust with a meringue made from sweet cream. Pure satisfaction, his eyes said it all. A big smile came over Julio's wife as Cooper grinned and patted his stomach. *No wonder Julio is always so happy…and rotund*, Cooper thought. *Mmmm…*

"Dolce is the best cook on the island," O'Grady volunteered.

O'Grady explained, seeing Cooper's puzzled look, "Dolce is Julio's wife. You should taste her guava cake."

"I can't wait," Cooper said, "but not tonight."

CHAPTER THIRTY ONE

THE SHIP HEAVED AS a swell rolled under. A slight breeze from the northeast pushed the early morning haze inland. They would up anchor and get under sail as soon as the water barrels had been brought back aboard after a thorough scrubbing. Something Beau Cannington had supervised himself. Fruits and vegetables had been brought on board with the last of the sun's light the previous evening. Cooper had a degree of anxiety as the time for getting underway approached. It would not be Buck taking the ship out as Cooper had come to trust. No, Buck was now the captain of *Thunderbolt*. *SeaFire's* new first mate was the former British officer, Virgil Culpepper. He was a tall, freckled, red-headed man. He reminded Cooper of Mac.

"He passed muster," Buck had said, after meeting with the man. He had also said, "Talk is cheap. Right now, we only have his word he's a deep water sailor. That and O'Grady's guarantee that he is. He's a womanizer of some renown."

Cooper had to laugh at Buck's words. When Virgil was approached, he seemed ready to make a change. Buck presented the articles for Virgil to review, and he looked to see what his shares would be. After seeing the Letter of Marque, something no one else had asked to see, he signed his name with a flourish.

They started their patrol today; it would be three ships setting sail. Tina Hai and the *Southern Cross* would be joining them in a loose association. She would not share in any prizes other than what she captured but Buck and Cooper had decided having three ships attack a convoy meant there'd be more problems for escorts to deal with. Also, through Tina and Julio's help, they had developed a ready market for the cargo of any prizes and possibly the actual ship itself on occasion. A win, win situation as both Cooper and Buck saw it.

A week later, *SeaFire*, *Thunderbolt*, and *Southern Cross* passed south of Cuba under easy sail. It was already hot with the sun beaming down from a cloudless sky. The deep blue of the sky seemed to penetrate the sea so that it too matched the sky's blue. Any misgivings that Cooper might have nursed in regards to Virgil Culpepper being a seaman were long gone. He was a good seaman and officer. He'd first sought out and established a relationship with Johannes Ewers, the master. After that, he'd met with the other officers and the ship's professional men. On a Royal Navy ship, they'd have been called the warrants. He was quick to compliment Buck but added he did some things different. Not necessarily better than Buck, just different. Most of the men had served with Mac, and having done so, many of Culpepper's ways and Mac's were very similar. Ox had voiced his unwillingness to make a change that the new first mate had made.

"You idjet," Banty snarled. "He's got his reasons for making the changes."

"What are they?"

Shaking his head, Banty snarled again, "The biggest is he said so. The second is, it'll probably keep you from getting yore big arse fed to the fishes." Ox understood this and made no more comments.

On one occasion, when Culpepper was dining with Cooper, he volunteered, "Captain, have you noticed how much better *SeaFire* sails at night?"

Cooper had noticed. They'd gotten away from British patrols a few times by being a better nighttime sailor than the British ships. It could be something particular to American built ships.

Culpepper went on, "The air is heavier at night, I'm told. We can sail much closer to the wind in a light breeze than a heavy wind. More so than any ship I've previously sailed on."

Something to keep in mind, Cooper mused.

"Sail ho! Deck thar." The foremast lookout called down. "Directly off the bow."

"A dollar for Johnson," Cooper shouted, so the entire crew could hear.

The crew cheered at the prospect of prize money. It had been two weeks and this was the first sighting of anything beyond a local island trader or fishing yawl. The wind was off the larboard quarter. As the order to clamp on all sail was given, Johnson called down again.

"It's a bleeding convoy, Cap'n."

SeaFire's speed had noticeably increased with the added sails and she seemed to leap over the wave crests. Signals were sent to *Thunderbolt* and *Southern Cross*.

"They're headed to Bermuda and probably on to Halifax," Culpepper advised Cooper. "I wouldn't doubt the admiral at Bermuda hasn't sent out a patrol to intercept the convoy and give them a bit of extra protection."

A flurry of signals was seen as *SeaFire* and her consorts closed with the convoy.

"They'll scurry now," Turner, the second officer volunteered.

"Shall we go to quarters, sir?" asked Culpepper.

"I believe the time is right," Cooper replied.

"Ship coming about," Johnson called down again. "She's sailing to the end of the convoy."

"Towards us," Ewers added.

Looking at the helmsman, Cooper ordered, "Alter course two points to starboard."

"Aye, Cap'n."

A far off rumble was heard. "Signal gun," Culpepper said aloud.

They were now closing with the rear of the convoy. *Thunderbolt* and *Southern Cross* had worn ship and set out for independent action as had previously been agreed upon. The escort ship was a brig. As she attempted to tack, to come up to *SeaFire*, she stalled.

"She's in irons," Ewers clapped.

The crew moved like demons but it was too late. It was the first time Cooper had ever witnessed a ship in irons. He'd heard Eli, Mac, and Ewers talk about it, but now he'd seen it firsthand. Every sail was aback.

"She's in the eye of the wind," Culpepper explained. "Her captain probably just lost his command," he continued. "Clear away the forward guns?" Culpepper asked.

"Aye," Cooper replied. "Have Buster sent to the tops."

Men moved to get boats readied to board prizes. Axes, cutlasses, and pikes were placed in each boat.

"The forward guns are ready, Captain," Spurlock bellowed.

Quang was there with Cooper's pistols and sword. As they came alongside the first merchant ship, the starboard bow chaser went off, narrowly missing the ship's jib boom. The sails came down immediately. *SeaFire's* crew gave a cheer only to be silenced by the bosun, Diamond. The order to sponge out was heard from forward.

"Mr. Ryker, gather your boarding party and prepare to take possession of our prize."

"Get in the royals and stays'ls?" Culpepper asked.

"Aye, Mr. Culpepper, we are among them now."

Johnson called down from aloft, "A two decker is headed our way, Cap'n."

Headed our way, rather than bearing down, meant they had some time. Without being asked, Culpepper took a glass from its holder on the binnacle and climbed up a shroud several feet. Propping the glass on a ratline, he found the two decker, and then after examining her, he climbed down.

"An old fifty, Captain. We can take another prize and then alter course before she'll bring her guns to fire."

"Thank you, Mr. Culpepper."

"Happily," Culpepper said with a grin. The new first officer seemed to enjoy fleecing his former country.

Once again the forward gun spoke almost before the echoes of Cooper's order to fire was given. This ship was not as large as the first ship.

"Put us alongside, Mr. Ewers. We'll board her."

The ship hove to meekly. Grappling hooks shot out and as the ships came together, Mr. Diamond and his party went aboard, quickly taking control of the ship.

Johnson called down again, as *SeaFire* took in her grapnels, "The two decker has worn ship, Cap'n."

Smiling Cooper looked at Culpepper. He'd called it almost to the minute. "Alter course, Mr. Ewers, and lay us alongside the big Indiaman."

The big ship was on the larboard side of the convoy and was trying to distance itself from the rest of the convoy.

The first officer spoke, pointing to a large Indiaman, "Take that one and her hull alone is likely to make us rich men."

CHAPTER THIRTY TWO

THE INDIAMAN PROVED TO be a fast sailing ship for her size and tonnage. However, she didn't have the speed to outdistance the fast and nimble *SeaFire*.

"*Thunderbolt* is pulling away with her prizes."

The snapping of a glass made Cooper turn his head. Culpepper was looking at their fleeing cohorts. "The lady captain has two prizes herself," he said. "She's defiantly a daring soul."

"Aye," Cooper agreed, but couldn't help but think Virgil Culpepper's interest went further than a professional interest. "Forward gun ready, Mr. Spurlock," Cooper yelled.

"Aye, Captain. Ready and willing."

"Lay one alongside her if you please…but don't damage the timbers or we'll have to take it from your share of the prize money." This caused a chuckle from Spurlock's gun crew.

BOOM! The forward gun spoke, sending forth a spout of orange flame and a black nine pound ball. The shot landed so close alongside of the chase, that it sent spray aboard the ship.

"He didn't damage her timbers but he peeled her paint," Banty yelled.

Turning to Cooper, Culpepper swore. "Damnation, Captain, but our gunner knows his business, I believe."

Cooper smiled, "That he does, Mr. Culpepper."

"Deck thar!" Johnson called down. "That ship be flying that flag you hates, Cap'n."

"Are you sure?" Cooper called back, not believing his luck.

"Aye, Cap'n. Yellar with a black F."

Hearing this, Cooper called to his gunner. "Put one across her bow as soon as possible. If she doesn't heave to, drop one amidships...the repairs will come out of my shares," he added. Another cheer went up.

"You've a happy crew, Captain."

"They always are when we're putting money in their pocket," Cooper chimed.

BOOM! Spurlock had fired again. "Sponge out," Cooper heard Spurlock ordering his crew to prepare to fire again.

"That bilge sucking whoreson is veering to starboard," Ewers, the master exclaimed.

"Watch that she doesn't present herself to give us a broadside," Culpepper warned.

"Mr. Turner," Cooper addressed his second officer. "Should that sodomite turn broadside, give her a taste of *SeaFire's* metal."

"Aye, Captain," Turner replied with a smile. He was anxious to put his guns into action.

Culpepper spoke, as Turner turned away, "A bit eager, that one."

"Aye, most eager," Cooper replied.

"She's luffing," Johnson cried from aloft.

"Put up your helm," Cooper ordered the helmsman.

"You've got the fat cow," Culpepper volunteered in an excited voice.

Cooper was not sure. "Where's the escorts?" Cooper called up to Johnson.

"The two decker is at the tail of the convoy," Johnson replied. "Don't see the brig, Cap'n."

"Not surprised," Ewers said. "Probably got rigging to repair."

Cooper nodded. Watching the Indiaman, he spoke to the helmsman again, "Bring her a point closer; easy now. Mr.

Culpepper," Cooper addressed his first officer, "Make sure the swivels and the carronades are loaded with grape. I don't trust this one to act like a gentleman. Mr. Spurlock, let go one closer across her bow. Mr. Turner, open the larboard gun ports and run out, but don't fire…unless they fire, and then blast them to hell."

"Aye," was the officers' solemn reply.

The gun crews threw themselves at the guns, hauling on the side tackles pulling the guns across the deck. The sound of the guns as they rumbled forward across the deck was ominous and finite to Cooper's thinking. Each gun captain raised his hand indicating his gun was ready. Spurlock fired the forward gun with smoke and flame billowing forth, and then the smoke, bitter and acrid, drifted back. Cheers went up from Spurlock's crew.

"She's struck," the gunner called back.

Cooper smiled, "We'll see. Lay us alongside, Mr. Ewers."

The Indiaman's bulwarks rose above *SeaFire* but they'd swing across on lines rigged forward and aft. The two decker escort ship still in his thoughts, Cooper figured this would lessen the time they had to wait to make their escape.

"Keep your eyes on that escort ship," Cooper called to Johnson.

"Aye," the reply came down.

Cooper, still not satisfied with the ship striking her colors, spoke to Culpepper, "This ship belongs to my cousin. Therefore, the likelihood of treachery is high. Don't let the men become lax at their station."

Culpepper was a bit puzzled by Cooper's comment. That he'd attack a family owned ship said a lot for their relationship. He'd query the master later, but for now he'd keep the crew alert.

"Mr. Turner," Cooper spoke to his second officer. "I know normally this would be your prize to take charge of, but I'd appreciate you relinquishing that honor to me, sir."

"Certainly, Captain, by all means."

Climbing up in the shrouds, making ready to go across, Cooper felt his heart skip a beat. It couldn't be...but it was. There on the deck of the Indiaman was his nemesis. The object of his hatred...Phillip.

Calling to Banty, who was just below him, Cooper ordered, "See a bosun mate and get me a bosun's starter." Banty was taken aback by his captain's orders, but he'd do as ordered.

The starters on board *SeaFire* were made out of woven rope with a cane handle. Before the ships had even come together, men were swinging over to the Indiaman. Standing, hands clasped together at his back stood Phillip, with his dandy beside him. He held, under his arm, a cane with an ornate silver head. He was wearing a white wig that the wind had gotten the best of, causing hair to hang down to his eyes. The wig had been powdered with a reddish color. His silk shirt was ruffled at the top and cuffs. His britches were black and his waist coat was red. He looked a dandy. A man behind him wore green with green feathers sticking out from his hat.

"Well, cousin," Phillip spoke. "You've picked a beastly day to go about your barbaric endeavors. " He took the cane from under his arm and set the end down on the deck. Leaning forward, he peered at Cooper's face and then said, "My, my. Father did leave his mark upon you, didn't he?"

Livid with rage, Cooper lashed out with the starter, tearing flesh from his cousin's face from his temporal area to his chin.

Crying out in agony, Phillip slumped to the deck. As he did so, his dandy friend, with the green hat and feathers, pulled a pistol, aiming it at Cooper's face but before he could pull the hammer back, a shot rang out. The dandy stumbled to the side a step. A black hole just above his ear had appeared. A surprised, bewildered look came across his face. He took another side step as his eyes glazed over and he collapsed alongside Phillip.

"Dudley…Dudley," Phillip called, and then taking his bloody hand from his face, he pulled his dead friend to him.

Cooper looked at his ship. Buster stood on the platform where he was stationed. He made a motion between a wave and a salute. Cooper saluted back. The backwoods marksman had just proved his worth.

"Banty," Cooper called to his seaman. "Keep your eyes on my cousin. I'd not desire that he should be killed but should he make a threatening move, put a ball in him."

"Aye, Cap'n," the seaman answered, still in awe over the way his captain had struck out. So this is the man who'd pained his captain. *I should go ahead and kill the bugger*, Banty thought. Otherwise…

CHAPTER THIRTY THREE

IT WAS TWO DAYS since the convoy had been raided. A coastal trader was sighted and stopped. The passengers and crews from the captured ships were placed aboard the coastal trader. The captain was paid for his troubles and promised he'd take the people directly to Jamaica. The ships then made a rendezvous as had been agreed upon. Would it be better to take the prizes to Puerto Rico, New Orleans, or try for Savannah? Culpepper felt with the prizes being captured from the south, the British would likely send out patrols in that direction and probably even into the gulf. Tina wanted to head back toward Honduras but agreed if they could make Savannah, she'd have a better market. It was settled, they'd head northeast.

Sitting in his cabin after Buck, Tina, and their first officers left, Cooper found himself with misgivings about his handling of his cousin. He wanted retribution, yet he was not a murderer. He'd killed men, but only when necessary. He'd marked Phillip, much as he, Cooper had been marked by Uncle Lawrence. He didn't blame his uncle. It had been Phillip, who had lied and caused his uncle to strike him…to mark him. It was now Phillip who had been marked. Would he harbor the same burning hatred? The same need to strike out? Had he put his family, his wife in jeopardy? Had he put those he loved in danger by sparing his cousin's life? Downing the last of the brandy, he'd been twirling in his glass, he had the sinking feeling he'd made things worse.

Slamming the glass down on the table, shattering it, Cooper cursed. "I should have killed him."

Josiah, standing in the pantry, felt his captain's pain...his despair. Captain Cain had treated him well. Better than any he'd served. He'd do his best to watch his captain's back. He'd talk to Quang. Between the two of them, they should be able to keep Cooper's backside safe. Should a person come at Cooper, face-to-face...well, that would be their sad luck, he decided. He'd yet met the man who could best Cooper with blade or ball.

HOMECOMING...WHAT A GLORIOUS DAY it was. The people of Savannah spread the word. Captain Cooper Cain aboard the privateer, *SeaFire*, and his cohorts were returning from another victorious cruise with prizes strung out a mile. It was another black eye for the Redcoats, who plundered American ships, taking their seamen. The pride in Cooper had spread so that neither he nor his men could buy the first drink at any tavern or common house.

Maddy and Suzanne Bledsoe were in town when they heard the news. Leaving her items on the shop's counter, she rushed out to her carriage and ordered, "To the waterfront."

The streets were so congested she cursed the bloody laggards who got in her way. She'd just made it to the company warehouse when Cooper stepped out of the door. John Will, Michael Brett, Cooper, Buck and some woman in seaman's attire had all gathered in front of the door. Seeing Maddy, Cooper rushed up to her. The embrace and kiss was passionate; so much so, that Maddy flushed when she realized so many smiling faces were watching her. Putting her hand to her mouth, she muttered, "Oh."

THE REUNION WITH MADDY was all a man could ask for. What she lacked in experience, she made up for in eagerness. Cooper was totally amazed when Maddy instigated something new. When she'd finished her administration, she rose up and smiled. "Liked it, didn't you?"

"Was there any doubts?"

Maddy smiled and put on an exaggerated tone like a jack tar. "Me thinks you did. It be like you fired a full broadside."

Cooper pulled her up to his chest and slapped her naked rump. "Me thinks you've been talking to somebody," he said.

"Oh several," Maddy admitted. "You can learn a lot from the twins, Suzanne has the most wonderfully vulgar book with illustrations and Debbie has her share of tales."

Cooper acted shocked, "Is that all you women do, when us men are gone, talk about sex?"

"Not all the time, but I want to be able to please my man. I don't want to be such an ole prune that my husband beds some mistress like Mr. Harwood does. Did you know that Mrs. Harwood won't even take off her clothes when he's around?"

Cooper asked, "Who told you this?"

"Their maid told the cook who told Priscilla, who told me."

"I see."

"Cooper, you don't think me naughty, do you?" Maddy asked.

"Yes, absolutely, wonderfully so," Cooper replied.

It was Maddy who was silent now. "Josie said that she and Jessie used to take turns doing that…that it drove you crazy with desire."

Cooper didn't speak for a moment and then said, "It doesn't bother you to know my past with the twins?"

Maddy sat up and Cooper's eyes fastened on her jutting breasts. She took his chin and lifted his head so that he was eye to eye with her. "Look at me, not my wares, Sir Pirate. What happened between you and the twins was before I came along. Try it now, and I'll cut off your bullocks."

Cooper smiled. Maddy pulled his head to her chest, to her breasts. Cooper couldn't explain the pleasure he felt as his wife held him close. "In truth, Coop, you could have had your way with me when you killed that pirate. I wanted you then. Had mother not been there, I'd have taken you myself. I knew it was you who would have my maiden head. I told mother as much."

"Damnation, Maddy. What if she'd told your father, he'd have shot me?"

Maddy lay flat with Cooper's head still on her chest. She didn't respond to Cooper's comments but said, "Your time now, Sir Pirate. Your wench demands to be pleasured."

DAGAN LISTENED INTENTLY AS Cooper told of his meeting with Phillip. When Cooper finished, he said, "I couldn't commit murder, as much as I hated the sodomite, I couldn't just kill him outright."

"I never considered or thought that you would. You can and have taken a life if needed. Should your family be threatened, you'd not hesitate. It's a quality that sets you apart from the rogues that follow you. But you understand that when you take a life, you also affect others as well. You kill one's dreams. You might be taking away a husband, a father. You kill the dreams he shared with his family. You might be taking the bread from their mouths; you take away the means for a family to live. Killing should never be taken lightly or without forethought. No, Cooper, I see hard times ahead for you…dangerous times. Last night, I saw you hold out your son to me. It's the first vision I've had in a long time but this one was vivid and woke me up. You go about your business, Cooper Cain. I will take care of Maddy. That's my vow."

Cooper felt a relief. "We are eating with Eli and Debbie at the inn tonight," he said. "I'd appreciate it if you'd accompany us. Tina Hai, Buck Jewell, and my new first officer will be there."

"Aye, I'll come. I think your new officer will be in for it soon. I saw the way Jessie looked upon him."

"He has a reputation as a womanizing rogue, a real blade as they say."

"Not for long," Dagan said. "I can see the splice already being woven."

CHAPTER THIRTY FOUR

IT HAD BEEN A month since *SeaFire*, *Thunderbolt*, and *Southern Cross* had weighed anchor and put to sea again. During that time, they had taken only two prizes. Those had been taken to New Orleans with Cooper's second officer, Lamar Turner, in overall command.

"Don't let Jean LaFitte fleece you," Cooper warned.

Cooper had expected Turner to be gone two weeks. It was now the fifteenth day. Cooper, Buck, and Tina Hai had sailed past Havana, enroute to Puerto Rico, and then turned southwest past Jamaica and were approaching Grand Cayman. Once through the Yucatan Channel, if no prizes were taken, Captain Tina Hai would come about and make for Roatan. Cooper was considering it...if only Turner were back.

They had planned on keeping the smaller of the two prizes to use as a tender for the other ships. However, more pressing now was the barometer. The glass had been falling for three days. What the master called a steady fall causing him to predict a storm was in the making. Captain Hai and Buck Jewell pulled alongside of *SeaFire*. If a gale approached, they'd have to run for it. Tina wanted to turn more southerly and make for Roatan. They'd never keep station anyway, if the gale was a blow of any size. It was agreed that she would go it alone while Cooper and Buck awaited the return of their newly captured tender. If things worked out, they'd make for Roatan after rendezvousing with Turner.

The wind had already freshened before the *Southern Cross* was over the horizon and out of sight. Cooper felt a pang of guilt for not following his lady friend captain to what was hoped to be a safe port. The wind was at gale force by noon, battering *SeaFire* with the same intensity as the enemies' cannons. Dark gray clouds rushed by overhead dimming the sun's glow. The horizon would go bright as lightning flashed. Each time the flash seemed to be closer. The long, low rumble of thunder grew as well. McKemie, the carpenter, Diamond, the bosun, and Spurlock, the gunner, all met in Cooper's cabin along with Culpepper, the first officer and Ewers, the master. As the men gathered, Cooper could picture Buck Jewell going through the same procedure aboard *Thunderbolt*. Ewers brought a chart with him, laying it out on Cooper's table. He spread it out and laid his divider, plotters, and an old quadrant on the corners to keep it from rolling up.

"We should be through the channel, meaning the Yucatan Channel, before the next watch," Ewers said. "Sooner if the wind continues. It's open sea then into the gulf, if the storm plays out. Should it be prolonged…" The master left the sentence unfinished. They all knew the answer.

"We've got everything battened down as possibly can be," Diamond volunteered. "We've double catted the anchors, also. The hatches are secured and ready to batten down, and all gear has been stowed. We've ran lifelines, both forward and aft."

When Diamond finished speaking, Spurlock advised the group that the big guns and especially the bruisers, meaning the carronades, had been lashed tight with double lines.

McKemie was next, "No more than the usual amount of water in the well. As you know, we gave a thorough inspection of the hull while we were in Savannah."

Culpepper was last to speak. He seemed to be going over a checklist in his mind for a moment or two. He then spoke, "We've taken in the jib and set the fore topmast staysail. As the wind has freshened, I have had the hands take a second reef in the topsails and a single reef in the courses." He then paused again. "If the wind gets up anymore, we can take in a third reef. We may also haul up and furl the mainsail. We've sent up and hooked pendant tackles and preventer braces. I've had the yards pointed toward the wind and secured and hoisted clear of the caps. Spare spars and yards have been brought on deck and lashed down. The boats have been made secure and I've had spare axes securely placed by the mast." Culpepper paused again and then added, "Pumps have been cleared and we've brought up extra relieving tackles ready for hooking."

Cooper was satisfied that they'd taken all the precautions they could from the maintop to the bilges, now all that remained was the wait. As the wind picked up some more, Cooper noted Ewers had put two men on the helm, each with a rope tied around his waist. The wind was now howling. Culpepper had set storm sails, hopefully they would hold. The rain pelted against Cooper's tarpaulin making a tapping sound. Between the howling wind and the tapping, Cooper couldn't hear a thing.

Turning so that his back would be to the wind, Cooper noticed Quang standing there. To tell him to go below would have been useless, so Cooper didn't attempt to speak. Where the wind had pushed his face back until his eyes were near slits, it now tried to push his entire body.

Forward, a crash was heard and the ship slewed to starboard. The helmsmen were thrown to the deck, but Johannes took the wheel. Grabbing a life rope, Cooper fought his way forward. The bowsprit had broken off. Only the rigging lines held it against the bow, causing the ship to cant.

"Axes," Cooper shouted to Quang.

Before the Chinaman could turn, Culpepper was there, holding two axes. Keeping one, Culpepper handed the other one to Quang. Together they chopped with all their might, each knowing the ship would not last long with waves slamming over the bow as they were. Quang's rope parted first with a loud snap. One side was done, but the strain caused a forestay to part. How much strain could the forward mast stand deprived of the support from the stays? Cooper was not the seaman that Culpepper was, but he knew full well that they were in imminent danger of losing the topmast and topgallant mast. Culpepper continued to chop as Diamond came forward with a party. Hearing the crash forward, Culpepper had called all hands prior to coming to Cooper's aid.

Culpepper was still chopping and ordered Diamond, "Get your men to clearing away that debris." He then looked at Cooper.

Seeing the look and realizing the need, Cooper nodded, "Give the ax to Quang and then heave to."

Diamond's party had attacked the hanging bowsprit, knowing their lives depended on clearing away the wreckage. Diamond had a kedge anchor dropped and then pulled up into the debris, hooking the bowsprit to save, if possible. Rigging a tackle and hoisting on the line attached to the kedge, the wreckage was pulled free of the water. Straps were then hooked to tackles around the lower aspect of the foremast. With the bowsprit secured to the foremost, lines were run to the cat-head. Once the debris had been cleared from the water the ship righted itself, making control of the ship more manageable.

Culpepper approached Cooper, "We've got to secure the spars and send down the topgallant mast and house the fore topmast."

Cooper involuntarily looked aloft. The wind had abated in the last few minutes but it was far from calm.

Seeing the concern in his captain's eyes, Culpepper spoke again, "If we don't, Captain, we stand to lose a lot more..."

"Aye, you're right, Virgil, see to it." As Culpepper turned, Cooper called again, "Virgil."

"Yes, Captain."

"Banty is the best topman we have."

"Thank you, Captain."

The hands were mustered below the mainmast and Culpepper told the men what needed to be done. Seasoned men, every one of them. No grumbling and no shirking. The men went at it with an energy that only comes with the knowledge that failure to get the job done could end up with the loss of the ship and all aboard. The wind had calmed even more, but was still a force.

"You've a seaman in the first officer, Captain." This was from Johannes Ewers. The master was impressed with Culpepper. To impress the master was something, indeed. Looking from Ewers to the wheel, Cooper noted two new helmsmen. "I had to send Johnson down to Dr. Cannington. The wheel spun when the bowsprit carried away and broke his arm." Cooper nodded.

Culpepper was headed Cooper's way. "Banty says we have a guest, Captain."

"A guest?"

"Aye. He thinks we have a British frigate bearing down on us."

Cooper had a sinking feeling. Had the bowsprit not carried away, they'd have probably been able to out sail the frigate. As it was, there was no way. The damage also cut down on the maneuverability, so to think they could out fight a frigate was insane.

"Have they seen us?" Cooper asked.

"Aye, Captain, it appears they have."

"Huh, well it was bound to happen the way our luck has run today," Cooper replied.

Culpepper forced a smile on his face, but thought, *it was fun while it lasted.*

CHAPTER THIRTY FIVE

THE BRITISH FRIGATE HAD reduced sail and the royals were down. Cooper picked up a glass and swept it over the British ship. Sail handlers were aloft but none of the gunports were open. *They're ready, but only their forward guns appeared to be manned,* Cooper thought to himself.

"One false move and we'll see a full broadside," Virgil said, as he walked up to his captain.

Cooper continued to scan the frigate with his glass. The ship seemed familiar to him but why? As the glass moved to the quarterdeck, Cooper swore and let the glass fall from his eyes. "It seems we meet again," Cooper said to himself. "I don't have Dagan and Faith, this time, to get us out of our predicament."

Cooper realized he'd spoken aloud when Virgil said, "Beg your pardon, Captain."

"The British ship's captain is known to me, Mr. Culpepper. This should be interesting. Mr. Ryker!"

"Aye, Captain."

"Haul down our colors. Quang!" Cooper spoke to the ever present Chinaman. "Bring me my best sword."

Quang nodded and then hurried off.

WHILE THE WEATHER HAD moderated in the last half hour, the frigate's boat pitched heavily as it was rowed to *SeaFire*.

"Let's make a show of honors as the captain boards our ship." Several crewmen glared at Cooper. "No use inflaming the already bad situation," Cooper growled. Not used to the men's reaction, but understanding it. "Banty," Cooper called, "aloft with you and let me know…quietly if either *Thunderbolt* or *Southern Cross* are within sight."

The little seaman scampered off and was climbing the ratlines as the British boat came alongside. Diamond was there with his bosun pipe and Culpepper called the men to attention. Diamond had honors sounding by the time the British captain's head was level with the entry port.

When the captain stepped on deck, Cooper stepped forward, removed his hat, and gave a slight bow, and then spoke, "Welcome to the American privateer ship, *SeaFire*, Captain Hawks."

Surprised at his reception, Hawks returned the bow and took Cooper's outstretched hand. "I wasn't expecting such a peaceful reception, Captain Cain."

Cooper smiled, "I'm always peaceful when there's no use being otherwise." He had spoken with a smile and Hawks returned the smile. Cooper took his sword from Quang and handed it to Hawks.

Hawks shook his head no. "Keep your sword, Cooper. I didn't capture you, the elements did. Do you have what you need to rig a new bowsprit until we reach port?"

"Aye," Cooper replied, and then added, "now that the weather will allow."

Hawks nodded and moved a bit as others in his boat came on deck…a midshipman and a squad of marines. Hawks came to attention and spoke in a formal tone, "I regret to inform you, Captain Cain, that this ship and its men are now a lawful prize of *HMS Racer*. Should you give your parole, I will allow you to continue in command of your ship until we reach Grand Cayman, where I will turn you over to the authorities."

Banty had silently come down from aloft. He coughed to get Cooper's attention and shook his head no.

"I will give you my parole for as long as we are under your immediate authority, Captain Hawks. I shall be honor bound to try to escape, after that."

Both men eyed one another and shook hands, with Hawks saying, "Until Grand Cayman."

"Captain Hawks, may I give you a bit of refreshment," Cooper asked.

"Thank you, Captain, but first, Mr. Locklear."

The midshipman stepped forward, "Yes sir."

"Get the key to the weapon's locker, and then collect the crew's weapons."

"Aye, sir."

Cooper spoke to his first officer, "Mr. Culpepper, see that the men offer no resistance."

"Aye, Captain."

Hawks followed Cain to his cabin. "Josiah, something for our guest," Cooper said.

Out of sight from the men, Hawks took the offered seat and then asked, "How's Maddy?"

"She's fearful of this war's effect on our future, even with Dagan's assurance that things will work out."

"How is Dagan?"

Cooper smiled, "He lives with us now. We actually built a small cottage next to our house. He has a young girl, Priscilla, who takes care of things for him while he watches over Maddy. I tell you, Captain Hawks..."

"Richard," Hawks interrupted Cooper, "let us be friends. Call me Richard when we're alone."

Cooper nodded and replied, "My friends call me Coop."

"Coop, it is then," Hawks said, and smiled. "I remember when we were at Dagan's birthday party at the Tavern and you walked in and Maddy squealed 'Sir Pirate'. I thought Sir Gabe would die. Lord Anthony and everyone else laughed. Do you remember that, Coop?"

Cooper was laughing now. "I was sure his Lordship would have me swinging from the yardarm by sunrise."

"No, not after you rescued Faith and Maddy, not to mention Sir Richard Basnight." Hawks smile faded. "You've naught to worry if you're taken by one of Sir Gabe's ships. There's others patrolling though, Coop, and you've wrought bloody hell among the merchant convoys. Were you taken by one of the other captains, you might find yourself looking at a noose." Hawks paused for a moment. "We met up with a mail packet yesterday that had sailed from Bermuda. The gossip is your cousin has put a reward of a thousand pounds to any man who brings him your head."

Cooper gave a sigh, "I should have ended it when I had the chance." He looked at Hawks and continued, "I should have killed him for what he did to me, but even in my anger, I couldn't kill the man who caused this." He touched his scar. "I'm not a murderer, I've discovered."

Hawks had heard Cooper's story from Maddy's brother, Jake. A knock was heard. It was Midshipman Locklear.

"The weapons have all been collected and secured, sir."

"Thank you, Mr. Locklear," Hawks replied, and then winked at Cooper. "Now, young sir, I shall leave you in command of our prize. Captain Cain has given me his parole so I think you will have no worries. You will follow us in to Georgetown. Should you need any assistance, I'm sure my friend; Captain Cain will do all in his power to satisfy your needs."

"Your friend, sir?"

"Aye, Mr. Locklear. Did you know that our commander, Vice Admiral Sir Gabe Anthony, is actually Captain Cain's father-in-law?"

"But sir," the midshipman said, his mouth agape. "He's an American."

"He was born British, but Mr. Locklear, you'll find that war will often provide some strange situations. Until Grand Cayman, Captain Cain." Cooper nodded. "Mr. Locklear, you are now in charge. See that the marines are looked after."

"Yes sir."

"Good, then I bid you adieu, young sir. Captain Cain."

Cooper smiled, "Captain Hawks. I will give your regards to Dagan and Maddy when I next see them."

"Thank you, sir, that's most kind."

As Hawks went down the battens to his boat, Locklear looked at Cooper, "Let's get underway, Captain Cain."

Cooper saw Johannes and Virgil look his way. "Do you not think it best, young sir, that we allow your captain time to return to his ship, so that we don't capsize his gig?"

"Oh! Yes, Captain certainly."

CHAPTER THIRTY SIX

LIGHTS WERE APPEARING IN the windows of the houses and shacks that made up the little town the Crown had proudly named Georgetown. Across the way a fort...Fort George, stood overlooking the harbor. The ugly black snouts of cannons poked out from their embrasures. Several fishing boats were pulled up close to the shore and off to starboard *HMS Racer* was anchored. The crowing of a rooster and cluck, cluck, clucking of chickens roosting in a shed that was near the water could be heard. The soft groan of two fishing boats shifting on their lines and grinding together added to the early morning noises.

Prevailing winds and currents meant that most ships coming from Jamaica or other Eastern Caribbean islands, or even Europe would pass the Cayman Islands. Therefore, many stopped at Grand Cayman. Water cask from ships could be cleaned and filled at the well near the harbor steps. Quantities of fish and turtle were also readily available.

"Morning suh." This was said by one of the five marine guards sent aboard *SeaFire* by Hawks.

"Morning," Cooper greeted the marine. "Looks like it's going to be a beautiful day."

"Aye, that it does, suh."

"Have you been on the island?" Cooper asked.

"No, suh, but Cap'n Hawks said we'd be here long enough to take on water and provisions. So it's likely, I'll get ashore for a bit to stretch me legs."

"I see," Cooper said. "Are you headed back on patrol then?"

"Not as such. We got orders to head back to Antigua. The Jamaica squadron will take over this area."

"Are you looking forward to that?"

"Aye, suh. I has a woman there, that is, if she ain't hooked up wid some sergeant or such."

"Let's hope not. You seem like a decent fellow."

"Thank you, Cap'n." The marine cut his eyes and then held his head down. "I best go, Cap'n, here comes the admiral. Good day to you, suh," the marine said and smartly did an about face to continue his rounds.

Cooper turned as Locklear walked up. Admiral...hmmm... said a lot as to how the men felt about the midshipman.

"Hope he was not bothering you, Captain Cain." So formal, Cooper thought.

"No, young sir, we were just talking about the sounds that greeted the sunrise."

"Yes, I see. Some are very delightful."

"Just so," Cooper said as he walked away. "Just so."

Josiah appeared at the companionway and stumbled as he stepped over the coaming. The noise caused both the marine guard and Cooper to look. "I sorry, sir," Josiah said. "I should be able to remember to lift my feet higher."

Seeing the captain's man, the marine guard continued his rounds. *While he was a friendly sort,* Cooper thought, *he takes his duty seriously. To think otherwise would be amiss.*

"Can I help you, Josiah?"

"Yes, Captain. Do you think if possible I may go ashore and purchase some eggs today? It appears they have chickens very near."

"That will depend on what our captors have in mind, I'd think," Cooper replied.

"Oh dear me," Josiah muttered. "That captain was so nice, I forgot we were prisoners, as it were."

Cooper smiled. "Captain Hawks and I have met previously. However, we are being turned over to the local authorities until a decision is made as to how to dispose of us. It appears our captain is being relieved by another ship. We may well be taken to Jamaica, once he arrives."

"I see, sir, since we are in a quandary as to our future, I shall forget about fresh eggs for now. Would a pastry be sufficient or do you want more, sir?"

"A pastry for now, I think."

"Coffee or cocoa, sir?"

"Coffee."

"Very well, sir." As Josiah turned to go, he paused. "Captain, have you heard what our first officer calls eggs?"

Cooper thought for a moment. "I don't believe I have."

"Cackleberries, Mr. Culpepper says cackleberries when he speaks of eggs."

A laugh was heard, behind Cooper. "Pardon me, suh." It was the marine sentry. *He's quiet too*, Cooper thought.

"I see you find it as amusing as I," Josiah said to the marine.

"That's enough, Private, be about your duties instead of wasting time with our prisoners," Locklear, the midshipman, barked.

"Suh!" The marine responded, coming to attention but not before giving Cooper a look that didn't hide the marine's resentment of the midshipman.

THE WATER IN THE harbor was flat, almost like glass as the fresh heat of a new day grew. Pelicans wheeled and crashed into the still waters as breakfast was spied. To the east, the sky was a molten gold. Virgil Culpepper took another swallow of coffee, letting it loosen phlegm that accumulated in his throat as he slept. He hacked, coughed it up and spit over the side.

McKemie, the carpenter, and his assistants were already forward working on the bowsprit. The young midshipman, Locklear, not having been told otherwise, watched as McKemie and his crew in a well thought out and professional manner cleared away the remaining wreckage from forward. The broken bowsprit was hoisted up and inboard. The lines were cleared away and after a thorough inspection found that a cannon ball was the culprit for its being carried away.

"We had to have taken a hit that we didn't realize," McKemie explained to Cooper.

A shadow loomed over the kneeling men so they looked up. It was Culpepper. "Boat approaching, Captain," the first mate advised.

"Thank you, Mr. Culpepper." Cooper turned back to McKemie, "Any thoughts on when repairs will be completed?"

"If we put our mind to it and find no more damages, I'd say by sunset."

Cooper looked McKemie dead in the eye, with a look that said more than the spoken word…a look of urgency. "See to it then, if you will, Mr. McKemie."

McKemie was no fool. It had to be ready soon…very soon.

"Mr. Locklear."

"Yes, Captain Cain."

"A boat is approaching. One aboard is definitely Captain Hawks."

The boy had been so absorbed in McKemie's repairs, that he'd not noticed the approaching boat. He looked for a marine, wondering why they'd not warned him. Cooper tried to hide his smile. Locklear would find that it would take more than his pretty blue uniform to gain respect from those he commanded.

A show of thoughtfulness or a kind word earlier that day may have brought him a warning of the approaching boat. Locklear was now about to be embarrassed by not having things ready for his captain.

Taking pity, Cooper called to his bosun, "Mr. Diamond, muster the crew and prepare to render honors to our guest."

"Aye, Captain."

The boat was not challenged as would be done on a Royal Navy ship, but the crew was in formation and Diamond piped honors when Hawks made his way on deck. He was followed by a man dressed as if he may be of some importance. Hawks introduced the man to Cooper, after shaking hands with him.

"Captain Cain, it is my pleasure to introduce you to Mr. William Bodden. He is the Chief Magistrate for the island."

Cooper shook Bodden's hand and said, "Were it not for the circumstances in which we meet, I would say it was a pleasure, sir."

Bodden was quick to smile, "I understand your feelings, sir, and wish they were more pleasant indeed."

"Would you like to go below?" Cooper asked. "I'm sure that we can persuade Josiah to bring us a glass."

"Just a moment, if you will, Captain." Bodden then took a package from a man who had accompanied him aboard the ship.

Bodden shook his head and Captain Hawks said, "We'll follow you, Captain Cain."

Once in the captain's cabin, Hawks spoke, "If you will have your man bring us three glasses, Coop, we will delve into Mr. Bodden's welcome offering." Puzzled, Cooper called for the glasses. Hawkes opened the package to show a liquid concoction.

"You may need to stir it," Bodden advised.

Hawks turned it back and forth a few times and poured each a glass. "Don't ever let Maddy taste the stuff, Coop, or she'll become addicted."

Cooper took a small sip, looked appreciatively and took another larger swallow. "That's good."

"Aye, see what I mean," Hawks returned.

"We call it coconut rum. I also have a jar mixed with pineapple," Bodden said.

"I'll warn you, Coop, while it tastes great, a glass or two will put you arsehole over tea kettle."

Cooper's reply was, "Hmmm."

Bodden smiled and added, "Your father-in-law, Sir Gabe, will attest to that."

After the first round was finished, a jar of the pineapple was opened. Bodden got down to business, as this rum was poured. "We have petitioned the admiral in Jamaica for a constant naval presence in these waters. He has indicated the first suitable prize taken would become that ship. Captain Hawks will depart on the evening tide for Jamaica where he will inform the admiral that a suitable prize has been taken."

"Captured," Hawks interrupted. "I just captured a storm damaged ship."

"Er…yes, quite right. Your ship is to be made our prize, none-the-less. Captain Hawks was honor bound to inform me your parole was only until you reached Grand Cayman. Unless you will extend your parole to me, sir, I'm afraid I will have to have you incarcerated."

Hawks, who had been toying with his glass, at this point spoke, "I had considered taking you aboard *Racer* and on to Antigua, where you could be put under the custody of Sir Gabe. I have no assurance, though, that the admiral in Jamaica wouldn't have you removed from the ship."

Bodden spoke again, "One thousand pounds is a significant enticement, be you a jack tar or an admiral." He was speaking of the reward Cooper's cousin had posted on his head.

"I'm sorry to say, Mr. Bodden, I cannot give my parole."

"Captain Hawks was certain you'd say that, Captain Cain. As unpleasant as it may seem, I do hereby arrest you in the name of the Crown."

"You have been most gentlemanly, Mr. Bodden, so please no apology for doing one's duty. I would like to inform my first officer, in your presence of course, if you don't mind."

"By all means, sir, and you may have your man bring any personal items that would make your…stay more comfortable."

Cooper was about to decline, but thought it might be good for someone to know where he was being held. Culpepper was sent for and soon arrived. Cooper explained his being taken away. He then added, "Keep the men busy, Mr. Culpepper. Idle hands stand to make for an unhappy crew."

"Aye, Captain. I'll keep them at it right enough."

Bodden tried once more, as they made to leave, "Our gaol is nothing more than a stone house with a set of bars for a door and one window. I will have a bed put together for you. I promise, sir, should you reconsider and give your parole, I will do everything in my power to see no harm comes to you and will put you on the first ship to English Harbor."

"Were it that easy, sir, I might take you up on the offer," Cooper replied.

LATER, JUST BEFORE THE sun went down, Cooper watched out his single window as *HMS Racer* was put to sail. *So long, Richard,* Cooper said to himself. *I'm glad we didn't meet broadside to broadside.* His thoughts were interrupted by a noise. It was a couple of men bringing in a small bed as promised by Bodden and a small table that hadn't been mentioned.

When the workers had brought in the table and bed and left, the guard called. He handed Cooper a jar of liquid and a glass. "A present, suh."

"From Mr. Bodden?"

"No sir, a Mister Vallin. He says he'll stop by later."

"I don't believe I know him," Cooper said.

"He was in the navy wid Sir Gabe." *Ah, another connection to his father-in-law,* Cooper thought. "Ahem...," the sentry wanted to speak but seemed uncomfortable. "I'm told you are a gentleman, sir, and while you won't give your parole, I'm told should nature call, as long as you give me your word you wouldn't try to escape, I can let you out to...ah...take care of business. If you don't give your word...well, you'll just have to shat in your pants."

Cooper couldn't help but laugh, which caused the guard to laugh. "Before it comes to that, you'll have my word."

CHAPTER THIRTY SEVEN

H MS *Racer* HEADED OUT to sea, and the captain had no idea the friendly little fishing yawl, with its owner seated at the tiller and waving farewell, was anything but what it seemed. Buck Jewell sat at the tiller and the boy at the nets was the owner's son. The owner was being held aboard *Thunderbolt*, with the promise of gold and his vessel back, upon Buck's safe return. However, if the son didn't play his part right, the father himself would become fish bait. With this knowledge, the boy had acted most appropriately. As the yawl passed close to where *SeaFire* was anchored, Johannes Ewers got a glimpse of the man behind the yawl's tiller.

A slight nod was given by Johannes and returned by Buck. As the yawl came about and headed just off the coast of the Seven Mile Beach, *SeaFire's* master approached the first officer. Culpepper listened as Johannes spoke in a low voice and then each moved along. The word had been passed that help would be forthcoming. Meanwhile, the crew was to act very subdued and polite to their guards.

COOPER HAD LIT THE candle he'd been given and after melting a bit of wax onto the small table that he'd been given; he stuck the candle into it. As the wax cooled it made the perfect candleholder. The sun went down and a breeze came through the window causing the candle's flame to flicker, creating shadows on the bare coquina walls. The walls were rough and various shells, oyster and small seashells, were visible. It was not smooth as that made by Gus, Cindy Veigh's man. Maybe this was more a tabby rather than coquina, Cooper theorized.

"Evening, suh!" Cooper heard his guard speaking, so he rose and headed toward the entrance.

"You may let me in, guard; I assure you we are in no danger."

The guard looked very unsure but Vallin had been a Navy captain and was a member of one of the richest families on the island. If anyone denied Captain Vallin, it wouldn't be him. Besides, no one said the prisoner couldn't have visitors.

Cooper stepped back as Vallin entered. After a greeting, Cooper said, "Your choice, bed or chair?"

Vallin smiled, "Your accommodations are a bit sparse, worse than the captain's cabin on a sloop."

Cooper smiled at this. "I'd offer you a glass but I only have the one cup."

Vallin smiled, "I've made do with worse."

"Aye, then we'll share some of the coconut rum I was given by your Chief Magistrate."

"Mr. Bodden," Vallin volunteered. "William is a great host." Again the men smiled at the comment…host indeed. Vallin's smile left his face and he became very serious. "I just left the Bodden residence. You, Cooper Cain, have caused a dilemma. You have married into the Anthony family. I was one of Lord Anthony's officers, first lieutenant to Sir Gabe. Both men have spent time here and even provided protection for the island during the last war. The island feels it owes a debt to the Anthony's. I owe being a captain to Sir Gabe. It's been a quandary as to how to deal with you. I'm sure you've heard a substantial reward has been placed on your head by your cousin."

"I've heard," Cooper muttered.

"The thought among our people is that once Captain Meriweather arrives in his ship, you will be taken from our custody." Vallin paused. "The Anthony's still have lots of friends. One of the staff at the Admiral's Headquarters overheard a conversation between the admiral and Captain Meriweather. He quickly carried a message to one of our merchant captains who delivered the message to William Bodden. Captain Meriweather had to replenish his ship before sailing. Had they known you were here, I'm sure the replenishment would have waited. You also must know that Captain Hawks is duty bound to report your capture to the admiral. If Meriweather has not already set sail, you can bet he will as soon as Richard Hawks makes his report. Since we can't find any fair and legal way to keep you from Meriweather, we'll do it illegally. Once a British ship is spotted, a group of brigands will over power the guard, take his keys, taking care not to bust the lock as they are hard to replace, and take off with you to parts unknown."

"I assume that I'd eventually end up as Sir Gabe's prisoner."

"Aye, that would be my thoughts. Were you to give Sir Gabe your parole, I'm sure Maddy would find her way to Antigua."

"My men?" Cooper asked. "They sail under a Letter of Marque."

"They would become prisoners of war. They are in no danger of death, Cooper. Those that would give their parole would probably never be taken from the island." Vallin stood, "It's as much as I can offer, Cooper."

Cooper stood and shook Vallin's hand. "I'm grateful to you, sir, more than you know, but I must think about my men."

"You may not have that luxury, sir," Vallin said, sounding a bit put off. "I would think it better for your men were you not here to inflame the Navy."

"Aye," Cooper acknowledged. "There is that."

THE RAIN STARTED OFF as a mist and then picked up until it was a steady drizzle. It wasn't a hard rain, but it didn't take long for the marine guard's uniform to become soaked. A slight breeze off the ocean came along with the rain, and this caused the guard more discomfort. He was not only wet, but also chilled as well. The midshipman in charge of the marine detail aboard the privateer ship didn't notice. He was in Captain Cain's cabin enjoying the captain's wine. Any other bloke would have noticed the weather, and had the guard changed every couple of hours, but not Locklear... 'Admiral bleeding Locklear', as the middy was called. The guard recalled how he'd made a slip and called him 'Admiral' when speaking with Captain Cain. The good captain didn't correct him. He just smiled. He was a real captain.

The men aboard his ship all seemed to like him. That's the difference between the volunteers of this ship and the pressed men in the bloody Royal Navy. The Americans all volunteered, they had a choice. The marine felt a cold drop of rain plop down his collar and run down his spine causing him to shiver. *Damn this rain and damn Locklear's bloody soul.*

He searched for a spot that provided some relief from the wind if not for the rain. He thought to hell with it and stood just inside the companionway. It was the only place that gave a poor marine any relief from the rain or wind. He'd keep an eye open and should 'Admiral Locklear' open the cabin door, he'd say he thought he heard a sound. Besides, who'd try escaping in this weather? The marine thought, after a moment, *that the men had acted differently that afternoon...friendlier. Did they have something planned? If they did, he wouldn't care. Had he brought it to the shat for brains Locklear, he'd have berated him. Almost hope they do have something planned*, he thought. The blame would be on the middy...

Admiral Locklear, not some lowly private.*I wonder what time it's getting to be* .

The privateer's men didn't keep a strict watch like the Royal Navy did unless they were at sea. Thinking on this, made the private more morose. He'd have to depend on Locklear keeping time and deciding when it was time to change the guard…gawd what a miserable stinking night it was.

CHAPTER THIRTY EIGHT

THE SAME WEATHER THAT created such misery for the marine guard proved the perfect cover for Buck Jewell. *Thunderbolt* was anchored just off the coast. The rain clouds had darkened the sky even more than it already was at quarter moon. He took several men in the fishing yawl but also towed two of the ship's boats. Once they boarded *SeaFire*, the boy sailing the yawl would go back with one of Buck's men, pick up his father and their pay and be off; but only if the correct password had been passed. Otherwise, the boy's father would never see the sunrise over Grand Cayman. With the guard taking refuge in the companionway, he didn't hear the whisper of voices nor feel the slight bump as the yawl nudged alongside the entry port.

The forward men swarmed up the chains and over the bow. Buck Jewell could not have picked a better night or easier boarding. Nobody was on deck. His initial elation suddenly became suspicion and he grew cautious. He eased toward the companionway to look down, when he saw the marine. The guard leaned against the door and seemed to be asleep or daydreaming. He motioned to the sailor with him to use his belaying pin on the man.

THUNK!!! The marine collapsed with Buck catching him as he could and easing the dead weight to the deck. He whispered to the seaman beside him, "Unbatten the hatches and free our men." He then called two more men to him, "Quietly find the rest of the guards. They are probably in the mate's cabins. Don't fire a pistol unless it's absolutely necessary." The men nodded their understanding and went to find the guards. Buck was left with just his cox'n, Talon. They eased down the ladder and opened the door to the captain's cabin.

They came face to face with Josiah, who was on the verge of speaking when Buck put his finger to his lips and shushed him. They ducked into the pantry where Josiah said, "One man lounging at the captain's table."

Buck winked at Josiah and motioned Talon to follow. He stood in the center of the cabin a full half minute before Locklear realized that he was not alone. He lunged for his dirk but came up short as Talon put his cutlass at the boy's throat.

"I wouldn't," Buck hissed. "I'd hate to leave a mess in the captain's cabin for Josiah to clean up." Locklear, ever so slowly, leaned back away from the dirk. "Where is Captain Cain?" Buck asked.

"He's in the gaol," Josiah volunteered. "I can show you."

The men went back on deck, with Talon's cutlass in Locklear's back. The one marine guard was still out but the others were bound securely.

Buck saw Culpepper and walked over to the first mate, "Get your ship ready to sail, Virgil. We'll be back as soon as we get Captain Cain."

"I'll go along, sir," Buster Reynolds, the marksman, said.

Buck nodded and said to Virgil, "I'll leave our midshipman in your care. He'll be our hostage, not much of one for sure, but maybe he's someone's son or nephew."

"Not bloody likely," one of the marines snorted.

"Drown him then, if we're not back soon."

"Aye," Virgil replied, seeing Buck's wink.

The men shoved off, with Talon at the tiller. Josiah was pointing the way and they ground up on the beach one hundred yards down from the gaol.

COOPER HAD DRAGGED HIS cot as far away from the open window as possible and still the ocean breeze blew in the rain. He looked at his sentry and the man was worse off than he was…wet and miserable. He walked to the front and called to the sentry through the bars.

"I know you must be miserable. Come in out of the rain. Lord, man, you're shaking. Come on in. You can have the chair and I'll sit on the cot."

"I can't chance it, suh, but thank you for caring."

"Look, you have the gun," Cooper pleaded, feeling sorry for the man.

"Aye, that I does, but the powder is too wet to shoot, I imagine."

Cooper thought a second, and then spoke, "Listen, both Mr. Bodden and Captain Vallin have asked for my parole. If I give it, they know they can trust me. So here's a bargain, unless I'm rescued by persons unknown, I give you my parole not to try to escape while it's raining."

The guard stepped closer to the bars. "What does you mean by persons unknown?"

Cooper gave a sigh, "I have men on my ship and possibly men on the other ships close by, or even possibly men on this island who might try to rescue me. I have no knowledge of such an attempt, but it could happen. With that possible exception, I promise you I will not try to escape."

"I believe you's a man of your word," the guard said. "I also knows that the magistrate and Cap'n Vallin sets store in yo family. But, suh, it took me a while to earn my stripe, so I'll just stand close and get by best as I can. It wouldn't be the first time I's been wet."

Cooper sighed once more and stepped back. The guard was a black man who'd earned his 'stripes'. Something he was sure not many blacks had achieved. He admired the man's devotion but wasn't sure he wouldn't get sick from it. Cooper turned and walked back to the little window in the rear. He saw the boat as he peered out, and then lost it in the shadows. When the little bit of a moon peaked out of the clouds, he saw it again. He watched as the boat was beached and men rushed from it. He knew one was Buck and another was…yes, it was Josiah. They were coming to rescue him. Hopefully, they wouldn't have to kill the guard. He continued to watch. The tall lanky one looked like Reynolds.

He sat down; suddenly glad the guard hadn't taken his parole. Should he distract the guard, he wondered. It might save his life but would the man believe he knew nothing of the attempt. *What did it matter*, he thought, but realized it did. He leaned forward as much as possible but could no longer see anyone. He could stick his arm out and signal but the shore was nothing but boulders and the sea sloshed among them so he just sat and waited. They wouldn't come from that direction.

He heard a startled voice, a few moments later, and rushed to the gaol door. "Don't hurt him."

"He ain't hurt, Cap'n," Buster Reynolds volunteered.

The keys were removed from the guard's belt and Cooper thought the click as the cell door was unlocked was the sweetest sound. Cooper stepped out and the guard was pushed in the cell with his hands tied behind his back.

Cooper said, "Wait," as a seaman went to put a gag on the guard. He called Buck over, "Captain Jewell, answer my questions for this man, please. How long has it been since we were in contact with one another?"

"Days, sir."

"Did I have any knowledge that you would attempt to rescue me today or any day?"

Buck had caught on, "No sir, none in the slightest."

Cooper then turned to the guard. "When I spoke to you of parole earlier, I had no knowledge of Captain Jewell's plans. I give you my word of honor on that."

The guard managed a smile, "I believes you, suh. Least I'm outta the rain."

Cooper smiled, "Between us, I'll have the gag tied loosely if you promise to not raise the alarm."

"Wouldn't do no good, suh. Ain't nobody venturing out in this rain until time to relieve me."

"Fair enough." Cooper nodded to the seaman, who applied the gag and gave a wink. They hurried back to the ship, once Cooper was free.

"Ready to get underway, Captain," Virgil Culpepper volunteered.

"Let's be about it, then."

The men went aloft and soon *SeaFire* was gliding out to sea. Banty was suddenly sliding down a backstay, dropping to the deck, and rushing up to Cooper. "Ship approaching, Cap'n. Looks to be a frigate."

"It's the ship they're expecting. You came in the nick of time, Buck. Mr. Culpepper!"

"Aye, Captain."

"Have the larboard guns loaded but not run out. Make sure the powder isn't wet and have some slow match lit and in the tubs ready."

"Aye, Captain." *Ain't this a hell of a mess,* Culpepper thought. *But this time is different. The captain will fight this time.*

Cooper turned and spoke to his master. "Out of the kettle and into the fire, Mr. Ewers."

"Aye, Captain, but she's fit to fight this time."

"Thank you, Mr. Ewers that was well said."

CHAPTER THIRTY NINE

C APTAIN."

"Yes, Mr. Ryker."

"What do we do with our prisoners?"

Seeing his cox'n was standing near, Cooper replied, "Take Quang with you and put them in a boat, and then set them adrift."

Ryker smiled, "Adrift they'll be, Captain." *Small punishment,* Ryker thought, *for the superior attitude the midshipman had shown during his time as warden.* "I'm sure 'Admiral Locklear' will find a way to get them ashore, Captain," Ryker replied to Cooper.

He'd heard the comments made by the marine guards as well, Cooper thought. As Ryker and Quang departed, Cooper's attention went back to the matters at hand. If the frigate's captain was aware of meeting *SeaFire*, he didn't show it.

Whereas, the British ship had lanterns showing, *SeaFire* was completely dark. There were also a few lights showing at Fort George and Georgetown. The lookouts undoubtedly had their attention focused on the shore. However, that would change soon enough. It was only another minute when Virgil Culpepper stepped up to his captain.

"Men are at their stations, Captain, and the guns are loaded but not run out."

"Thank you, Virgil, and not a moment too soon, I might add," Cooper responded. Taking the night glass from his eye, he handed it to his first mate.

There was a rush of activity around the enemy frigate. A moment later, a man appeared in white britches and white shirt, but no coat or hat.

Virgil handed the nightglass back to Cooper, "I think their captain just came on deck."

Although the man wore no coat or hat, he had an air of authority about him. Someone, a midshipman most likely, brought the captain a speaking trumpet. His voice carried across the way.

"What ship is that? Heave to!"

"By whose authority," Cooper called back.

"The Royal Navy," the captain replied in a testy voice, not believing anyone would question his authority.

Cooper thought a second, and then shouted across the way, "What ship is that? How do I know you're not a privateer?"

"By God, sir," came the harried reply. "I'm Captain Royce Merriweather of the frigate *Recourse*. Now heave to or I'll put a broadside into your ship."

"Very well," Cooper replied. "You've identified yourself to my satisfaction." In the night glass, Cooper watched as Merriweather tossed the speaking trumpet to a midshipman. *Smug bastard*, Cooper thought. "Time to wake up the island, Mr. Culpepper. Run out and give them a taste of *SeaFire's* metal."

Culpepper's teeth showed as he grinned, "Aye, aye, Captain."

Cooper put the night glass back to his eye and watched as someone saw *SeaFire's* gunports open. The man set off the alarm and suddenly men rushed to the rails. The captain rushed forward shouldering someone aside. His mouth was agape as one by one of *SeaFire's* larboard battery belched forward, the orange flame lighting up the night. Large sections of *Recourse's* bulwark jumped skyward. Cooper watched as one large section was torn away. It was only then that he realized the rain had stopped.

Buck approached Cooper, as the last gun fired and *SeaFire* had sailed past into the night, "Think she'll give chase?"

"No, I think they will rest and lick their wounds."

"Aye, my thoughts as well," Buck replied.

"Set a course to *Thunderbolt*, Mr. Ewers," Cooper ordered. "I think we'll go to New Orleans, Buck, and then maybe home. I'm a bit concerned that my cousin may try to take his revenge on my family."

Buck rested his hand on Cooper's shoulder. "No reason not to collect our prizes and head home. It won't be long before the convoys will end until the hurricane season is over."

Cooper nodded, but didn't reply as he headed toward his cabin.

"Captain."

Cooper turned to his third officer, "Yes, Mr. Ryker."

"I fear one of our guards was left aboard, sir. It appears he's been nursing a headache."

Cooper looked at the man. "So Locklear left you?"

"Aye, suh."

"I can't take you back. If you'll give me your word that you'll not try to harm the ship or hurt any of my crew, I'll take it. Once we pass a likely vessel, we'll put you aboard; otherwise, we'll take you with us to New Orleans."

"You has me word, Cap'n."

Cooper nodded. "Mr. Ryker!"

"Yes, Captain."

"Have Dr. Cannington look at our guest. He seems to have a rather large knot on his head."

"Yes sir."

Josiah handed Cooper a glass as he entered his cabin. "Brandy, sir, it's just the thing for what you've been through the last few days."

"Thank you, Josiah that was thoughtful."

A DENSE FOG HUNG over the Crescent City of New Orleans. Cooper had wondered about the name Crescent City and while having dinner with Eli Taylor and Jean LaFitte, he inquired about it. LaFitte replied, "The town was built at a sharp bend in the Mississippi River around 1718. The Crescent came from the sharp bend of the river."

Stepping under a shop awning and pausing a moment, Cooper took his handkerchief and wiped the moisture from his face. His cox'n wiped his shaved head and face with his hand and slung the moisture to the sidewalk.

"We should have taken the hotel's carriage," Cooper volunteered. Quang smiled at his comment but didn't speak.

They were going to the bank where they'd meet Mr. LaFitte and finalize the sale of recent prizes and cargoes. Looking about, the fog was so dense; Cooper couldn't even make out the store fronts across the street. It would be worse along the waterfront and possibly the bayous connecting Grand Terre to New Orleans.

"He'll be on time," Quang muttered, a long sentence for the Chinaman.

Cooper's mind reflected, as they walked, over the last several days after they escaped from Grand Cayman and the rendezvous with *Thunderbolt*. The next morning, they sighted the *Southern Cross*. Captain Hai, this time, was in company with another ship, a schooner. The captain of this ship was Morgan MacDonald. He was a tall man with a full head of graying hair. He also had a gray beard and a ready smile. When MacDonald and Tina Hai came aboard for a quick introduction and refreshments, Cooper did not miss the casual way their hands touched or their closeness in his cabin. He thought to himself, *I wouldn't doubt Julio Villarreal might be performing a marriage ceremony before long.* After some discussion, a loose agreement was made to sail along in a pack, so to speak.

"A wolfpack," MacDonald had said, "preying on the sheep that's preyed on our country for too long."

Hai and MacDonald now had their ships at anchor in Barataria Bay. However, neither of them felt inclined to take a pirogue to New Orleans via Bayou LaFourche, spending the nights on snake and gator infested little islands or chenieres.

Quang interrupted Cooper's thought process when he nudged him and spoke softly, "We are being followed."

Cooper never missed a step but asked, "You're sure?"

"Yes."

The bank was only a block farther but the fog still blocked out the building from sight. When they came to where they needed to cross the street to go into the bank, the Chinaman volunteered, "Quang stay." He ducked around the corner as Cooper continued across the street.

Cooper heard the rush of feet, behind him. He turned in time to see a pistol being leveled at him. The villain pulled the trigger but there was a muffled flash instead of a bang. The man grabbed his chest and made a half turn, stumbled, and caught himself falling with an outstretched hand. He attempted to get up but fell on the brick paved street dead. Cooper ran over as Quang used the toe of his shoe to roll the man over. Stooping over, Quang pulled his blade from the man's chest. A sucking sound was made as the blade pulled free. He wiped the blade on the man's coat and stood up.

Cooper looked at his cox'n, "Thanks."

"Quang waited too long," his cox'n said. "Man had time to shoot." The Chinaman twisted his hands in a motion like ringing a neck. He seemed distressed that the rogue had time for his ill-fated attempt.

"See if he has any identification," Cooper said.

Quang looked through the man's pockets but found nothing but a few gold coins. "He paid killer," Quang said, handing the coins to Cooper.

"You keep them," Cooper said. "Why was he shooting at me? Can't be robbery, I haven't even been to the bank."

"He not know," Quang guessed. "Lucky powder was damp, gun not shoot."

"Aye," Cooper acknowledged. "But why?" Looking about, Cooper could see no one. "Leave him," he told his cox'n.

They crossed the street and entered the bank. LaFitte stood from the chair he was sitting in and met Cooper. "My man saw a flash," he told Cooper.

"We'll talk later," Cooper answered, seeing the banker walking to them.

CHAPTER FORTY

COOPER WAS WEARY AS he sat in Eli and Debbie's suite at Hotel Provincial. He stared at the fire in the fireplace. No doubt, Otis had ordered it to help drive out the dampness. Outside the French doors that led to a private patio, a man stood guard…one of LaFitte's trusted men.

Cooper sipped at a snifter of brandy trying to drive away the weariness. It was not just simple fatigue from exertion. He had dealt with that many times since taking to the sea. No, it was different; it was a soul-deep weariness. It went to his very core. He felt disheartened; yet another attempt had been made on his life. The would-be assassin fired from the corner of a street, this time. Young Reynolds' reaction had been swift and accurate… too accurate. His shot pierced the rogue's heart. He was dead before he hit the ground. A search of the body only turned up one hundred dollars in gold coin, which Cooper promptly gave to Reynolds. There was no telling how long the man had lain in wait. As Cooper and his group had started across Charles Street, the man had called out, "Cooper Cain." When Cooper turned, the assassin fired. The ball whizzed by so close to Cooper's ear, the buzz made him lurched sideways. Before the man could pull a second pistol, he was dead.

Buck Jewell had wanted to leave New Orleans at once but Cooper said no. He'd not be intimidated by these would be assassins. A shadow passed by on the wall and Cooper whirled toward the French doors, but it was only the sentry.

The room was dark except for the flickering flames from the fireplace. Cooper stretched out in his chair and propped his feet on the hearth. A small table sat at his right hand and next to it another chair. It was not as thick and padded as the one Cooper sat in, although it was a match in other ways. It was...dainty. The word came to Cooper's mind. It was a woman's chair. This was where Eli and Debbie had spent many an evening together. This made Cooper think of Maddy. In his heart, he felt that he should be at home sitting next to Maddy and later making love to his beautiful woman.

Buck Jewell came to his mind. He was, no doubt, keeping company with Mary Esther. She was a beautiful lady in her own right. Ava Katelyn, Mary Esther's daughter, was also a pretty little lady. She was very smart, very polite and friendly. Buck was a lucky man. If things continued as they were, Cooper expected a wedding announcement soon. Would Mary Esther move to Savannah or would Buck take up residence in New Orleans?

New Orleans was a city in fear. Fear of an attack by the British. The governor had put out a request for help. He'd sent letters to everyone, including Andy Jackson. A most capable general, everyone said, especially those in lawyer Edward Meeks circle. A most capable man, *hmmm*, so was Admiral Sir Gabriel Anthony, Maddy's father. A pang of guilt went through Cooper, just as the heat from the fireplace penetrated his boots. Snatching his leg back, he saw smoke coming from the sole of his boot. *Damnation*, he thought, *I don't need to worry about an assassin, I'm about to do my own self in*. Taking off the boot, his foot cooled quickly.

Above the fireplace, on the mantle, lay several pipes. Reaching up, he took one down. Opening a jar sitting on the small table, Cooper packed the bowl of the pipe with a nice smelling tobacco. It was a bit dry, but that would not distract from the flavor and it would burn better. Taking a splinter from the wood box, he set it on fire from the flames in the fireplace. Puffing, he soon had the tobacco glowing. He tossed the splinter into the fire and grabbed another piece of wood and added it, as the other logs had burned down. A cigar to dip into the brandy would have been nice but the pipe was not unpleasant. He sat back and watched the new log catch fire, as his thoughts returned to Maddy's family, Sir Gabe in particular. Without Sir Gabe's significant influence, he'd no doubt be in a Jamaican gaol or prisoner aboard some ship. He may even be dead, with his cousin's reward offer. Thinking on it, Cooper realized his cousin's reward offer was undoubtedly the basis for these continued attempts on his life. A sudden chill and Cooper's body gave a shudder. Was Maddy safe? The fear seemed to engulf him and Cooper started to rise. He'd call his crew together and immediately return to *Thunderbolt*.

He swallowed the remainder of the brandy in a gulp. Calmness spread over him like the burning liquid that ran down his throat and into the pit of his stomach. Dagan was there. He would not allow any harm to come to Maddy. Dagan would know. He'd protect her as he had her father before her. A voice seemed to speak to him, "Finish your business and then go home." Yes, he'd finish his business and then go home.

COOPER HAD MET WITH Eli's agents in New Orleans. He'd signed the contracts for disposal of the goods that they'd captured and, with Meeks in hand, had made sure all war supplies were documented and accounted for to be sold to the government. Other articles and the ship they'd captured would be taken to Savannah where they'd be purchased by Eli's partners at the Savannah Import, Export Merchants and Ship Chandlers. The proceeds would then be paid out to those investors in the privateer venture. It would all be done legally and above suspicion by any of the partners.

Buck Jewell had made his appearance after being absent for the last week. He had a big smile on his face. Cooper shook the outstretched hand as Buck gave him a big hug. "She said yes, Coop. She actually said yes."

Playing the devil, Cooper asked, "Who said yes to what?"

"You scoundrel of a sea dog. Mary Esther has consented to be my wife."

Cooper smiled now, "Congratulations, Buck. Have you set a date?"

"Not really. We both want to wait until after the war but I want to list her as my beneficiary should anything happen to me, Coop."

A somber look came over Cooper, "Aye, Buck, it's always best to take care of all the possibilities. We will sup at the Hotel Mayronne when we get to Barataria. My treat, a celebration."

"Or a funeral pyre." Looking to see, who'd spoken, Buck and Cooper turned and shook hands with Pierre LaFitte. Cooper had met Jean's brother some time back. He'd given refuge to Quang, who was now his cox'n and friend. "I've been looking for you, Coop. Jean has put out feelers, as you know, about who has been responsible for these attempts on your life. We now have a name, one M'sieur Antoine Roche. He is a dealer in death, though this has never been proven. He has a den in a gambling house and bordello. A place filled with rogues, male and female. The man is smart, but...I happen to know he's on his way to purchase slaves from Jean. Usually young female slaves, who after a couple of years no longer look young."

"Why does Jean sell them to him?"

"He doesn't, M'sieur. This sale was to lure the cat from his den so that you could face the man without fear from the local authorities."

"When did he leave?" Cooper asked.

"Within the last hour, but don't rush, my friend. His pirogue will be manned by a group of cutthroats and blackhearts just as evil as Roche."

"Damnation," Cooper cursed.

"Patience, my friend, the journey will cool your flames so that you can deal with the man as you should. Anger will only cause you to make mistakes. Think on what you learned from your instructor. Jean Paul de Giraud would caution you to face your foe with a cool head on your shoulders. I must also warn you M'sieur Roche is a villain to be sure, but he has left many men staring up at the heavens when he leaves the Oaks. He is in his own rights a superb swordsman."

Cooper ingested all of this, knowing that Pierre was right. He had to put away his anger, while realizing he should have killed his cousin when he had the chance.

CHAPTER FORTY ONE

DAGAN SAT ON A bench watching a mother hen scratch about and cluck until her biddies came running. Priscilla and Rosa were picking figs from a tree to make preserves. He had come to enjoy figs on a hot buttered biscuit. Some days he'd make breakfast out of two fig covered biscuits and coffee. Out of the corner of his eye, he spied Brand. Brand was a young black teenage male. His parents worked for Eli Taylor but the boy wanted to be on his own, so Luke, Cooper and Maddy's overseer, had hired him. He was supposed to be apprenticed to the blacksmith. As Dagan watched, though, he realized the boy's reason for coming over had little to do with the blacksmith and more to do with Priscilla. They were both at that age.

Watching, Dagan saw Priscilla give a furtive glance toward Brand when she thought Rosa wasn't looking. "Girl, get yo' mind on these figs and off that boy," Rosa snapped.

Dagan smiled, caught in the act she was…oh well, such was young love.

"Uncle…" Maddy was calling.

"Over here on the bench," Dagan answered.

Maddy rounded the corner with a yellow kitten in her hand. "She's the runt and it seems like the others push her away from the tit," she said, with obvious concern in her voice.

"Let's get a box and put her in it with the mama cat so the other kittens can't push it away. If that doesn't help, we'll feed her," Dagan said.

Maddie smiled, "I've named her Buttercup."

Dagan smiled, "That's a good name." As he spoke, he saw Luke over by the blacksmith's shop. He had motioned to Dagan, but not called out. Something was up. "You go find a box," Dagan said to Maddy. "We'll see if we can't turn Buttercup around."

Maddy hurried off and Luke walked over to Dagan. "I was just down at the General Store and one of Eli's hands told me that two men had been asking the whereabouts to the Cain Farm. They said they were old friends. Mr. Driggers, the storekeeper, didn't think they looked like old friends and neither did Colonel Bledsoe. He asked the men their names and volunteered to give it to Captain Cain when he saw him. The men said never mind and walked out. The colonel told the hand to come find me but I drove up just as he mounted his mule."

"They look like seamen?" Dagan asked.

"Not according to Mr. Driggers. He said they looked like river bottom trash."

Dagan nodded. "I think it's best that we don't alarm the women." After a pause where Dagan appeared in deep thought, he added, "Have the blacksmith keep a gun handy. He see's most of what goes on in the yard." Looking at Luke, he continued, "You carry a pistol at times. Start carrying it all the time now and I'll do the same."

Their conversation was interrupted at that time as Suzanne Bledsoe came up in her buckboard. She and Maddy were going to Savannah.

"I think you need to follow along with the girls to Savannah." Dagan gazed across the yard and then added, "Take Brand with you. He will accompany Maddy and Suzanne. I've seen him throwing his knife at targets. He's pretty good with it. Take him aside and tell him he's to protect the women with his life if need be. Big strong boy that he is, he'd run off most just with his size.

I'll go talk with Eli and see about getting a couple of armed men from the warehouse to help keep watch."

Luke did as he was told while Dagan had a horse saddled for him. This was what Cooper had feared. He'd spared his cousin's life…yet by doing so, the man was not content. He was out to hurt Cooper any way he could, even if it meant killing an innocent woman. *That will not happen, not as long as I've breath in my body*, Dagan thought to himself.

Two men, hidden at the edge of the riverbank, watched as Maddy and Suzanne rode out in the buckboard followed by Brand on the mule. As the men made to move, a man on a horse rode by. He was armed with a pistol and a musket.

"Let's move," the one rogue whispered.

The other rogue held back, "I don't know, Sam. I suddenly got a bad feeling about this."

"You didn't have any bad feelings when you got that gold piece, and there's thirty more when the job is done."

"You can't spend thirty more dollars if you're dead," the man whined.

"For God's sake, Marvin, this ain't the furst person we kilt."

"It's the furst woman," Marvin throwed back.

"Shh! Get down."

Another man rode by, but unlike the others, this one stopped. Even though he could see no one, it was evident that he sensed a presence. Speaking softly, yet loud enough that Marvin and Sam could hear, Dagan spoke, "A man's soul is cursed when he attempts to take an innocent life. Judas hung himself realizing what he'd done for thirty pieces of worthless silver. Your soul, like Judas', will be consigned to the far reaches of hell if you continue." Dagan sat on his horse silently, not speaking another word for a long moment, and then he rode on.

"That's it, Sam, I'm through with this," Marvin said.

Sam looked at Marvin. The man was ghost white pale and sweating. Sam pulled his pistol, "We made a deal, Marvin. We took a man's money. You don't think he'll let us back out do ya? You are in it, Marvin, whether you like it or not. I'll do the killing if you want, but you are in it."

Marvin gulped; he'd seen Sam kill a man over a dollar whore. He had no doubt Sam meant what he said. "I'll go," Marvin agreed, "if you do the killing."

Sam smiled. He thought, *after her, you'll get yours, Marvin.* Smiling still, he also thought, *I'll get the entire fifty dollars for myself.*

IT WAS LATE. MADDY had let the mama cat nurse Buttercup in the crate by the fireplace and was putting the cat out to go to the other kittens. She put a piece of an old blanket in the crate to keep the kitten warm since it didn't have the other kittens to snuggle up too. She turned the lantern out when she entered her bedroom and climbed into bed.

Across the farm, all was dark, but not everyone was asleep. Dagan sat looking out his window. Not up close where he could be seen but further back. He was able to see the back entrance to Cooper and Maddy's house and the big window to their room. Earlier, he'd seen a shadow dart across the yard, headed toward the blacksmith shop. As he watched another shadow emerged, it was Brand. He'd been waiting on Priscilla. Dagan smiled, so the two had taken their relationship a step further. Were they lovers yet? Dagan didn't think so, not that Brand wasn't ready, but Priscilla wouldn't be willing…not just yet.

Dagan glanced at the clock. It was almost eleven p.m. On a farm, where most folks were up at dawn, they went to bed early. What was it Rosa had said, "She went to bed with the chickens so that she could be up before the roosters." The moon was bright, not quite a full moon but close. Over by the corral, a horse whinnied. A slow, deep growl was heard from one of the dogs. Dagan continued to watch. Then with a low growl coming from its throat, the dog was up and walking toward the corral. Something was thrown through the air and landed with a splat not far from the dog. The dog stepped nearer and then wagged its tail and started eating. Meat, Dagan decided with sadness. He realized that it was probably laced with poison. The damnable rogues had come prepared. Next to the blacksmith shop nothing stirred. Brand and Priscilla had surely heard the dog. Hopefully, they were not so carried away with their romance that they were oblivious to the sounds, to what was happening. There was silence now. Another splat as more meat was tossed into the yard. The big cur was the only dog on the place. He'd remedy that, Dagan decided.

The cur continued to eat but wobbled on his legs, and then with a whine he fell. The meat was probably well laced with strychnine, to act so quickly. Honey had most likely been added to cover the bitter taste. Regardless, the cur now lay silent, dead.

A few minutes later, a shadow appeared. The shadow became a man. A man…not men, but a man. It was said that there was two men.

Brand stepped out from the blacksmith shop at that time. He had been watching. "Hold it right there," he said. "One twitch and you're a dead man."

Dagan, while cocking his pistol, eased his door open in time to see the second man lift his musket. Brand had no idea he was being set up for the kill. However, the unmistakable sound of the click as the hammer on the musket was cocked made Brand freeze.

Brand calmly spoke then, "He may get me but you're a dead man."

Marvin was suddenly spooked, "You hear that, Sam?"

Sam didn't reply. He just raised his musket to take aim. Unknowingly, he'd just lost the chance to ever speak again. Dagan, with his arm outstretched, squeezed the trigger. A round hole appeared in Sam's temple. He never made a sound. He just crumpled to the ground.

Marvin watched in horror, and then made to run, before he realized something had struck him in the chest. "Oh God," he screamed as he sunk to his knees. He could see lights coming on from the houses in the little clearing, as he looked up.

Dagan rushed over, "Save your soul. Tell us who sent you."

A slight smile came to Marvin's face. "Save my soul?" he asked.

"Yes," Dagan replied. "Tell us who sent you. It will be easier for you."

"Didn't want to kill no woman," he said. He coughed and blood appeared on his lips. "Sam threatened to kill me if I backed out."

"Sam's dead," Dagan responded. "Now, who sent you?"

Marvin gagged and spit out a mouthful of blood. "I'm dying," he said.

"Yes," Dagan replied. "Who sent you?"

"Frenchie…"

"Frenchie who," Dagan asked, trying not to finish the man off.

"Roche," Marvin managed as his eyes glazed over.

"I hope he's at peace now," Luke whispered.

"Aye," Dagan responded. He then turned to Brand, "Didn't you know there were two men?"

"Yes," Brand replied.

"Why didn't you wait to see where the other man was then?"

"I thought I'd draw him out before they got close to Miz Maddy."

"You never thought that you might have been killed," Luke threw out.

"Oh no, suh, I never paid that other man no mind," Brand replied. "Mr. Dagan was there."

CHAPTER FORTY TWO

Hotel Mayronne looked out of place for Barataria. It stood out in the middle of the business district. It was of such standing, it could have competed with any of the prominent hotels in New Orleans. The restaurant had not only the island's only chef, but one that any restaurant would have been glad to have. Bernard, the fierce-looking doorman who kept out riff-raff and broke up any quarrel before it started, was missing tonight. In his place was a man who reminded Cooper of Ox...a large, powerful man. His head was shaved. A tattoo or tattoos took the place of hair and covered his shaved head and neck. He's been to the Orient, Cooper decided.

As Cooper, Buck, and Virgil Culpepper climbed the steps of the hotel, Cooper quickly came to realize that while a different man occupied Bernard's stool, the same old blunderbuss was cradled in his arms. It was a very menacing looking weapon. As the three men entered the hotel, several of *SeaFire's* seamen loitered about. Seeing them, the doorman frowned. He recognized the beginning of trouble when he saw it. But as long as they didn't attempt to bring it inside, it was none of his concern. He watched as two others showed up, and then a third. These were men he knew. Johannes Ewers, Spurlock, and Diamond were all good men with a head on their shoulders. They were here to protect someone, more-than-likely. Was it the young captain with the terrible scar down his face? He pushed his thoughts to the back of his mind as other men climbed the steps. He was only concerned about what happened inside.

A PERT LITTLE WAITRESS came over to Cooper's table. She had just enough cleavage showing to interest her male customers and ensure a good tip but not enough to classify her as anything other than what she was. She was quick, energetic, and had a ready smile. She responded quickly to a couple of Virgil's comments, giving as good as she got. Cooper ordered a beer, not wanting anything to dull his senses. A tray of shucked oysters had just been cleared away when a plate of fish and shrimp arrived. The men had started on their main course, as Jean LaFitte and Antoine Roche entered.

Cooper nibbled at his food but didn't eat enough to make him sluggish. He'd just finished his beer, paused, gave his friends a look and then stood up. Did Roche know him on sight or just by name? LaFitte and Roche looked up as Cooper approached their table. A smile creased LaFitte's face but a frown covered Roche's. He knows. LaFitte stood up as he would to greet any guest.

Cooper shook the offered hand. "My humble apologies, M'sieur LaFitte. I mean no disrespect to you at all, sir, but the man seated at your table is the lowest form of humanity I know. He is a dealer in death. He hires would-be assassins rather than face a man in an honorable way. How do I know this? One of his men talked before he took his last breath. A dying man seldom lies, as you know, especially when he's trying to prepare his soul to meet his maker."

Roche had risen by this time. Cooper took a half step forward and dared Roche, "Tell me it's not true." Yet, before the man could speak, Cooper gave the man a violent slap with his glove. "I'll be outside," Cooper growled. "We'll finish this tonight. You choose the weapons. I'm sure M'sieur LaFitte can accommodate us."

Roche was fuming. "I'll run you through," he snapped.

"So it's to be blades," Cooper snarled. As he started to withdraw, he paused, "You have my most sincere apologies again, M'sieur LaFitte. Please allow me the honor of paying for your meal." LaFitte stood erect and gave a short bow, with the hint of a smile on his face.

Roche's hand darted inside his coat as Cooper turned away. The simultaneous click of hammers being cocked arrested his movement and he drew out a silk handkerchief. He looked at LaFitte and said, "Would you act as my second and arrange a time and place?"

LaFitte replied, "I think that's already been decided, M'sieur Roche. The man awaits you outside."

Torches had been lit and a circle cleared. Roche's men, being outnumbered two to one, stood very innocently at the edge of the circle. A group of *SeaFire's* men had surrounded them and Spurlock demanded their weapons, which were handed over to Banty and McKemie. Tankards of ale were pushed into their hands.

"We wouldn't want you to be overcome with thirst, you turd suckers," Skeeter snarled.

"I may need to relieve myself," one of the men, bolder than the rest, said.

"You turns your back then and pisses where you stand, you poxed son of a goat molester." Where Skeeter came up with his remarks, no one could guess, but everyone laughed except the man Skeeter had spoken to. "You sees that even your friends know what you be."

Footsteps were heard coming from the restaurant. "You have him riled," Virgil volunteered to his captain.

"That was my intent."

LaFitte and Roche soon came down the steps. A glass of brandy was in Roche's hand. Diamond stepped forward holding several of Cooper's collection of blades.

"If one of those is not to your satisfaction, we'll allow M'sieur LaFitte to obtain more choices," Cooper said.

Roche may have been a lot of things, but he certainly knew his steel. He chose one of a matched pair and stepped back. Cooper nonchalantly took the other one and faced his foe. He would kill the man. He couldn't risk reprisal. He'd made that mistake with his cousin. None of the niceties of a fencing match would be observed.

Roche knew little of the man he faced. He'd been contacted and agreed to have the man killed. Had he taken the time to look into the boyish captain's background, he'd have found out he was not facing just another foe. No, the man he faced now had been trained by a master swordsman. A fact that he was about to discover. Most of Roche's duels had ended quickly. He was the aggressor. He charged his opponents and overwhelmed them, while enjoying the fear on their faces just before he ran them through. He gulped down his liquor and tossed the glass aside, and then charged Cooper.

The clink of steel on steel sounded and the glint of torchlight on the blades flashed. Rather than back up in fear, Cain merely parried and did a smooth sidestep. The look of confidence was still on Cooper's face. *I'll wipe away that look*, Roche thought as he engaged Cain again. It was Roche who became over confident, as Cooper took a step back. He increased his intensity and attacked once more. The rasping sound of blade sliding off blade filled the circle. Others came closer and watched the duel...attack, coun-terattack, and then a riposte. Roche was sweating and breath-ing hard. He'd felt a burning sensation and was shocked to see that the wetness he felt in his hand was his own blood. Taking a chance, he paused and looked at Cain. The man had not even broken a sweat and was breathing calmly. Roche, for the first time felt fear. He knew he would die this night. Cain had only been toying with him.

Cain stood quietly, allowing Roche to rest. Roche gave a half nod to begin again when Cooper spoke, "How does it feel to know the death you ordered will result in your own?"

Roche screamed out an incoherent curse and charged. He thought he had Cain as he charged but then he stopped. He felt sick. Something wasn't right. The lightning fast blade of Cain had come under his guard. Cain had been ready for the move. He'd beat aside Roche's blade and let the man impale himself..

Roche looked down at the hilt buried deep in his sternum, and felt the length of the blade sticking out of his back. A hushed silence took over the crowd as they watched in awe. One of Roche's men was the first to speak.

"He wasn't so great, not against a real swordsman."

Cooper looked at Roche's men. "Who knows where Roche kept his correspondence…his papers?"

"That would be Lacy. She helped with all of that."

"Mr. Spurlock!"

"Aye, Captain."

"Take several men with you…enough so nobody will attempt to stop our search. Take…your name man?"

"Haskil."

"Take Haskil with you. I want every paper gone through. I want to know where Phillip is hiding. When you return, we'll hunt down Phillip and bring this to an end."

"Aye," Spurlock answered.

Turning to Buck, Cooper smiled, "You go with them and let Mary Esther know we will be sailing soon. Have your first mate get the ship ready to sail."

"Aye," Buck replied.

"Would you care for a brandy?" Jean LaFitte asked.

"I think it would be in order," Cooper responded, and thanked LaFitte.

CHAPTER FORTY THREE

SEAFIRE CAME TO AS her best bower went plunging down in the anchorage below the hill at Savannah. Cooper was excited to be away...to see Maddy, and to make sure that she was unharmed. His senses told him that she was fine. Dagan was there. He'd never allow harm to come to his niece if he could prevent it.

Spurlock had gone to New Orleans with one of Roche's men. When they entered the club, Spurlock noted the sign proclaimed the place as 'Pleasures.' "I'm not sure a busted noggin or getting poxed would be considered a pleasure," he quipped to his men. A few chuckled, but most knew they were here on business, and that might include busting a few noggins themselves.

Lacy saw them, a rough group of hard men, as they entered the club, Her face paled and her hand went to her mouth. She darted toward a door but Banty was quicker and got there before her, blocking her entrance.

Spurlock spoke, "All you people here, keep your arses firmly seated and there will be no harm to anyone. Move...and it's likely to be taken as a threat." He punctuated the word threat. What he left unsaid made its point.

The men returned to their drinks and cards. The wenches stood aimlessly behind the men at the tables. Spurlock and Banty went into the office with Lacy. The office was searched but produced little. Roche's man had said he slept upstairs. A back door in the office led to a outside set of stairs. In the small apartment was another desk and safe. The lock on the desk was broken. Bits and pieces of different schemes and enterprises were found, and also a lot of damaging information. Somewhere, prominent men were being blackmailed due to gambling debts or other indiscretions. Spurlock put them in a pile for the captain. He'd know what to do with the information. They still were not finding anything that would be helpful.

Spurlock turned to the safe. "Open it," he said to Lacy.

"I don't know the combination," she replied.

During the search of the room, it was evident that a woman spent a lot of time sharing the suite. Spurlock looked at the woman, who stared back defiantly. Realizing that she only understood one type of persuasion, Spurlock turned to Banty.

"You have your skinning knife? The one you used to scalp the wench that stole your purse."

"Aye," Banty replied and whipped out a blade from its scabbard. The blade was long with a sharp needle point. As he stuck his finger to the tip, a drop of blood appeared. Banty gave an evil grin. "The size of her mellows is just right to make a new purse. My last tit purse wasn't tanned long enough and needs to be replaced."

Spurlock smiled at Banty's words. He had played the game well. The girl, seeing him smile, mistook his thoughts and folded her arms across her chest. Fear was apparent. Spurlock crossed to the door, "I'll go have a wet. When I return I want the safe open...and Banty, keep the mess confined to one room, not all over the place like last time.

Lacy screamed as Spurlock opened the door, "No. I don't know the combination but I know where it is." She crossed to the little desk and pulled a small drawer all the way out and then she turned it over. On the bottom was the safe combination. Lacy took the drawer over to the safe, flipping it over to see the combination. She deftly twirled the knob and a few seconds later the safe was open. A quick survey of its contents ensued.

"I have it," Spurlock exclaimed. "The sodomite is in Bermuda."

The safe contained numerous documents of ownership to various buildings and a few thousand dollars in coin and paper money.

Spurlock took the money and handed it to Lacy, "Turn your joint into an honest establishment. When I come back, I'll take a look. If it's not…Banty still has his knife."

The girl was flushed and she didn't speak but nodded.

THEY WERE NOW IN Savannah. Cooper was met at the top of the hill by John Will. "How's Maddy?" Cooper asked, foregoing the usual pleasantries.

"Well," John Will said. A sigh of relief escaped Cooper. John Will continued, "We've sent a rider to catch Eli. He was here earlier. Come to the office for a bit of refreshments."

Cooper had just finished his first drink when the sound of a horse and carriage was heard. Eli came in with a big grin on his face. "I've sent for Maddy," he said as he greeted his protégé.

"Thank you, but let's talk before she arrives. I've much to say. Our venture was successful but I'll speak on that later." Cooper then laid out the attempts on his life, his duel with Roche and the discovery of his cousin's whereabouts.

"Bermuda!" Eli did some quick calculations in his head. "I've made the voyage in four days, with the right winds, but it usually takes five or more days. It's too far to have a spy return with any information that might be helpful."

"Aye," Cooper replied. "It would be wise to have a man in place to keep us informed, however."

Eli did not reply and seemed deep in thought. He was silent so long that when he puffed on his cigar it had gone out. Cooper, now used to Eli's ways, did not interrupt his train of thought but allowed himself a refill on his glass.

Eli spoke finally, "If Phillip is on Bermuda, he is likely waiting for passage to England. The other possibility would be to Antigua. But with his last reception being less than warm, I suggest he's headed to England. We could put a man at Bermuda, and have you waiting along the return route to England. We have a sloop, a Bermuda sloop, built from Bermuda cedar. She was used as an island trader before the war. She will not be suspicious with so many of her type entering and leaving port. That's it. We'll put a man on the island with the sloop at his disposal. You will lay off the island a day's sail. If Phillip sails, you will be informed fast enough to take him. If he's staying on the island, you will know that as well. I will see things are set up with *Stinger…Stinger* is the name of the sloop."

Cooper could think of no other plan or alternative, so he nodded as he made for the door. "Another time, Eli."

The sound of a carriage arriving outside had caused Cooper to look out the window. Maddy jumped down unladylike, and asked, "Where's Coop?"

"In the office," a hand told her.

Cooper was at the door to meet her. *Another time*, Eli thought as he smiled, *another time, indeed.*

COOPER AND MADDY TOOK turns washing each other's back. "Mmm," Maddy moaned as Cooper massaged her back, neck, and then as his hands slid to her breast as he kissed on the back of her neck and nibbled at her lower ear. She leaned back, splashing water out of the tub onto the floor. Cooper leaned forward and kissed her forehead, the tip of her nose, and then found her lips as he continued to fondle her breasts. As his lips pulled from Maddy's, she rose up to him and they kissed again. This time the kiss was longer. Their bodies were so close that Cooper could feel the thump, thump, thump of Maddy's heart. She stepped out of the tub as Cooper grabbed a towel and started drying her off. A kiss here and a kiss there followed the drying.

"Me thinks you're ready to do battle again," Maddy whispered, using her best seaman like language.

"What makes you think that, dear lady?" Cooper asked between kisses.

"Your cannon be locked and loaded," she answered.

"Hmm," Cooper replied, picking up his wife and enjoying the closeness of her nude body entwined in his. "Let's come about and be on with it," he said as he toted Maddy to the bed.

"Aye," Maddy whispered.

CHAPTER FORTY FOUR

THE FOLLOWING WEEK WAS busy and went by fast. Maddy, realizing that her and Cooper's lives were in danger, was more passionate than before. She knew her husband was frequently in harm's way. That was the nature of the sea and more so being at war. It was something she understood, as long as she could remember it had been that way. First it was with her father and uncle, and then her brother and now with her husband. But this was more sinister. No one in her family, and certainly not herself, had ever been singled out for murder.

Dagan was right. Cooper had to flush out his cousin and put an end to it. If they were to have a life together…a family together, it had to end. Dagan had said there'd be no more attempts of her life. Was it part of his 'knowing' or wishful thinking? Luke had agreed with Dagan. Once word had gotten out, that one of the community's ladies had been in danger of an assassin, they rose up in protest. A stranger would be watched closely. If a person was passing through, they'd be hurried on their way. To have an attempt on one of their own lives would not be tolerated, even if a few innocents did get bruised up a mite.

Dagan was at ease with his beliefs that the danger to Maddy was past; so much so, that he was going to Bermuda on *Stinger*. He would be a known person to many of the naval personnel making the task of getting the sloop in and out much easier. The captain of *Stinger* would be Robert 'Dutch' Gooden. He was an old sea dog who'd smuggled contraband to the Americans for years without getting caught.

SeaFire met the new day under easy sail as a gentle breeze and a blue sky with puffy white clouds greeted them. Off to larboard, the Bermuda sloop, *Stinger*, was pulling away on a different course bound for Bermuda. *SeaFire* would pass to windward, along the route that convoys sailed between Jamaica and Falmouth, a route of some 3,700 miles or so.

Mr. Ryker was taking in *Stinger*, when the master walked up and volunteered, "She's a fine ship, young sir."

"Aye, Mr. Ewers. I don't think I've seen her like."

"I'm sure you haven't, but you will," Ewers replied. "More and more people are discovering her qualities. She is especially longed for by privateers. She's a better than average sailor and she's fast. Her high raked mast and those triangular sails give her the ability to sail upwind. That advantage means if she's after a prize and help comes, she can cast loose the prize and make a quick getaway."

Ryker turned to the master, after putting down his glass, and said, "I'm going to have one of those ships one day, Mr. Ewers. Mark my words, I'll have one."

Johannes bit back a smile, "I believe you, young sir, I surely do."

A quick shower had come up, so Cooper went down to his cabin. Josiah came in with a glass of cider. "That's the last of the cider, Captain. It will be lemon juice or wine in the afternoon now, sir."

"Either," Cooper replied absently.

It had been a week since *Stinger* left to sail on to Bermuda. During that time, Cooper found himself to be impatient, almost to the point of rudeness — something that he detested in a man. As Josiah made to slip away, Cooper called him back.

"Get yourself something to drink," Cooper said. After pouring himself a glass of sherry, Josiah sat at the captain's table. "I apologize for snapping," Cooper started.

"That's alright, Captain. We all know these attempts on you and Maddy's life has to play on a person's mind." Cooper smiled, so the crew was overlooking his ill behavior. "Were the members of our privateer venture satisfied with their documents, Captain?"

Cooper sat up, "They were, as a matter of fact, Josiah. Captain Taylor noted the duplicates had been done in a 'fair hand'."

Smiling, Josiah took a sip of his sherry. "It was our stowaway, Captain. I put him to work."

"Our stowaway, you mean the marine?"

"Aye, Captain."

Cooper had completely forgotten about the man. "He knows how to write, does he?"

"More than that, Captain. Our marine, his name is William House by the way, once worked for a printer and engraver. He became very good at his trade…too good. His talents for engraving various black market items and his skill for making keys from a clay impression were in high demand until he was caught. He got out of a window as the magistrate's men came in the front and back doors of the shop where he worked. He ducked in a tavern to hide out. His friend told him he needed to join the army but the lass at the tavern said they always check the army barracks. He needed to volunteer for the Navy or the Marines. He chose the marines, and let on that he was running from a pretty lass with an angry older husband. He was trained in Portsmouth and went to his first ship. He's been a marine for two years now."

"Does he desire to be sent back to the British?"

Josiah looked at the tint of his sherry as the sun shining through the skylight reflected on his glass. "I do believe, Captain, that he is very content to be away from Admiral Locklear." Josiah said this without emotion, but as he and Cooper looked at each other, they both burst out in laughter.

Skeeter nudged Banty on deck, "Hear that, mate. Cap'n seems to be coming out of his 'dull drums'."

Banty snarled, "Probably told you'd been left in Savannah."

Skeeter looked puzzled for a minute and then replied, "Up yours, matey." When Banty turned with a smile, Skeeter smiled also. "You're a piece, Banty, you know that."

CHAPTER FORTY FIVE

AGAN WALKED ALONG THE waterfront with *Stinger's* Captain Gooden. As with most ports with a naval presence, Dagan noticed and spoke to half a dozen old mates and comrades. No one seemed surprised to see the old sea dog nor questioned his presence. Bermuda had grown in importance since Dagan's last visit to the island. It was now the primary Royal Navy headquarters and dockyard in the western Atlantic.

The navy, since the first war with the Colonies, had spent a great deal of time charting Bermuda's reef. A deepwater channel was found. The discovery of this channel, which gave access to Hamilton Harbor, caused the navy to abandon its properties around Saint George and move to the west end.

Dagan had learned the harbor had been named, like the city of Hamilton, after Sir Henry Hamilton, who was the Governor of Bermuda when the harbor was founded in 1793. The two men, stopping in a tavern for a wet and information, sat next to a window, which allowed for a bit of breeze to pass through. Before long, Dagan noticed an old gunner's mate walk behind the bar. Standing, Dagan whispered for Gooden to remain seated.

"Is there any real spirits to be had or is it just the horse piss ye serve here?"

Anger swept over the old gunner's mate. He whirled around, slamming his hand down on the bar with a loud bang. Whatever words he planned to speak died as he recognized the smiling face of an old shipmate. "Dagan...as I live and breathe. I figured you'd long since joined the lost souls in Old King Neptune's kingdom."

"He's tried a time or two to lure me to the deep but I've still got me sea legs and cutlass." After a few minutes, Dagan leaned close, "Sark, I'm after a man who's tried to harm my niece, Sir Gabe's daughter as it were."

Sark was now all ears. "Do you needs help to send him to Hades, mate?"

"Not yet," Dagan replied. "We want to hurt 'is purse before I runs him through."

"What be 'is name?" Sark asked.

"Phillip Finylson. He's as foul as they come. I've looked about but realize he'd not be where I'd expect." Dagan leaned in close again. "He prefers the 'windward passage'. I need to know where it is the sodomites gather."

Sark had a disdainful look on his face. "Only one place his kind gathers. The Molly house. I'd help you burn it down were you to say the word," he spat.

"Not yet," Dagan responded.

"The place doesn't even have a sign on the door. I'll give you a map to guide you. Dagan, just remember this. They keep look-outs posted so they can clear out if an effort is made to do away with the devil's den."

Dagan thanked his old mate and motioned to Captain Gooden as he stepped out the door. "I noticed you haven't forgotten the seaman slang," Gooden stated.

"I find it advisable to always communicate according to the person's level," Dagan replied. Glancing down at the crudely but accurate map Gunner Sark had drawn for him, he memorized it and gave it to Gooden to review.

The place in question did not have a sign, as Sark had said, but somebody with a good hand had painted a beach scene with flamingoes on the sand on the outer wall.

"Looks new," Dagan volunteered.

"Aye, the pink flamingo," Gooden japed.

They'd just gone down a street where they had to step over a filthy looking beggar. The street was worse looking than the beggar. Windows were dirty or boarded up. Foul smelling gutters were clogged with trash. A single dog, missing most of its fur and so gaunt its ribs stuck out, limped along sniffing in the trash.

Dagan looked back, as the dog passed. He nudged Gooden, "Time to go."

The beggar had disappeared. He was likely a watch, one of the lookouts, Sark had mentioned. At the end of the block, two men stepped out and seemed to be waiting. As they passed the next house, an unmistakable odor permeated the air.

Dagan grasped his friend by the upper arm, "In here."

"What's that smell?" Gooden asked.

"Opium," Dagan answered. "Once you smell it, you'll never forget it."

"It's something like a sweet perfumery smell...or a burnt flower," Gooden said.

Before Dagan could speak, an elderly Chinese man stepped from behind a curtain. "You smoke...you lay with young girl?"

Gooden volunteered, "We want to buy...to take with us."

"You no smoke here?"

"No...on ship."

"Ahh, we sell. You want lay with young girl?"

Dagan, glancing out the door, could see the two ruffians were now outside. He pushed inside and behind the curtain. "We buy. We see young girl," he said.

"Ahh…" the Chinese man made a motion to follow him.

The smoke was much thicker, almost a fog. Men lay about, some with naked Chinese girls, some alone. Passing by a smaller curtained off cubical, Dagan saw a half-dressed white woman, propped on a pillow and smoking a pipe. Light shone through cracks around a door as they continued to walk towards the rear of the building. Dagan turned to his friend, who gave the briefest of nods. He'd seen it as well.

The old man stopped and pointed toward two pallets, "You wait here. I go get yâpi´an."

When the old Chinaman walked away, Gooden said, "Let's go."

The two men hurried away, making their way out the door and into the bright Bermuda sunlight. Blinking to restore their vision, they realized they were a block over from the street they come down.

"I had to get out of there. I was getting sick," Gooden admitted.

"I was feeling it, as well," Dagan said, and then added, "We're not going to find out anything this way. Our best bet is to get back to the waterfront."

"Do you think those rogues will venture inside the opium den?" Gooden asked.

"I doubt it. When we don't come out soon, they'll figure we went in to smoke. Did you notice the woman in the cubicle?"

"Yes, she certainly wasn't some tavern wench."

"She's somebody's wife or daughter, who's gotten addicted to opium…or as that old Chinaman called it yâpi´an. She could be the daughter of some Honest John merchant. They often take their families with them to the Orient."

"Wouldn't doubt it," Gooden answered.

BACK AT THE WATERFRONT, the two entered the "Brass Monkey". A cute serving girl was there replacing Sark. She mentioned the owner wouldn't be back until the following day.

"Do you have rooms?" Gooden asked.

"One…or two," the girl said, leaning over the table to get the candle holder. In doing so, she managed to give Gooden a nice view of her more than ample wares. The move also added innuendo to the question, one room or two.

"Two, if you have them," Dagan volunteered. Pleased, the girl turned but let her hand glide over Gooden's shoulder. "Dutch, I believe you have an evening of entertainment ahead of you."

Gooden smiled but didn't speak. Instead, he motioned with his head. Dagan, following Gooden's motion, saw a man with tight aqua colored knee-length breeches worn over white silk stockings. He also had a matching aqua colored tailcoat cut high over the top of his breeches. His collars were turned up and a ruffled cravat was worn at his neck. His shoes had high-elevated heels and aqua colored bows adorned the front. He had a brilliant white wig and carried a cane that had an ivory handle. *A sword cane*, Dagan thought. The tavern girl returned with two tankards of ale. Seeing the men looking out the window, she peered out herself and then chuckled.

"Lord Phillip," she said with a chuckle.

"Lord Phillip," Dagan repeated.

"Aye," she laughed. She leaned forward and whispered, "He practices buggery." Both men turned toward her. "He keeps young boys, usually slaves, and makes them do despicable acts." As if reading Gooden's mind, she added, "If they fail to satisfy or he…ruins them, he gets rid of them. He sells some of them. He's cut the throats of a few of them," she added without being asked.

"Who is that man with him?" Dagan asked.

"Captain Temple. Some say this is his last cruise. He was a captain for Phillip's father, who was a firm but fair man. I hear he can't abide Phillip, but he has to make this last trip."

"Where are they headed?" Gooden asked. "Could be they need a mate."

The girl stood back, eyeing Gooden. "I didn't take you for a mate," she said.

"He's not. He's a captain," Dagan stated. "We have a hand that's ready to be a third mate."

"If he's young, I wouldn't put him aboard that ship," she said. "Captain Temple will drop in at times. You might ask him if you are here." As she made to leave, Gooden dropped a coin down her low cut front. She quickly reached in for the coin. "A guinea," she squealed. She gave him a long wet kiss. She pulled away and whispered, "Your room has an outside entrance to it. Leave the door unlocked."

Dagan smiled, "Yes, it appears you have plans for the evening. I only have one question, Dutch. What does she see in you that I don't have more of?"

Dutch Gooden saluted with his tankard. "Years, Dagan, years. For her…too many."

CHAPTER FORTY SIX

Watching the chain of islands fall astern— Hinson's, Marshall's, Long, and finally Hawkins, *Stinger* sailed a course toward Antigua. Dagan knew Gooden would hold this course until Bermuda was well over the horizon. They'd then come about and make for their rendezvous with *SeaFire*.

Dagan had bumped into Captain Temple the next evening after learning who he was. "My pardon, Cap'n," Dagan apologized. "My timbers not so steady as she used to be, so it's a lubber's life for me now."

Recognizing an old salt, Temple took no offense and after Dagan bought the captain a round, the two set down and shared sea stories and the evening meal. Dagan told him who his nephew was and stated that he was looking for a ship where he could take passage to English Harbor.

"I wish I could be of service," Temple said, "You could share my table if we were headed that way. We're bound to Nova Scotia, to pick up a cargo of timber to take to England."

"Aye," Dagan said. "Not much timber left in England for building and nothing useful for ship building."

They talked of Portsmouth, Kent, and Devonshire, where the captain was from. After an hour of small talk, Temple related the fact that this was his last voyage. He then spoke about Phillip. "A man's sexual habits are his own," he said, matter-of-factly. "I had a first mate once that I was sure leaned that way. But it's more. The man is cruel…evil and cruel. He is not the man his father was."

"Then why make the voyage?" Dagan asked.

"I ask myself the same question," Temple replied. "In part, because I hate turning my ship over to some Molly house cat-amite, who doesn't know the difference in a hawsehole and a arsehole."

Dagan had to chuckle at this.

"SAIL HO!" DARBY CALLED down. "Off the larboard bow."

First Mate Virgil Culpepper stood calmly. He'd been on *SeaFire* long enough to know the crew was well seasoned. When Darby had more, he'd call down. In a few minutes, Culpepper was rewarded for his patience.

"She be a sloop…looks like *Stinger*."

While the first mate showed the patience of Job in the bible, the same could not be said for Cooper Cain. He'd been on deck and then back to his cabin. He drank a glass of claret, almost gulping it down, much to Josiah's dismay.

"Sir, claret is a beverage to be savored, not some…some grog like drink to slosh the gullet with." To waste the finest Bordeaux was appalling to Josiah.

Cooper ignored the comment but held out the glass to be re-charged. He did drink this glass more slowly knowing he was under the watchful eye of Josiah. "Pour yourself a glass," he said to Josiah. He could hear the men, from the deck, talking excitedly.

Stinger was alongside now. Downing the remainder of the deep purplish-red colored liquid, Cooper made his way back on deck. Dagan had just made his way through the entry port.

Shaking Cooper's hand, he said, "To Maine…Machias, Maine."

"Mr. Ewers!"

"Aye, Captain. We'll see to it."

SEAFIRE PLOWED THROUGH ONE wave after another. The men held firm as they went about their duties on deck. It was as if the ship had to climb over a rolling mountain and then sink beneath the wave's crest. The slap of a halyard overhead drew Virgil Culpepper's attention. The wind had picked up so that a whistling sound was heard in the shrouds and riggings. The sky looked leaden as dull, dark gray clouds passed overhead. Virgil noticed the master, Johannes Ewers, had just added another helmsman to the wheel. A spar groaned overhead.

"I fear we have a troubled sea," Virgil commented to the master.

"Aye," Johannes agreed. "I believe we've caught the edge of a squall. She'll handle it, though. No need to pipe up the sail handler yet."

Virgil smiled at this. Not if you were to ask the captain. He was on a mission. He wanted every knot that *SeaFire* had to give. Dagan had reported Phillip was headed to Maine. To Machias… or a bay before you get to Machias, that was called Little Machias Bay. He was to pick up a load of timber there to take back to England. Dagan had discovered that smuggling was a thriving business in Northern Maine. More so since the war had started.

It seemed there was a large group of people loyal to the Crown near Passamaquoddy Bay. They lived on the New Brunswick side, yet they did a lively business with the Americans on the Maine side, even though trade was forbidden by both countries. While the trade was forbidden, little was done to stop the smuggling. "You have to be very unlucky to get caught," Captain Temple had said.

There had been much discussion in regards to entering waters where British warships were constantly on patrol. It was too risky to sail into the area in *SeaFire*, and while *Stinger* was commonplace in the islands, they'd never get past close scrutiny in Nova Scotia or the Bay of Fundy. Therefore, they'd sail to Freeport and get a fishing boat...maybe even George Jewett's *Lazy Susan*. They'd then sail north from Freeport to Machia's Bay. If a fishing boat was spotted by one of the English privateers that used the Port of Eden, or a British warship, it would likely go unchallenged.

These plans were full of holes. They'd make a dash for shore and go the rest of the way overland if they were challenged by a warship or privateer. Also, there was the slim chance that they'd overhaul Phillip's ship. If so...well, that would make things a lot simpler.

CHAPTER FORTY SEVEN

A BRIGHT MOON REFLECTED OFF a silver sea. Forward on the fo'c's'le, Leon had his fiddle playing a sassy tune. At the wheel, Ox was listening intently as Goose was telling a tale of his rendezvous with some tavern trollop while at Barataria.

Ox's eyes grew wide when Goose got to the business part of his story. "I thought me nutmegs would bust when she let 'er cat-heads fall from 'er blouse." Ox watched intently as Goose closed his eyes and tilted his head back as if reliving the moment. Giving a shiver, Goose opened his eyes again. "That was one fine piece of mutton."

Johannes, who'd been at the binnacle, slammed the little door shut at this time. "Ox, I'd appreciate it if you were to limit the object of your desires to just the wheel and steer small. And you…you whoremonger, get forward or you'll have a watch you aren't scheduled for."

Cooper smiled as Goose hurried off toward the music. Ewers had seen the captain and while it didn't hurt for the men to break the monotony while on watch by talking, Goose's tale was so juicy that Ox had let his mind drift away from his duties. He, Johannes Ewers, would not have that on his watch.

"Casco Bay by dawn, I'm thinking, Captain," Johannes volunteered, as Cooper walked over to him.

Cooper acknowledged the master but thought, *damnation*. *SeaFire* had sailed as hard and fast as she could be pushed and yet no sign of Phillip's ship. Giving a sigh, he made his way to his cabin. Seeing Dagan with a deck of cards, he asked, "Shall we call the good doctor and Virgil, and see if they would enjoy a rubber of whist."

Dagan smiled. He knew that Cooper needed something to occupy his mind. Whist would be a good distraction. Josiah rounded up the other two and the cards were cut to see who would be partners. The two highest cardholders would partner as would the two lowest. Josiah brought in some brandy, and without asking Dagan went to Cooper's desk and returned with four of Gus' cognac infused crooks. A candle was passed around to light the cigars.

Cooper growled, after seeing Josiah lick his lips, "Get yourself a cigar and a glass of brandy. You can keep score. But if I don't have a sack of apple tarts by eight bells of the forenoon watch, you'll be cast away."

"Don't worry, Josiah," Dagan said. "He'll not carry out that threat. You've spoiled him."

"All of us that get a chance to share the captain's table agree," Doctor Cannington said.

"Aye," Virgil added.

"Deal dammit," Cooper snarled. "Just deal."

THE FIRST SET OF sails spotted heading into Casco Bay was a fishing vessel, not much longer than a Royal Navy cutter. The second came into view as the sun was burning off the dawn mist.

Banty, at his usual station when entering port, called down from the mainmast platform, "Fishing yawl approaching. Looks like the *Lazy Susan*."

"Heave to, Mr. Culpepper. Let's let Captain Jewell come alongside." Cooper then turned to his cox'n. "Quang, have Josiah fix up some hot cocoa. I recalled that was the good Captain Jewett's morning pleasure."

Quang ran down the companion ladder as Cooper went to the entry port, sure that George Jewett would recognize *SeaFire* and him. He didn't have long to wait. Jewett called out a greeting to Cooper and came aboard when invited. Cooper introduced Jewett to Dagan and the three men went below to Cooper's cabin.

George Jewett enjoyed a cup of hot cocoa and a pastry as Cooper brought him up to date on the situation with Phillip. Jewett listened without interruption. When Cooper had finished, Jewett pushed back from the table and took out his pipe. He packed it full and then taking an offered splinter of wood from Josiah, he lit the splinter from a candle, using it to light his pipe. He puffed a few times, creating a cloud of smoke. Once the pipe was well lit, he blew out the splinter and placed the remnants in the small plate his pastry had been on.

Jewett then took a breath and spoke, "You would never reach Machias in *SeaFire*. You maybe could in the *Lazy Susan*, but space would be limited for the number of men you are liable to need. No, you need a larger ship but one less likely to be stopped. What you need, Coop, is the *Summer Wind*. She is a ten gun sloop used as a smuggler and she's known well by the Quoddy rogues. Zach Carter owns her and he lives not far from me. I take it you're putting my services under hire."

"Aye," Cooper responded, knowing that Jewett would need the income if his fishing were interrupted.

"Good," Jewett said. "Let me come about and we'll head back to Freeport. There are other ships in port so your men need to be on their best behavior. One is the *Maryland*, she's a twenty gun Navy sloop. You know how rowdy sailors can be and we don't need any of our taverns wrecked." Dagan couldn't help but smile at this.

"I can promise my men won't start anything," Cooper replied. "I can't say they won't finish something if someone else starts it."

"Fair enough," Jewett said.

JEWETT WAS AS GOOD as his word and, after a quick meeting with Zach Carter, an agreement was reached. Once the business was completed, the cargo in the vessel would be his along with a guarantee of one thousand dollars should the cargo not have net that amount. If the ship could be taken without undue damage, she would be given to Captain Temple. That was something Dagan put forth, and it was agreed upon with the understanding the ship might not be saved should certain conditions prevail.

The *Summer Wind* could carry, in addition to her crew, sixty extra men. Cooper would leave *SeaFire* under the command of Virgil Culpepper. Cooper would take the second officer, Lamar Turner, Spurlock, Diamond, and Quang. He'd then call for volunteers. He was sure he'd have more than he needed, so he would leave it to Turner to pick the men from the volunteers. They'd leave on the morning tide. Until then, Cooper would get a good evening meal and then try to sleep.

COOPER WENT TOPSIDE TO have one of Gus' cigars, after eating a meal that made him groan when finished. Dagan walked up as Cooper sat on the taffrail,

"Tomorrow will finish these attempts made on your and Maddy's lives," Dagan said.

Cooper nodded and then fetched a cigar from his pocket and gave it to Dagan. Once Dagan had lit up, Cooper looked at his friend. "Should I fall tomorrow…"

Dagan stopped him, "You will not. I feel that. You need not fear, Cooper Cain. Maddy will be cared for. You've seen to her financial future and her family will see to the rest. You will be there when *SeaFire* drops anchor in Savannah."

Cooper smiled and said, "Thank you, old friend." Suddenly, the cigar lost its taste. Cooper threw it into the water below. As he stood up to go below to his cabin, he looked at Dagan. "Tomorrow, I will kill Phillip. God as my witness, I didn't want it to come to this. If he's there…tomorrow, he dies."

CHAPTER FORTY EIGHT

THE *SUMMER WIND* MOVED like a ghost across the water of Casco Bay. Under reduced sail, her canvas filled with the predawn breeze.

"He knows his business, that one," Diamond whispered to his friend, Spurlock.

The ship was silent except for the slow creak of the ship's timbers and a faint groan in the riggings. Zach Carter, captain and owner of the sleek sloop, stood by the wheel. No doubt, he'd made this trip hundreds, maybe thousands, of times but nobody knew what may rise up out of the dawn's early mist. A man was stationed forward by the rail, a rag in his hand to wipe away the sea spray.

Zach Carter was tall, a touch over six feet. He had broad shoulders ad blondish brown hair with a beard to match. His eyes were bright blue, and one of the first things you noticed about the man. Cooper could easily see Carter as a Viking standing on the deck of a long boat. His sailing master stood beside the binnacle box. His feet were planted solidly on the deck. As Cooper watched, the master gave an "Ahem." When he did that, a sailor scurried forward a few feet. Shortly after the "Ahem", the master spat a mouthful of tobacco over the rail.

Dagan, standing by Cooper, smiled, "Yonder sailor moved upwind quickly enough."

"Aye," Cooper agreed.

While the men moved about freely, a certain amount of tension was noticeable. Cooper's men were trained, seasoned fighting men. But being on an unknown ship and placing your trust in men not known to you played on one's nerves. When volunteers were called for, every man aboard *SeaFire* stepped forward. It came down to picking the first sixty in line; not a completely fair way perhaps, but Cooper trusted every man to do his job. A lot depended on the unknown, and the situation that presented itself once they got there.

Zach Carter and his crew would do little other than transporting Cooper and his men, and then claiming and loading what plunder that was available. Sixty men were far more than was needed to overpower the crew on Phillip's ship. Most of them would not fight in the face of overwhelming numbers anyway.

Once the sun was out and the horizon was free of all but a few known fishing boats, Captain Carter turned the deck over to his first mate and invited Cooper and Dagan down to his cabin to break their fast and look over charts in and around Machias. To Cooper's pleasant surprise, the captain had warm apple tarts with a thick sweetened cream poured over the top and steaming hot coffee. The captain spooned sugar into his coffee and added fresh milk to it; not unlike the custom many in New Orleans subscribed to. After a hearty breakfast that saw Cooper put away four of the pastries with two cups of coffee, the table was cleared and Carter broke out his charts.

The entrance into Machias or Little Machias lay at the entrance into the Bay of Fundy. The area was heavily patrolled by the British. As Cooper peered down at Carter's charts, he first noticed that they were much more detailed than his. He wondered if his captured marine might not do a passable job of adding to his charts when they returned from this…this…meeting.

TWO DAYS HAD PASSED since *Summer Wind* had weighed anchor and set sail from Freeport and Casco Bay. Part of that had been spent eluding a small British frigate. Carter had put his ship into Penobscot Bay following a channel toward Camden, which was nestled at the foot of what Carter called Camden Hills. The frigate did not follow *Summer Wind* into the bay, but patrolled along the coast until the sun set.

"Yonder," Captain Carter said, speaking of the British frigate's captain. "He has decided we've made it home or to our destination. He'll head back to Halifax, I believe."

With the moon up over the bay and a leadsman in the chains on the weather side to call out the depth, *Summer Wind* made sail. After the leadsman called out the deepening depths, Carter called him back on board. The rest of the trip was uneventful.

In the first dogwatch, Carter approached Cooper, "The master says we'll be at the entrance of Little Machias toward the end of the next dogwatch. Do you desire to sail into the bay and come alongside of your cousin's ship or block the entrance of the bay and take boats the rest of the way in?"

Cooper thought for a second and then asked, "Is your ship known to the smugglers?"

Carter thought for a moment now. If the answer was yes, then he'd be admitting to the act of smuggling. In this instance though, it mattered not. "Yes, *Summer Wind* is well known."

"I'd suggest sailing in and coming alongside Phillip's ship then, if he is indeed here."

"Too late for misgivings," Dagan said, joining the conversation. "He's there, I can feel it." Both men nodded.

It would attract less attention by sailing in, than a ship anchored at the entrance of the bay. Also, the men would be fresher from not having to row. Tired men would not be at their best if called upon to fight.

Cooper called Turner, his second officer, over and explained the plan. "Make sure the men have white armbands on as we've discussed."

"Aye, we don't want to cut down one of our own," Turner said, in agreement.

Two chests of weapons had been brought aboard along with a keg of powder and a case with wadding and balls.

"The men you trust with pistols divide what we have among them. Arm the rest of the men with cutlasses and tomahawks."

"Aye, Captain. We'll be ready."

"Thank you, Lamar, I know you will."

CHAPTER FORTY NINE

SUMMER WIND GHOSTED ALONG under a gentle zephyr. She was a dark ship, with not a light showing. Captain Carter had reduced sail in preparation for entering the bay. He did so in a deliberate way. That he'd sailed into the bay previously was obvious by his lack of the precautions normally taken when entering a strange bay or harbor.

They were now under topsails, jib and spanker. In the distance, lanterns were seen, obviously hanging at different points aboard a ship. A large fire was going on shore and the silhouettes and shadows of men moving about were visible. So far no alarm had been raised. They'd glided by a couple of fishing boats tied up on the larboard side of the bay. If anyone was watching they must have recognized the ship, that or they were asleep.

"Too early," Dagan said, when Cooper mentioned the possibility.

Summer Wind continued to grow closer and closer. Captain Carter positioned men with grapnels on the starboard side. They were ready to heave their hooks when the word was given.

Captain Carter spoke to Cooper and Dagan in a whisper, "Not long now." He then called his first mate. "Mr. Nelson, get ready forward, hands aloft."

"Aye, Captain."

Once the hands were aloft and the time for silence was over, Carter called out, "Ready, Mr. Nelson."

"Brail up, back the fore-tops'l. Back the main tops'l." As the mate barked out his orders, the sail handlers went about their business in a professional manner. Carter had a crew well-seasoned.

Cooper had his men mustered to starboard, along the rail, behind the men with the grapnels. They were also keeping out of the way of Carter's crew as much as possible in the confines of the small ship. Cooper looked at his men, each with a determined look. They were ready to risk their life and board their foe when the word was given. Not one of them had asked why or what do we get out of this. Each man was fiercely loyal to Cooper. He felt emotion swell inside him as he looked at his men.

A shout was heard from ashore. The alarm was set. "What ship," A voice rang out.

"*Summer Wind*...on a private matter with yonder ship."

As no further challenge came or gunfire erupting, Cooper felt they'd recognized Zach Carter and took his word for its purpose.

"Grapnels away!"

The call startled Cooper, his mind on the recent challenge. The grapnels flew through the air, thudding on the other ship's deck. The men then pulled hand over fist until the hooks bit into the bulwarks of Phillip's ship. Boarders swung over with pistols and cutlasses, before the ships were even pulled together, ready to keep the grapnel lines from being cut. As the two ships were pulled together, Cooper's men leapt across the small divide in mass. One or two men, at first, made to resist but once they were knocked silly, the resistance vanished.

"What's the meaning of this?" It was Captain Temple.

"Where's Phillip," Cooper demanded.

"He's just gone ashore," the captain replied. Cooper went to the entry port, without another word, and down the planking to the shore.

Captain Temple then saw Dagan. "You!"

"Easy, Captain. Let's go to your cabin. No harm will come to you or your men as long as they don't take up arms. If you have a brandy, I will tell you what this is all about."

"You...you lied to me," Temple swore.

"No, Captain, everything I said was and is true. Now let's go below so we can talk." Temple nodded.

As they were about to enter the companionway, Dagan stopped before he stepped over the coaming. "Mr. Turner, I'd take a party of men ashore in case the captain needs assistance. Six men should be enough left aboard."

Cooper couldn't help but notice that the sharpshooter Reynolds, the only man with a long gun, was the first down the planking. He was followed by Spurlock, Ox, Diamond, and Turner. The rest of the men bunched at the entry port, waiting their turn.

BY THE TIME, COOPER rounded the shore in front of the ship; Carter was stepping out of a boat and shaking hands with a smuggler. He was apparently the head man. Cooper looked about and could see stacks of timber waiting to be loaded aboard Phillip's ship. Several barrels were stacked, off to the sides, with sail cloth thrown over the tops.

The man Carter had been talking too walked up to Cooper. "I'm Jeb Sharp. I understand this is a private family matter, and that you do not intend to prevent any agreed upon transactions between...us and yonder ship."

"That is correct, Mr. Sharp," Cooper replied.

Sharp called out, "Smitty, bring Mr. Finylson forward."

A voice rang out, "That's Lord Finylson." This was not Phillip who spoke.

A second passed and then Cooper did hear his cousin's voice, "That's alright, Desmond, they don't go by titles here."

Smitty looked at the two and then spit. "The only Lord we recognize is the one in 'heben."

"You've come to get your just desserts," Phillip snarled. "I heard we missed our chance at your wife as we did you, too bad really. I'd have put her up for every poxed bastard in the world to have his way with her."

Cooper smiled. He knew he was being goaded. "Wasting your breath, Phillip, but I do remember stories from women you tried to have. They all said you didn't have the nutmegs for the job. It's a pity really. But for your treachery and lies, I'd never have been able to enjoy breaking you. Now, not only will I take your last ship, I'm going to kill you."

"No," screamed Desmond. He charged Cooper with a long dagger. He got no closer than Buster Reynolds, who stuck out his long rifle and tripped the man. Before he could gain his feet, Ox kicked him in the head, knocking him unconscious.

Phillip screamed an obscenity. "As soon as I'm through with Cooper, you are next, you ape."

"Never mind him, Ox. He will not get past me," Cooper spoke calmly.

"No worries, Cap'n. Whether he gets past you or not, he's got nothing that'd stop me from squeezing this arse bandit's head until his skull crushes and his eyes pop out like grapes." Ox's words hit home.

Phillip suddenly realized the fear of death. He knew should he make it past Cooper, he'd never get past Ox. The big man could carry out his threat, even in death. Why had he wronged Cooper, he wondered. He never expected his father to go so far as to scar his cousin. The excitement and joy he felt at the time now seemed so distant. The despair, wreckage, and ruin of the once mighty Finylson Shipping dynasty were now reduced to one ship. Had this venture succeeded, he could have moved on, bought another ship and stayed away from Cooper's sailing grounds. Now, if only he'd not put a reward out for Cooper's wife, he might have gotten by with his life. He would pay for that night so many years ago, when he had lied to his father about Cooper and the twins. They never offered him their friendship. *I should have killed them*, he now thought. I shall kill Cooper, and his friend, with a ball to the brain, and then those twins. Touching his vest pocket, the weight of the derringer gave him hope…his secret ace in the hole. If need be one barrel for Cooper, the next for the ape of a man.

Smiling and sensing a degree of infallibility, a smirk creased his face. He wanted blades; he wanted to show his cousin that he'd mastered the art of fencing. He'd killed several men in duels, some of them lasting only a few thrusts. Would Cooper offer him his choice?

"Since you have so offensively called me out, dear cousin, do you wish to choose weapons as well, or should we abide by the rules of honor?" Phillip asked.

Cooper looked at the man in disgust, "You have no honor, Phillip, you showed that years ago. But as you will be dead in a matter of minutes, I'll play the part of a gentleman. So yes, you may choose the weapons."

"Rapiers," Phillip responded at once.

"I'm sorry, cousin, I left mine aboard my ship."

Phillip smiled, "That's of little consequence. I have brought mine. If one of my crew were to be allowed, he could get mine out of my cabin." Cooper agreed and a man was sent to get the blades.

When the man returned, he carried only two blades. "These were the only two of equal length and same appearance," he explained. Phillip made a motion for Cooper to choose his blade.

"Thomas Gill rapiers," Cooper said, as he took one of the blades. It felt good in his hands. Say what you may, Phillip knew his blades.

Thomas Gill was one of the most recognized manufacturers of blades. They were located in Birmingham, England. He had a contract to produce military officer's swords, as did many other English sword smiths. He also produced well made and well designed blades for the English gentry.

"I assume you are satisfied with your choice," Phillip snarled.

Cooper gave his cousin a hard look. "I am."

"Will it be rapier and dagger or rapier and cloak?" Phillip asked. "We have no buckler or shield."

"Your choice," Cooper said.

"Let it be rapier and dagger," Phillip hissed. He walked over to Desmond, who had regained his consciousness and was sitting up but had the barrel of Buster Reynolds long gun inches from the small of his back.

"Is that necessary?" Phillip asked, pushing the long rifle aside and helping his lover to his feet. He then reached over and picked up Desmond's jeweled handle dagger from the ground. "It's a pity, it's not you I'm fighting," Phillip growled.

"Pity for you," Reynolds said. "I don't play with blades. I'd blow a hole right through your heart before you even got close."

Phillip said, turning to Cooper, "I see you've got yourself surrounded by the dregs of humanity."

Looking at Desmond, Cooper responded, "No, Phillip, I could never compete with you in that area." He then pulled out the long dagger Quang had given him, with the stallion head on the handle. Cooper then turned to his men, "No matter the outcome of this fight…should Phillip win…he is to be let go unmolested."

A murmur of disapproval went through his men. "I want your word on it," Cooper said.

"As long as there's no foul, you have it," Cooper's Second Mate Turner responded for the group.

CHAPTER FIFTY

SHARP HAD A CIRCLE made by putting long poles with torches on them, to provide the light. Men then gathered around the laid out circle.

"This is a duel," Sharp said. "Should a man fall by any means the other will allow him to regain his footing. The duel will then resume. Toe the line," Sharp called out.

"Should you die, I will have your wife serviced by every poxed bastard I know," Phillip hissed.

"Ox," Cooper called out, "kill Desmond."

Ox grabbed the man by his head and snapped his neck before Desmond had a chance to respond.

"Damn you to hell," Phillip screamed as he charged. Phillip's comments had been made to unsettle Cooper. It was now Phillip who went off unhinged.

Rapiers were made for thrusting and in his anger, Phillip came slashing left and right almost as one would do with a broad sword. The attack was fierce, but using both dagger and his blade, Cooper warded off blow after blow as he gave ground. The clang of steel on steel filled the night air. The men were now silent as they watched the battle.

Cooper could feel his arm growing numb as he defended himself. He had let Phillip continue, thinking he'd soon grow tired with his onslaught and give him an opening. Though they were close to the same height, Phillip outweighed Cooper by forty pounds. Cooper could feel the strength in his cousin's rage coupled with the weight. Men moved aside as Cooper backed up from Phillip's attack.

Phillip, seeing how close Cooper was to the edge of the bay, went from a slashing attack to a lunge. Cooper parried the lunge easily enough but as he stepped back he fell into the water. Phillip raised his rapier to throw like a spear but the unmistakable sound of a hammer being clicked back froze him. Nothing was said as he backed away to allow Cooper to climb out of the water. As Cooper took off his waist coat, Phillip had a chance to see Sharp with a pistol on one side and Reynolds with his long rifle, was on the other side.

Phillip walked back toward the center of the circle. He was now confident of how the duel would end. He did not stop to think that not one of his attempts had even come close to scratching his cousin. As Cooper made it to the center, Phillip did not wait. "En garde," he spat out as he attacked again. He lunged this time, instead of slashing. His blade was beat aside by Cooper's dagger. A quick riposte answered the lunge only this time it was Phillip who backed away. A stinging, burning sensation was felt in Phillip's hand that held the dagger. Raising his dagger to parry a thrust, Phillip's hand felt wet. He dared not look. So his cousin had drawn the first blood.

Cautiously, Phillip now moved his blade against Cooper's, but every move was turned aside as Cooper disengaged. Tired of this, Phillip thrust forward with his blade and followed by a slash with his dagger. He heard material tearing, and he grinned when he saw he'd sliced a hole in Cooper's shirt. What was that he felt? Reflexes made Phillip look down at his white shirt now turning crimson. He now felt fear grip him as never before. He'd not even scratched his cousin.

"If you are through playing, Phillip, we will continue," Cooper said.

He's toying with me, Phillip thought. *He could have run me through when I looked down. Oh, God!* The doubt and regret he'd felt earlier was now engulfing him.

It was Cooper this time who called, "En garde."

Phillip was frozen in fear. He didn't move.

"Pret," Cooper called, meaning ready.

Phillip nodded. This time, it was Cooper who attacked. He lunged, and when Phillip parried, he slashed. Cooper thrusted as Phillip raised his blade. The point entered Phillip's shoulder. He felt a shocking sensation dance down his arm, causing him to drop his dagger. Blood poured down his arm.

Cooper stood, holding his ground. "Pick it up," he said.

"I…I can't," Phillip mumbled.

"Quang," Cooper yelled.

The Chinaman took a step forward. Flipping the handle around, Cooper tossed the knife, handle first to his cox'n. Seeing Cooper turn, Phillip lunged. Catching Phillip's movement out of the corner of his eye, Cooper tried to side step the attack. He avoided getting his stomach run through, but he was skewered in the side.

Cooper grabbed his side and growled, as Phillip withdrew his bloody blade, "You worthless piece of scum. Phillip, you are lower than whale shat." As he said this, Cooper now charged his opponent.

Phillip was no match for the ferocious onslaught. A slash across his forehead cut Phillip to the skull bone, causing blood to cover his face. He next felt a slash across his chest, but blinded by the blood that cascaded down his face, he couldn't see how bad it was. He backed and backed away further. When he felt a slice cut into his sword arm, he dropped his blade. He turned his back to Cooper, "You win…you win." He was trying, all the while, to get his derringer from his vest. If only he could see, he'd show the bastard. He had it; the handle was in his hand. The blood still made his vision difficult. He held his hand to his forehead to help stem the flow of blood. It was clearer now. Spinning around, he collided with one of the torches that had been set up. Falling backward, he grasped at the torch. He pulled the torch from the ground, and as he did so, he fell into the barrels of gunpowder. Hitting the barrels hard, Phillip's gun went off. This was followed by a flash and a boom. The boom knocked everyone to the ground.

Everyone tried to dig their bodies deep into the ground as barrel after barrel exploded until all four barrels were gone. The sky lit up with a bright blaze with flames dropping out of the sky and on the ships. Men worked feverishly stomping out small flames and using wet canvas to put out the flaming debris on the ships and stacks of timber.

When every flame was out, Sharp walked up to Cooper and Captain Carter. "Damme, if he didn't go out with a bang," he swore. Cooper just shook his head.

"Yes, he did," Captain Carter agreed. "I bet they heard that all the way to Halifax."

EPILOGUE

COOPER WATCHED AS VIRGIL Culpepper brought *SeaFire* to anchor. He could already see a man running up on the hill. No doubt to let people know that they were back. It had been almost three weeks since Phillip blew himself up. Cooper, or Dagan rather, had found in the aftermath, a chest in Phillip's cabin with three hundred and fifty guineas. Cooper divided the money up. He gave fifty guineas to Captain Temple, along with the ship and the timber. He also had Captain Carter draw up a document saying the ship had been captured by the American privateer ship, *Summer Wind,* and for the price of one hundred guineas, had been sold to the ship's captain. This was after the ship's owner had been killed in an explosion. Cooper then gave Carter a hundred guineas and he also paid Sharp one hundred explaining that even an English dandy could live well on one hundred guineas for a year.

"I know how much a hundred pounds are," Sharp said.

"A guinea is more," Cooper said, thinking the man wouldn't understand that a guinea was one pound and a schilling.

Sharp took Cooper's word for it and seemed satisfied. The other hundred guineas he had divided among the crew, even William House, the wayward marine who'd been knocked out when, with the help of Buck Jewell, the *SeaFire* had been retaken at Grand Cayman. While he was still officially a British prisoner, he'd made himself useful helping Josiah in his secretarial duties.

By the time Cooper made it ashore and up the hill, Eli Taylor was there. Cooper explained in detail the events. "We could have used Phillip's ship," Cooper admitted, "but that would have left Captain Temple without anything."

"You did what you thought was best," Eli said. "That's all there is to it; now that part of your life is closed. After the war, you can visit with your and Maddy's families in peace. You also don't have to worry about Maddy's safety every time you leave the yard."

Cooper winced as he moved. "How's your wound, Coop?" Eli asked.

"Not bad, mostly just sore. Doctor Cannington said I was lucky. It didn't get beyond the stomach muscle."

"You are lucky, Coop. You know better than to let yourself be distracted. You don't fight fair when your life is on the line, you fight to win."

Cooper had just finished his drink when Maddy drove up in the carriage. As he stepped out the door, he saw Virgil Culpepper and Dagan. "Our ride has arrived, Dagan."

"I see," he said with a smile.

"Virgil, once you have the ship in order, give the men a week off."

"No," a feminine voice said. "Give them a month off."

"You heard the boss," Cooper said, as he embraced his wife. After a long passionate kiss, they broke apart.

A bit flushed and embarrassed, Maddy spoke to Virgil. "I'd be flogged by a certain young lady if I failed to invite you to supper soon. Come over as soon as you can get free and we will schedule a time."

Dagan climbed in the front of the carriage, edging Brand over. So the young man had been promoted to drive Maddy around in their absence. "How's things with Priscilla," Dagan asked with a smile.

"Not good, Mr. Dagan. Her mama won't let her outta her sight more'n ten minutes."

Once Cooper and Maddy were seated in the carriage, Brand slapped the reins and clucked his tongue. Well-trained, the matched pair took up the strain and walked off at a quick pace.

After another passionate kiss, Maddy pushed Cooper back. "You rogue, you'd ravish my body in the back of a carriage going through Savannah with the top down."

"Aye, I would."

"Well, Sir Pirate, you'll have to wait until we get home to sample my favors."

"It will not be a sample...that I promise you," Cooper said.

"Humph, we'll see."

After they'd gone a bit further, Cooper pulled Maddy around to face him. "So Jessie is smitten with Virgil."

"I'm not sure she's smitten, but she is definitely interested."

It was Cooper now, who said humph.

"Not jealous are you, Coop?"

Cooper looked at his wife. It was no secret he, Josie, and Jessie had tasted each other's fruit. "No, Maddy, there'll never be any other woman but you. I was just thinking of Virgil's reputation back on Roatan. He was always one jump ahead of a husband or an angry father."

"So you will play the father figure?" Maddy asked.

"I don't know. We'll see where this leads."

SEVERAL DAYS HAD COME and gone. Cooper and Maddy were to-gether as much as possible and every night they fell asleep, ex-hausted from their lovemaking. Virgil came over for dinner and Cooper could tell Jessie had feelings for his roguish first mate.

The first dinner went so well, a second one was planned. When James and Josie invited Maddy and Cooper to dinner, Virgil was invited also. Virgil then took Jessie to a play in Savannah.

"It won't be long now before we hear an announcement," Maddy said after dinner.

"Aye," Dagan said. "I sees a bright future for the two of them; also for Buck Jewell and Mary Esther as well."

"And us, Uncle?" Maddy added.

"I've put Phillip behind me," Cooper said. "Like Eli said, that's a chapter in my life that's over, so we've no one to endanger our happiness now."

Suddenly, Dagan felt a shudder. Something deep within him seemed to send a warning.

"I'm glad," Maddy said, responding to Cooper's words. "Aren't you glad, Uncle?"

When Dagan didn't respond, Maddy spoke again, "Are you listening to me, Uncle?"

Dagan turned to Maddy, "I'm sorry. My mind was adrift."

"I said, aren't you glad that Phillip is gone so he'll no longer be a threat."

"Aye, child, that I am."

Cooper wondered, *but is he*. He'd seen Dagan's reaction. *Was it over…was the threat over?*

THE END